Insomnia

Insomnia

A Novel

Sarah Pinborough

HARPER LARGE PRINT
An Imprint of HarperCollinsPublishers

Lyrics by Tim Elsenburg.

An excerpt from the song "Candle Book and Bell," taken from the album *Motorcade Amnesiacs* by Sweet Billy Pilgrim.

HarperCollins books may be purchased for educational, business, or sales promotional use. For information, please e-mail the Special Markets Department at SPsales@harpercollins.com.

FIRST HARPER LARGE PRINT EDITION

ISBN: 978-0-06-321116-2

Library of Congress Cataloging-in-Publication Data is available upon request.

22 23 24 25 26   LSC   10 9 8 7 6 5 4 3 2 1

For Jessica Burdett.
Producer, dream-maker, friend,
and fellow sufferer of sleeplessness.
Thanks so much for everything.
SP x

The monsters were never
under my bed.
Because the monsters
were inside my head.

NIKITA GILL, "MONSTERS"

Trauma is a time traveller, an ouroboros that
reaches back and devours everything that
came before.

JUNOT DÍAZ, "THE SILENCE,"
THE NEW YORKER, APRIL 2018

Prologue

The other car comes out of nowhere.

There's no warning screech of brakes, not even a sideways *what the* glance through the window, just the hard *whoomph* of metal hitting metal at high speed, an explosion of energy, a symphony of disaster. The impact is so great that glass shatters instantly, dispersing in a sharp angry hail. The chassis ripples like water and the car lifts high, the worst kind of fairground ride, tumbling over, hard into the roadside ditch.

After that, a terrible stillness. A slight creak as the metal settles and then nothing. The radio is no longer on. There is no more excited conversation. In a matter of seconds everything has changed.

Small movements in the passenger seat. Contained, trapped, broken desperation. A scream that is barely a wheeze.

The other car, a bull of an all-terrain car, is still on the road, front end crumpled to a snout. The engine, surprisingly, is still running, an old man's rattling cough, but going all the same. For a moment, a longer moment than it took to destroy the universe of life in the other vehicle, the driver sits, trembling at the wheel. The sun is still shining, dappling through the trees. It's still a beautiful early morning and the road is still empty.

The road is still empty.

No witnesses.

Only one mile or so from home.

The driver leaves it to chance. To luck. The airbag has not deployed. If the car will go, the driver will leave. They won't look back. If it doesn't, they'll stay and face the consequences. Shaking hands shift the gears into first and then grip the steering wheel, suddenly aware of aches and pains coming alive from the impact. The car, a workhorse of a machine, grinds into movement, and turns, limping along the road. The driver does glance back. They can't help it. A hand rises a little from the figure trapped in the passenger seat. A cry for help.

The driver moans. They'll call an ambulance. From a phone box maybe. But there's no phone box on the short route. Someone will be along soon, though. This road gets busy by nine. Someone will help. They're sure of it.

1

TWELVE DAYS UNTIL MY BIRTHDAY

There's someone in the house.

It's not a complete thought, but something feral, more instinctive, and I sit up, suddenly awake, my heart racing. The clock clicks to 1:13 A.M. and I stay very still, listening hard, sure I'm going to hear a creak from the hallway or see a threatening shadow emerge from a dark corner of the room. But there's nothing. Just the patter of rain on the windows and the hum of night quiet.

My skin has prickled. Something woke me. Not a dream. Something else. *Something in the house.* I can't shake the feeling, like when I was small and the nightmares would grip me so hard I would be sure I was back in *that* night and my foster mother would run in to calm me down before I woke the whole house.

Robert is fast asleep, on his side facing away from me. I don't wake him. It's probably nothing, but still, I'm alert with worry. *The children.*

I won't be able to get back to sleep until I've checked on them and so I get up, shivers trembling up my body from my bare feet on the carpet, and I creep out onto the landing.

I feel very small as I look along the central corridor, the gloom making it appear endless, a monster's yawning mouth ahead of me. I walk forward—*I am a mother and a wife. A career woman. This is my house. My safe place*—and wish I'd brought my phone with me to use as a flashlight. I peer over the landing banisters. Nothing moves in the dark shadows below. No thump of burglars shifting possessions in the night. No menace.

A flurry of wind drives the rain hard into our cathedral feature window, startling me. I go to the end of the corridor, where it cuts into the wall, a perfect arch of black. I cup my hands around my eyes and press my face against the cold glass, but all I can make out is the vague shape of trees. No light. No activity. Still, I shiver again as I turn back and head down the L bend ahead to the kids' rooms. Footsteps dancing on my grave.

I feel better once I've pushed open Will's door. My little boy, five years old and at big school now, is asleep on his back, the dinosaur duvet kicked away, and his dark hair, so like mine, is mussed up from sweat. Maybe he's been having a bad night too. I carefully cover him up, but gentle as I'm trying to be, he stirs and his eyes open.

"Mummy?" He's blurry, confused, but when I smile, he does too, and wriggles onto his side. His sketchbook is under his pillow and I slide it out.

"No wonder you woke up," I whisper. "Sleeping on this." It's open on his most recent enthusiastic crayon drawing and I turn it this way and that in the gloom, trying to make out what it is. If I'm honest, it looks like a dog that's been run over. Twice.

"It's a dinosaur," Will says, and laughs and then yawns, as if even he knows drawing may not be his finest skill and he's cool with that.

"Of course it is." I put the notebook on the table by his bed and kiss him good night. He's almost asleep again already and probably won't even remember this in the morning.

I go to Chloe's room next and she too is lost to the

world, blond hair fanned out on the pillow, a sleeping princess straight from a fairy tale, even though, at seventeen and a staunch modern feminist, she'd be quick to tell me that fairy tales are misogynistic rubbish. I go back to my own room, ridiculing myself for having been so afraid.

I get back into bed and curl up, Robert barely stirring. It's only one thirty. If I fall asleep now, then I can get another four hours in before I have to get up. Sleep should come easily—it always has in this busy, exhausting, exhilarating life I lead, so I snuggle down and wait to drift. It doesn't happen.

At three A.M. I check my emails—a midnight congratulations from Angus Buckley, my boss, for my result in court yesterday with the Stockwell divorce custody hearing—and then scan the news on my phone and go to the loo. Robert almost wakes then, but only enough to mutter something unintelligible and fling one heavy arm over me as I get back into bed. After that I lie there, my head whirring with my schedule for the fast-approaching day, becoming more and more frustrated that I'm going to be facing it tired. I've got to be at the office at seven thirty and it's rare for me to get home before twelve hours later and that's only if I can get away without going for the obligatory drinks. There's no room for slacking. Especially not now. I'm in line to be the youngest partner in the firm. But I love my work, I really do.

I practice some yoga breathing, trying to relax every muscle in my body and empty my mind, which sounds so easy but normally results in my pondering stupid things like whether there's enough milk in the fridge or if we should change our gas supplier, and although my heart rate slows I still don't sleep.

It's going to be a long day.

2

ELEVEN DAYS UNTIL MY BIRTHDAY

Work is busy. By ten forty-five I've had two conferences, dealt with some billing, and returned calls to three more clients to calmly explain that I can't make the courts work any quicker, nor can I speed up responses from their partners' solicitors, however infuriating the delays might be, and that each time I have to call to reassure *them*, it's costing them money. People always seem to be hastier to exit a marriage than they ever were to get into one.

I check my mobile. There are three missed calls from a number I don't know, but whoever it is will have to wait. I've got something else to deal with first. Alison.

There's a knock at my door and I take a deep breath. Alison is never easy.

"Come in."

Alison Canwick is in her mid-fifties and of the mind-set that age in and of itself brings authority, and the fact that she's been a solicitor for a lot longer than me should supersede the fact that she's junior to me. If I make partner, she might actually kill me.

"Well done with the ex Mrs. McGregor." I smile as I wave her to a seat she doesn't take. "She must be happy with the result."

"As happy as someone can be when their husband of thirty years has run off into his sunset with a woman the same age as their eldest daughter."

Just take the praise, I want to say. Alison's forte is angry wives who want vengeance. I'm not even sure they all *do* want vengeance, but Alison fires them up to go for broke, just as she did herself when her husband left her for another woman ten years ago. Maybe if she stopped fueling rage in others, her own might fade. As it is, the McGregor result was all right, but it wasn't entirely in her client's favor. I only complimented her to try to smooth what I'm about to say.

"Well, yes, there is that." I sit even though she's still standing. "It's about your billable hours," I say, and her face tightens. *Here we go.* "You've been below eighty percent for two weeks now, and I thought I'd check that you weren't under any pressures that we don't—"

"I'm sure that stupid computer program doesn't always log everything right."

"Please, Alison, let me finish." That's the other thing. Alison is never wrong. Nor can she ever admit weakness. "I'm not pulling you up on it," I lie, "I just want to make sure you're okay. You're normally so good at hitting the targets." To be fair to her, that last is true. She's quite competitive and she might not always be on top of things, but she definitely knows we need to be at 80 percent minimum of our working hours being ones we can charge for.

"I'm fine," she says, disgruntled. "I'll make sure it's better from now on."

"Any problems, I'm here to help." The moment the words come out I can see it was the wrong thing to say. Her jaw tightens and her eyes flash with indignation.

"I'll bear that in mind." She squeezes the words out through gritted teeth.

A second knock at the door saves us both. Rosemary, my secretary, also in her fifties but someone who oozes warmth and joy at the world, comes in carrying a large vase of roses.

"Just look at these!" She takes them straight to the decorative table by the window. They are beautiful, at least twenty blooms.

"For me?" I'm confused. It's not a special occasion and Robert would never buy me roses. He knows I'd rather have a plant that carries on living instead of something that's condemned to rot even when it looks so beautiful.

Alison is lingering, curious, and I can't be bothered to tell her to leave.

"This was in with the bouquet." Rosemary hands me a card. Oh god, Parker Stockwell. *"Once again, thank you. And if you ever feel like that dinner, just call. Parker x."*

I groan and where Rosemary looks at me quizzically, Alison is all knowingly snide. "Let me guess, Mr. Stockwell?" She turns and leaves, with an air of victory somehow, which irritates me more.

"I wouldn't mind if he wasn't such a creep," I say as I look at the flowers. "Asking me out for dinner. I don't think he was expecting a no, even though I'm married."

"I should imagine he doesn't get many nos."

"True. But he's definitely not my type." I take a deep breath and cross Alison off my diary schedule for the day. "Maybe I should set him up with Alison." I laugh a little at the thought. "Why does she have to be such hard work?"

"She's jealous, that's all it is," Rosemary says. "You're younger, more successful, have a lovely family, and—ah, that reminds me—your sister called. She said she's tried your mobile a few times. She wants you to call her back. As soon as possible, she said."

Phoebe.

The flowers, and Alison, and my busy day, and my lack of sleep are suddenly all forgotten. Phoebe's called. I bring up the missed calls on my phone from the unknown number. A UK number. Phoebe. My sister. She's back. And the only thing I can think is . . . *Why now? Why so close to my birthday?*

3

I'm at the hospital. Ward fifteen. You'd better come.

That's all she said before hanging up and now that I'm here, I know why. She's tricked me into coming.

This is a private ward, but it's a *geriatric* private ward. I go past a couple of rooms and I can't help looking in through the half-open doors. In one a man, skin shrunken into his cheekbones, hair wispy thin, is silently descending into whatever comes next. In another, a patient is watching *Homes Under the Hammer* on a too-loud TV, and in the last one I reach there's a wheelchair folded against the wall and a woman is reading a magazine to an old woman, perhaps a mother or aunt, who's listening and carefully sipping a cup of tea. Snapshots of lives. I don't want to reach the room that holds the snapshot of mine.

"Can I help you?" A nurse makes me jump.

"I'm Emma Averell. I mean Bournett. I'm looking for Phoebe Bournett?"

"Emma? Patricia Bournett's other daughter?" *And there it is.* "Have you signed in?" She is loud and irritated and even the woman reading to her mother in the room next to where I'm standing stops and looks around. I step farther away from the doorway.

"I'm sorry, I—"

"Emma. Here."

Phoebe's standing farther up the corridor. My older sister.

Her hair's grown long and hangs free around her shoulders, and in her tunic top, skinny black jeans, and ballet pumps, it's hard to believe she's forty-two. But it's a disguise. There's nothing carefree about Phoebe, and a closer look at her face tells a different story. Lines are showing in her forehead and around her mouth, no longer gossamer threads, but sinking deeper, the fishhooks of time tugging her skin downward.

"You nearly gave me a heart attack, Phebes. I thought you were sick."

She studies me for a long moment. "It's uncanny."

"What?"

"You look so much like her. Like she was *then.*"

Why can't she ever say anything nice? *Hey, Emma,*

I've missed you. How's work? I'm so proud of you. No, she has to go straight for the jugular. As if she resents loving me. Sometimes—now for instance—I'm sure she does.

"I'm nothing like her."

"You don't remember." She shrugs. "But you *do* look like she did then." She frowns a little. "I mean, exactly like her. Quite disturbing."

I refuse to rise to the bait. "I left work because I thought you'd had an accident. If you're fine then we can catch up later." *In another couple of years probably.*

"You wouldn't have come if I'd told you."

"This is about her, isn't it?" She's right, I wouldn't have come. And nothing is going to make me stay.

"You mean Mum? She's not Voldemort. You can use the word." She nods toward a closed door. "She's in there. She smashed her head against a mirror in the night." She pauses as I take an involuntary step backward. "Repeatedly. She's got a life-threatening cerebral hematoma. I thought you'd want to know."

I look around and frown. "Where are the guards?"

Phoebe laughs then, a burst of sharp surprise. "She's a fragile seventy-five-year-old woman with a severe brain bleed who's barely done more than shuffle and mumble in decades. She's hardly a flight risk."

"They should still have someone here." I would feel

safer if there were guards. Someone watching the door. Childhood fears go deep.

"No one cares anymore, Emma." Phoebe, always so blunt. "About what she did. And it's a secure unit she lives in, not a prison."

Sometimes I Google the place. I've been doing it more often recently. I don't even know why; maybe it reassures me to know that she's still behind several sets of security gates and metaphorical bars. Hartwell House's Medium Secure Unit. *For patients who have been in contact with the criminal justice system and who present serious risk to others . . .* In a superhero film it's the kind of place that would be called "an institution for the criminally insane."

"Only because she was too mad for prison," I mutter. "And *I* care." Now it's me who's vehement. "I can't believe you made me come here. I've always been clear I never want to see her," I say. "Actually, I can't believe *you're* here." A thought strikes me. "How *are* you here?" How the hell would the unit have contacted her? I'm surely the easiest daughter to find. Phoebe doesn't even live in the country.

She shrugs, the noncommittal mildly annoyed shrug that normally means she's about to drop a bombshell.

"I've been visiting her."

And there it is. I lean against the wall. I should be at the office. I've got a full day. This is something I did not need. "What do you mean visiting her? When?"

"Not often. But over the past few months."

"Wait." Last we heard from Phoebe she was living in Spain and working for some property firm. "You've been back a *few months*? And this is the first time you get in touch? For fuck's sake, Phoebe." God, she makes me so mad. I'm too busy to be here and she should have known better than to make me come. I turn away, storming back down the corridor. The nurse is by the desk gesturing at the signing-in book. "Emma bloody Averell!" I shout at her as I pass. She can sign me in and out herself.

I lean against my car, the breeze cooling the anger burning me up inside. Visiting time must be over because people from all walks of life come past me heading to their cars. Some have been here to see their mothers, no doubt. I am the worst daughter in the car park. The worst daughter of the worst mother. But I'm not the worst sister. I can't even put my feelings into words. This is a proper kicker from Phoebe. Visiting *her*? And not even telling me she was back?

"Emma!" She's coming toward me. "Wait!"

"I can't talk to you right now, Phoebe, I just can't." I don't have the energy for a public car park confrontation with my own sister.

"I knew you'd be like this."

"Don't turn this around on me. I'm always here for you. *Always*. It's you who stays away."

"If that makes you feel better, then keep telling yourself that." It's her turn to flash an angry look. "And I've been there for you plenty of times too. Back before you had all this." She nods at my new car.

"What happened to the life in Spain? The job?"

"It was my boss's idea to come. They said it would be healing to spend time with her."

"But not with me." I'm cold and she's defensive.

"I really don't have to explain my life choices to you, Emma. I also knew you'd be shitty about me seeing *her*. As it is she was pretty catatonic just like she's been since then and—"

"I don't want to know about her. I don't care about her." I pull open my car door. *I'm nearly forty, too old to be so frightened of the monster.* "But you? You hurt my feelings, Phoebe."

"Oh, like you care about seeing me. Look at you. New car. New house. Flashy life. Always so busy. Saw that piece in the paper about you. Rising legal star. Your feelings aren't hurt. You just like to be in control of everything." She looks so bitter and I can't be bothered to go through our same old arguments again. "Anyway." She takes a step back. "She's in a very bad way," she says. "Maybe seeing her would do you some good. Give you some closure. Let all that fear out."

"I'm not afraid." I throw my bag onto the passenger seat and get in.

"Sure you are," Phoebe holds the door open momentarily, her dark eyes sharp, a hint of a smile on her lips. "You're forty in a week or so. You've always been afraid of that."

"Have a safe trip back to Spain, Phoebe," I say, before pulling the car door closed hard and quickly starting the engine. I can see her in the rearview mirror, watching me drive away, and I'm sure she's smiling.

How could she bring up my birthday like that?

She's a bitch. What a bitch.

4

I keep my eyes forward as I join the queue of traffic crawling toward the exit. Phoebe always said that turning forty didn't bother her, but she dropped out of a steady job and cut off contact—what intermittent contact we ever had—a while before hers and it transpired she went to a cooking retreat somewhere in Eastern Europe, which was the least Phoebe thing she had ever done, so she can say what she likes, it bothered her too.

She's been basically absent ever since. To me, anyway. And now, right before my own fortieth birthday, she expects me to suddenly, after all these years, want to spend time with our mother. I can't get my head around it.

It's lunchtime and the traffic heading to the roundabout is in a slow stop-start, disgruntled drivers moody in the muggy heat. I turn the air-conditioning up. I need to get myself together.

She smashed her head against the mirror in her room.

As I turn left, the traffic finally picks up. I try to focus on the mountain of work waiting for me at the office and how I'm going to have to lie to everyone about why I was at the hospital, because as far as they know my mother is already dead. I'm going to have to pretend Phoebe had an accident or something, but my mind keeps coming back to *her*. Our mother. The age-old jokes—*What are you scared of? Turning forty. Turning into my mother*— all terrifyingly true for me.

Forty has always loomed like a specter in my life— more so for me than for Phoebe, because Phoebe was never called the *mad child* by our mother. It was me she'd whisper to sometimes, that I'd go mad like her, hissed in my face as her fingers dug too tightly into my arms. That I had the *bad blood* too. It ran in the family.

Most of what I recall of my childhood with our mother are vague snippets except for that last day. Phoebe remembers more, but she was eight to my five. We were much more like sisters then. Bonded. And then that night came and broke us all up.

It's the morning I remember the clearest. The last morning. I can feel the rough carpet under my knees as we made a card with a big 40 on the front that Phoebe drew so carefully, and I colored in, and then her taking my hand, holding it firm as we went downstairs.

For a moment I'm back there, lost in the memory, and then a blaring horn pulls me into the present. Work. I need to get to work. But even as I park I can sense the ghost of my mother emerging from the darker corners of my mind, and can almost feel Phoebe's hand gripping mine, pulling me away from her.

"You look just like her."

I wish they'd both let bloody go.

"Funny is it? Wrecking my life?"

I've parked and got out of my car back at the office, and for a moment I don't realize that the angrily spat words are meant for me until I look up and see Miranda Stockwell, all sinewy nerves, blocking my path.

"Ms. Stockwell, if you have anything further you wish to raise, I suggest you contact your own solici—"

"You helped him steal my children from me!" Her face is red, a mess of makeup, as she slams her hands down on the hood of my car. I flinch slightly. Other cars are pulling in around us, so I'm not overly concerned that she's going to physically attack me, but having just avoided a car park fight with Phoebe, I have no intention of having one here with a client's ex-wife.

"No, Miranda." My voice is soft but cool. "I didn't

do that. You did. But things can change. If you get some help, then I'm sure you can reapply for—"

"Oh, now you're giving *me* advice?" She sneers. "Everyone thinks I'm crazy. You think I'm crazy." She hiccups a laugh. "He did well, didn't he? Turning me into a madwoman and you all went along with it. *Not stable* enough to look after my own children. Such utter bullshit."

I really have had enough of crazy for this morning, and this isn't any of my business. Not anymore. The case is done.

"I'm sorry." I'm wary but I do feel for her. I'd always rather parents split custody, but her erratic behavior made that impossible. "Speak to your solicitor if you want to contest it."

"Maybe I'll take the law into my own hands." She turns, stumbling slightly, and I realize that she's spent her morning drinking. "And we'll see how you like that, you *fucking bitch*."

She shouts the last words back at me as she walks away, and I lean against my car for a moment until she's rounded the corner. My head throbs. Well, at least the day probably can't get any worse.

It's only later, when I sneak off at the end of the day without going for the ritual Friday drinks at Harry's

Bar, claiming to having to check on Phoebe's sprained ankle, that I find that the day has indeed got worse. I'm so relieved to be heading home in plenty of time for Will's bedtime and to have an actual Friday evening with my family, and then I see my new car. *If you want to make partner, Emma, you have to look the part.*

The first thing that hits me is where the paintwork has been keyed all along one side, the jagged line clear against the blue, and then I see the note under my windshield. A piece of paper from a spiral notepad, the sort I didn't think people carried around with them anymore, especially not women like Miranda Stockwell, who I'd have thought wrote everything down in her phone or iPad, but who obviously did.

The word is scratched angrily in pen so hard the back of the paper feels like braille.

BITCH

I stare at it and then look around. No sign of her. No sign of any cameras. I take a picture of my car in situ with the scratches on my phone, not that I can prove anything, and then get in and close the door, tossing the note into the cup well. Great. Just great.

5

"Hey, where's Dad?"

"I don't know. His den, I guess. Is your brother getting ready for bed?" I ask.

I've just got home and am getting a glass of water in the kitchen, browsing the mail stuffed by the kettle—some new insurance Robert sorted out, although, looking at this eye-watering premium, I'll need to ask him why it's so much more expensive than our previous policies—when Chloe appears, hovering in the doorway, holding her iPad. She's taller than me now and blond, charming and confident. Her father's child.

"I've set up that Facebook event he wanted," she says. "Had to add some of the school mums and dads to mine so I could invite them. Think I got everyone."

"What event?"

"He didn't tell you? He said he was . . ." She turns and shouts down the hallway. "Dad? Dad! You didn't tell Mum?"

"Didn't tell me what?"

Three minutes later and I'm in Robert's den, standing in front of the TV, blocking Leeds taking a corner or free kick or whatever it was they were about to do that might give them a chance of winning. "A birthday party?" I say.

"Emma! Come on, I can't see!" Robert leans over, trying to look around me. I don't move and he finally pauses the game.

"I said I didn't want any fuss." I'm snippy. I can't help it.

"It's your fortieth. You've got to do something. And anyway, it's not a party as such, just a gathering. Life begins and all that." He frowns, irritated. "It was supposed to be a nice surprise. Why are you so *bothered*?"

I don't have an answer. I mean, I *do* but that's for me alone.

"You should own it." Chloe's half in and half out of the room, and I realize her existence at home is mainly spent in doorways these days, never fully committing to sharing time with us, always with one eye on a quick dash to the privacy of her room. "It's the patriarchy that makes women worry about getting older. You should embrace it. Your forties are going to be your decade of power."

"Well, maybe I should start *showing* my power by vetoing this party."

"*Mum*," Chloe throws one hand dramatically on a hip. "Come on!"

"It's only about twenty people," Robert says. "Nothing major."

"Fine." I know I'm beaten and Chloe's already had two responses on the Facebook event invite. If we canceled now it would look weird. "Okay. But you should have asked me first."

I can picture them rolling their eyes at each other as I head off to find Will, and I know I maybe overreacted, but my stomach is in a knot.

Forty. It's really coming. And there's nothing I can do about it. *Just a number,* I tell myself, as I feel the chill fingers of dread on my spine. *Just a number.* It'll be here and gone before I know it.

Will's just about finished finally brushing his teeth, a clown's smile of toothpaste around his mouth, when he pulls his lip down and studies his bottom teeth and then the top.

"No loose ones yet?" I'm not sure what he wants most, to have that first gap, like some of his friends, or a visit from the tooth fairy. Whichever, or both, Will's been feeling very short-changed by his still structurally sound molars.

He shakes his head, disappointed. "I thought my fuzzy head would make them wobble."

I touch his forehead. He's not hot and he doesn't look too pale. I look at his pupils, but they're both fine too. "Did you have a headache?"

"Just fuzzy."

"Gone now?" Maybe he's coming down with something. He hasn't had a bug for a while and is probably due. He shrugs, frustratingly noncommittal, and heads off to his bedroom.

He chooses *Paddington Goes to Hospital* from the box set of his favorites, and as we snuggle together, him under his dinosaur duvet and me laying on it, the book choice sours my pleasure of the moment. Paddington bangs his head with a boomerang and has to go to the hospital. *She smashed her head against the mirror.*

Will's warm and comforting on my chest and as soon as the story is done I hand the book over, so he can study the pictures and words by himself for a bit. It's good to have a few quiet moments before heading back downstairs for dinner. Chloe's going for a sleepover at her friend Andrea's, so it will just be me and Robert. He's going to ask how my day was, and however I answer, there's going to be a lie involved. I can't exactly tell him what happened with Phoebe, because as far as he knows—as far as he's ever known—our mother is dead. I told him the lie when we first met back when I was twenty-one, and Phoebe went along with it and I haven't regretted it. Would he understand if I explained? Probably. But I don't want my mother's story to be any part of my life.

I'll suggest a film. He'll nod off, or, more likely, I will. Whatever we do, I don't want to think about *her*. Or Phoebe. And yet here I am, thinking about them. I drift into the past again, to that last day, the family scrapbook in my head rolling fast through the pages.

"Mummy?"

I'm so zoned out I don't hear Will at first.

"Mummy," he says again, and his tone startles me back into the moment. He wriggles against me. "You're holding me too tight." And I am. I can feel the tension of my arm around him, my fingers digging into his shoulder. Squeezing far too hard.

"Oh, I'm so sorry, baby." I let go immediately, shocked and appalled. I've never seen him look at me like that before, with that confused wariness. I don't like it at all. "I was miles away. Do you want another *Paddington*?"

He smiles, sunshine after clouds, and I switch the

books out. By the time the bear has done *The Grand Tour*, Mummy's odd moment is forgotten and he's snuggled into me. *Mummy's odd moments*. I don't want to think about those.

We have sex. It's fine and practiced in a paint-by-numbers way, everything done in the right order so Robert and I both finish satisfied, the routine we've fallen into over the years. There's less sex now, and even less since Will was born and, awful as it sounds, when we finish, I'm already crossing it off my mental to-do list for the week.

Robert goes to the loo after me and in the lamplight I can see that the bedroom needs vacuuming and the laundry basket is overflowing. It's not that different downstairs. This, combined with his snappiness when I mentioned getting Will's gym clothes washed on the right day, and the general air of resentful distance that's crept in between us, is giving me the distinct impression that Robert isn't as happy being the stay-at-home parent the second time around as he was the first, but this was the deal we made all those years ago. He wanted this big house but it's my job that pays for it. Maybe we should think about getting a cleaner, but that's just more expense. There is a tension between us these days, that's for sure, and I don't know when it began, but now I'm getting irritated at him too. I'll vacuum in the morning, I decide. Just get it done, even though I can't help but wonder why it always has to be the woman who ends up sorting everything at home. But first, I need to sleep away this crazy day.

6

TEN DAYS UNTIL MY BIRTHDAY

I didn't sleep. I was still awake at four thirty, and then as daylight broke I catnapped for a couple of hours before all the noise in the house dragged me out of bed at seven. By the time we get to the barbecue at three I'm knackered.

"Emma, you look tired!" It's the first thing Michelle says as she opens the door to us and I want to poke her in her bright perfectly made-up eyes.

"Busy week," I say. "And I didn't sleep great."

"Have you tried chamomile tea?"

"I'll give it a go," I say, politely. Michelle is one of those women who has a suggestion for everything and in the main, they're pretty useless. I'm hoping I don't need to try it.

She leads us through to the kitchen, where the bifold doors are opened up onto their beautiful garden. "I find that works." She glances back. "With a splash of vodka in it."

I let Robert lead as we go to join the others. The school gate gang. They're Robert's friends more than mine, although as he points out, "the girls" are always inviting me to drinks or dinners or theater trips, but working ten- or twelve-hour days I rarely take them up on it.

"Matthew's on the trampoline." Michelle has one hand on Will's shoulder, casually caring, and I'm reminded of how blended they all are. After-school clubs, grabbing one another's kids when a hairdresser's appointment overruns, all that kind of thing. The life Robert leads that I know so little about. "And there's some Fruit Shoots in that ice box by the table tennis."

"Nice set up," Robert says.

"We see enough of them during the week, don't we?" Michelle hands him a beer.

"True enough. How did you get on with the last lot of spellings?"

"Oh, come on, that was just a mental glitch! I was full marks this week."

They laugh and I smile, pretending to be part of the group, as Will wanders over to the other side of the garden where the children are playing. Michelle's youngest, Matthew, is one of Will's best friends, but her seven-year-old, Ben, I'm less keen on. He's a bruiser and likes to be in charge. Today though, Betty's two girls are here and her eldest is ten and beautiful, so Ben will be doing whatever she tells him. There's a trampoline, table tennis, and a paddling pool all set up and ready to go, even though it's not too hot today.

As for the adults, there's only us, our glamorous and handsome hosts, Michelle and Julian, and Betty and Alan, the newest of the posse, recently moved from Scotland. They're all, the women anyway, in Robert's school WhatsApp group. Maybe I should tell one of *them* to remind him to wash the gym clothes.

"Wine, Emma? G and T?" Julian has set up a bar next to the large gas BBQ, where he has various pre-pared plates laid out. I can see prawn skewers, chicken satay, and fish parcels. I hope to god they've got sausages or something for the kids.

"Have you got a diet Coke?"

"Come on, have one drink. Celebrate." He pours me a glass of white wine.

"What am I celebrating?"

"The Parker Stockwell divorce. There was a piece in the local rag."

"Oh really?" It's a nice surprise and will go down well with the partners, who'll be pleased with the free advertising. Good for my promotion too.

"My company does some construction for him," Julian continues. "Not someone to be messed with." He lifts his glass. "So well done."

"Thanks." I'm a little surprised, because I'm usually in no man's land at these things. The men don't include me in their conversations about their work or golf or whatever else they talk about, and I can't really talk school with the women, so this makes a nice change. I glance toward the paddling pool.

"Chloe, could you go and keep an eye on Will for me? Just for a bit?" She's standing close by me, looking uncomfortable too.

"I'm a guest, not free labor," she says and then eyes my glass. "Although it looks like I'm going to be the driver."

"Ha, touché." Julian laughs. "Come on, I'm up for some Ping-Pong. I guess one parent should supervise these unholy monsters." He looks back over his shoulder. "Looking forward to your birthday bash, Emma. No children allowed, I hope!"

I force a smile at the mention of my looming big day and watch as Chloe nudges him, laughing.

"Okay, old man. Get your game on," she says. My daughter's teenage moodiness is reserved only for me, it seems.

"Challenge accepted." He looks to the others." Alan? Can you get those chicken burgers on for the kids?"

Chloe walks away, laughing at something Julian says, and then slaps him on the arm before they take their ends at the table. Even she's more at home with these people than I am, but then she's looked after most of the kids at some point—her penance for being the accidental baby of my youth—and if I'm honest I'm just glad she still wants to come out with us as a family.

As it is, by the time the burgers are cooked and the children are sitting on a blanket eating, I'm having a good time. The wine has given me a pleasant buzz and Betty has that great Scottish wry sense of humor that makes me think that in different company her jokes would be filthy and that would be a night out that could be fun. She's mercilessly mocking some of the other school mums, and even though I don't know them beyond their names, her comic timing has me laughing out loud. Maybe I could be friends with these women if I tried harder. I add it to the endless to-do list. *Try harder with the mums.* Perhaps I could have them over to ours. Or take them out for dinner—that would be easier.

"You had one, didn't you, Robert?" Michelle calls across and Betty's story stops immediately. "A battered old Land Rover? A while ago? They're very in vogue now." She's loud. Did she start on the wine before we all got here?

"Yeah, he did." I'd forgotten all about that boy toy. I bought it for his thirty-fifth birthday after I made senior associate. "It was jinxed."

"I only had it about six months." Robert drains his beer. "So, have you all responded to Emma's fortieth—"

"Jinxed how?"

"I'm exaggerating." I laugh. "It was old and cheap to be fair. But something was always wrong with it, and then Robert wrote it off. Just before we decided to move, wasn't it? I was away at a seminar and came back to find a bruised husband and the Land Rover sold for scrap." How had I forgotten about that?

"The steering failed and I went into a tree."

"Good job we got rid of it," I say, looking at my daughter. "Otherwise, that could have been your first car, Chlo. A little run-around for uni. Eighteenth birthday present."

Chloe looks distinctly unimpressed. "I'm thinking about a year out actually."

This is news to me, but she changes her mind with the weather, so while the others all start asking her why and recalling Interrailing around Europe and summers in Thailand and whatever else they were lucky enough to have done, I let it ride.

"At least you'll have an extra year before having to stump up the fees," Alan says.

"Could you sound any more stereotypically Scottish?" Betty says. "So rude! Sorry."

"This is Emma we're talking about," Robert says. "The money's already put aside. She'd saved for her first car by the time she was fourteen, doing paper rounds and Saturday jobs, remember." He finishes with a laugh and it niggles me, as if wanting a better life made me some kind of prude.

"Must be nice to have a wife who saves." Julian leans forward and refills his wineglass. "But then it must be nice to have a wife who earns. How lucky you are, Robert." He lifts his glass. "To Emma."

Michelle looks slapped and for a split second there's real hurt in her eyes before she composes herself again. "Thank you so much, darling." Her voice is brittle ice. "That's reminded me to buy some new shoes on Monday."

"Michelle works hard," I say. "Same as Robert. I bet your hours aren't any shorter than mine and there's no way I could do such long days if Robert had a proper job." Only as I finish the sentence do I realize that now it's Robert who looks appalled.

"Actually, Em—"

A shriek cuts through all conversation and I'm on my feet in a split second, heart racing. *That's my child.* A mother knows. The trampoline.

"He was supposed to be jumping! But he wouldn't!" Ben has his hands on his hips, standing on the trampoline. Will is sitting on the grass, crying. "I was trying to help!"

"Did you push him?" There's a safety net around the trampoline, but it's baggy and needs replacing. "Did you?" I glare at him and then quickly check Will over. No blood. Nothing broken. His tears are slowing down and I'm relieved that he's not hurt, just shocked. I turn my attention back to Ben as the other kids shrink back quietly.

"Get down here and apologize! That could have been nasty. What you did was mean."

"It was a bloody accident." Michelle is suddenly between me and her eldest son. "And don't shout at my child." She's swaying a little. We stare at each other, both holding back, both knowing how close we are to saying things we won't be able to take back and will probably—definitely—regret. She's drunk and I'm tired. It's time to go home.

7

"She's a bitch." Chloe is more irate about Michelle telling me off than I am.

"Oh, I'd have been the same if she'd shouted at Will." I'm in the back seat with Will, who's quiet but okay as he stares out the window, and with my daughter driving it's like we're in some kind of weird role reversal. "And you shouldn't call her a bitch. What happened to the sisterhood?"

"The sisterhood is about allowing women to be whatever they choose to be. She chooses to be a bitch." She looks at me in the rearview mirror. "It's also about sticking up for your mother."

She smashed her head into the mirror in her room.

"Hey look." Chloe sits up straighter as she turns the

car into the avenue, her voice excited. "Is that— Oh holy shit, is it Auntie Phoebe? On our doorstep?"

Oh god. Everyone turns, and even Will twists in his booster seat. There she is. Phoebe, standing, uptight, in the doorway. Our eyes meet and I think I see something there. A glint of vicious pleasure at my discomfort? Whatever it is, it's momentary, and then she's grinning and holding out her arms as if her visit is the best thing ever.

My heart is in my mouth as I watch my daughter rush to her, shrieking with excitement, while Will, at least still holding my hand, looks on shyly.

"Come here, Will," Chloe calls back. "It's Auntie Phoebe!" He lets go of my hand and before he can say no, Phoebe's swept him up into her arms and is planting a big kiss on his cheek. She can turn on the warmth when she wants to. Will hasn't seen her since he was three, so he doesn't remember her, and yet still he looks completely at ease, giggling in her arms as she blows a raspberry on his cheek. I feel betrayed.

"This is a nice surprise," Robert, looking equally as shocked as me, kisses her on the cheek.

"I was in the area, so I thought I'd drop by."

"You should have called," I say. "But then you rarely do." I smile as if it's a joke.

"Are you going to invite me in?"

What is she playing at? Why is she here?

"Of course." Robert swings the door open and Phoebe leads the way. She's wearing a T-shirt minidress over leggings and maybe she kept up the yoga after her birthday, because I have to admit she's looking really toned.

"Is that tie-dye, Auntie Phebes? So retro cool."

"The dress? Yes. You can have it if you like. I'll drop it in."

I wonder why she's suddenly dressing like this, like the art student she once was. She's not young or free. Neither of us is. She sells houses on the Costa Brava. She's probably got a wardrobe full of suits not dissimilar to mine, just cheaper. Why this pretense? Who's she trying to impress? Me? The kids? Robert?

"Are you back for a while then?" Chloe says. "We haven't seen you in *ages*! Please say you are. Isn't it great, Mum?" She looks at me as we reach the kitchen, Robert already getting wineglasses out and a bottle from the fridge.

"Sure is." I look at Robert. "I'll have a tea. I'll make it. I should get Will to bed too. Come on, monkey. You can see Auntie Phoebe another time." Will stays wrapped around my sister's leg, peering out at me from behind.

"Shall I take you?" Phoebe says, and Will nods, happy. "Okay then, let's go. Are you too big for a story these days?"

"Paddington!"

"Paddington it is, then." She scoops up my son again—she's definitely been working on her strength because he's not so little anymore—and then heads out to the hallway. "I'll be back for that wine though." Her eyes meet mine. "And a sisterly catch-up."

"I'll come and help. I want to hear about Spain," Chloe says. "Are you staying for Mum's birthday?"

"Oh, I wouldn't miss it for the world," I hear Phoebe answer as they disappear off, leaving Robert and me alone. For a moment there's a strange awkward silence and then he breaks it.

"She's looking good," he says as he fills the kettle. "Did you know she was back?"

"When does Phoebe ever tell me what she's doing?" I avoid an outright lie and rummage in the fridge for milk.

"I'm going to watch the game on catch-up. Leave you two to it." He picks up his wineglass and then pauses. "You don't seem overly happy to see her."

"Just tired. I wanted an early night." I try to smile reassuringly.

"She won't stay long," he says. "She never does."

We're in the main living room which we rarely use, but it's far away from Robert's den. Chloe's upstairs and

Will was apparently asleep before Phoebe had finished the story.

"The family seems well," Phoebe says after we've glared at each other in silence for a moment or two. "Chloe's so grown up."

"Why are you *here*, Phebes? And why didn't you text first to say you wanted to come over?" I'm too tired for games.

"You wouldn't have wanted me to come. And I had a sudden urge to see your children. Thought we didn't leave things too well yesterday."

To be fair, she's right. We didn't. But I don't really want her here either. Not with this other situation—*her*—hanging over our heads.

"All this business with our mother has made me think about family," she continues. "The past. Times gone by. How it might be nice to reconnect while I'm here." We sit in silence for a moment, all pent-up mutual annoyance.

"There's no change, by the way, in case you were wondering," she says.

"I wasn't."

"Of course you weren't." She looks at me with thinly veiled disgust. "Why would you give anyone else any consideration?"

"It's not anyone else, it's our mother. And I don't want to think about her now. Not this week."

"Ah, your fortieth birthday." She smiles then, a small, tight expression. "I knew that was bothering you. Makes you think of her birthday and the things she used to say to you, I suppose."

"You *suppose*?" Wow. What else does she think I'm thinking about? "And bothering is one way of putting it."

"But it's nothing real," she says. "Just in your head. Whereas our mother dying is actually bothering me. No, that's not quite right. It's upsetting me, which I know you'll find hard to believe, and I thought we could—"

"I told you I don't want to talk about her," I snap.

"Everything's always about you, isn't it? Heaven forbid we upset baby Emma." She gets up, her smile gone, and pulls out her phone. "I'll get a cab. I can see *I'm* bothering you by being here. Can't have me littering your perfect life with all our past."

"How am I suddenly the bad guy?" What gives her the right to come to my house and attack me? And what the hell does she know about my life? Apart from a year or so sharing a flat when I was at uni, we've barely spent any time together at all.

"Why does there have to be a bad guy?" she asks, hard nails tapping into some taxi app. "I was trying to connect with you because our mother—for all her problems—is in the hospital. Maybe dying. And maybe, just maybe, it might do us—do *you*—some good to confront that."

"I understand the past," I hiss back quietly, even though there's no chance Robert can hear me. "I don't need to revisit it. And that doesn't make me a bad person. And you think you know everything about—"

"Oh, come on," she cuts in, tone like acid. "Everything worked out fine for you, didn't it? After everything? Nice foster family, of course *everyone* wanted to foster little Emma—"

"That's not true—" I want to point out that one family pulling out at the last minute and then one family stepping in is hardly *everyone*, but she's in full flow and talks right over me.

"And so off you went to university and got your law degree and—thanks to me—met your wonderful, handsome husband and had your wonderful beautiful children, and now live in your *so* sterile but expensive house with everything planned and mapped out for the rest of your perfect life and you *still* don't even have the good grace to look happy about it or acknowledge that maybe I had something to do with it all."

She places her wineglass down carefully on the table, so carefully it's almost as if she really wants to smash it.

Crack. Crack. Crack. The ghost in my head whispers a memory and I shake it away.

"You never wanted a life like this," I snap. "A family. Children." I refuse to let her make me feel guilty. It's not my fault we had different foster experiences. And I've worked *hard* for this life.

"You don't know what I want," she says, her turn to be cold. "You never have."

Her phone beeps and she moves past me, now eager to be gone. Her taxi's here.

"Phoebe," I say, and she stops.

"What?"

"They don't know about *her*. You know that. I want it to stay that way."

"You thought I was here to tell them?" Her expression is unreadable. "It never crossed my mind." She laughs, hollow. "No wonder you're so obviously worried about turning out like Mum. Nothing paranoid about you, Emma," she says, her words dripping with sarcasm. "Nothing at all."

I don't think she even says goodbye to Robert, and within seconds it's as if she hasn't been here. Unreadable Phoebe. A ghost. She's my big sister and I love her, but I wish we could like each other more.

8

How can I still be awake?

I fill the kettle and lean against the kitchen counter, my forehead throbbing with tension and tiredness. Sleep is never normally a problem for me. I go out like a light. I've checked the children. There's nothing wrong in the house. What does that leave? Something wrong with me? *No wonder you worry about turning out like Mum. Nothing paranoid about you, Emma. Nothing at all.*

How long before that night, her fortieth birthday, did my mother stop sleeping?

I stare through the windows, but in the glare all I see is my own taut face staring back, another me, trapped outside in my reflection. It makes me shiver and I realize that anyone could be out there watching me. I flick the lights off as the kettle starts to bubble and after a moment of blackness my eyes adjust and moonlight casts jagged streaks on the kitchen tiles, the grainy white light fractured on heavy branches outside.

I go up close to the window again and peer out into the garden. This time it's a vista of black and gray monstrous shadows that fade into the ocean of night on the horizon. My eyes narrow. Is that—was that—a spot of yellow light? I blink and it's gone. If it was ever there at all. My heart beats a little faster. Is there someone outside? Is it Phoebe? Why would Phoebe be in my garden in the middle of the night? Or is it just a figment of my tired imagination? I blink. Nothing. There's nothing out there. I let out the breath I've been holding, and then look at the back door.

Our mother wasn't always mad.

I go to the door and grip the handle, turning it up and down. It's locked. I double-check. Still locked. The oven clock ticks over to 1:13.

No, our mother wasn't always mad. That's what Phoebe used to tell me anyway. She was weird, maybe. Mad, no.

The kettle clicks off behind me. Tea. That will

make me feel better. Something normal. Tea makes everything better, that's what they say, whoever *they* are. I'm unsettled after Phoebe's visit, that's what it is.

"Good luck with her!" That's what Phoebe shouted all those years ago when the Thompsons came to foster me. *"She's crazy! That's what our mum used to say! Emma's going to go crazy too! She's got the bad blood like me and your great-auntie Joanie!"* She was right. Our mum did used to say that.

I used to try really hard to remember our mother normal, but I could only ever remember her mad.

As I open the fridge to get the milk, the first thing I see is a tray of eggs on the shelf right in front of me and not tucked away on the side where they should be. *Crack. Crack. Crack.* The memory comes fast: the stench of rotten eggs, her bony fingers digging into my arms, her face lunging down from high above, warm, stale spit hitting my face as she hisses, *"I just want to slee—"* I slam the door shut. I don't need milk. I'll have chamomile.

I wish I could remember her not mad. I wish she'd always been mad. I'm not sure which of these would be better. The two thoughts rub friction between them. Cognitive dissonance. Why is the past always so much more alive at night? Ghosts, spirits, ghouls. Memories.

In the hallway, Chloe's jacket has slipped from the banister and is sprawled, an emptied torso skin, on the wooden floor. I crouch to pick it up, and as various lipsticks and coins and teenage junk fall out of the inside pocket, I put my mug down to gather it all back up.

When did she go mad? Why?

The last item returned, I'm about to get up when I realize I'm level with the under stairs cupboard. The air feels colder and the door seems huge from this position. A child's-eye view. I can see every brushstroke of paint on the grain of the wood underneath. My heart thumps as memory grips me again.

I want to open the door. I don't want to open the door.

How long before that night did she stop sleeping?

I stare at the door and almost through it to the void beyond. Why would she say I'd go mad? Because she was mad. It's a mad thing to say. I almost laugh at that. I sound like a Dr. Seuss cartoon. But still, I stare at the door some more. It's all I can see, as if it's the whole world, the whole universe, and nothing else exists. God, I'm tired.

My foot suddenly cramps and I stand up, gasping slightly with the pain. Once the initial stabbing feeling has stopped, I hang Chloe's coat up and sip my herbal tea. I instantly recoil, confused. The drink is cold and filmy. That can't be right. The kettle boiled. I remember it. Pins and needles creep up my numbing legs as the cramp fades. I look back down at the cupboard door as the only other alternative hits me. The drink cooled while I was staring at the door. I thought it'd only been minutes.

But how long was I *really* crouched there?

9

NINE DAYS UNTIL MY BIRTHDAY

I'm on my third cup of coffee and a mixture of jittery energy and abject exhaustion, so I'm not sure if I'm seeing my family through a filter of my own mood or whether they're all as grumpy as me this morning.

Chloe came downstairs for the whole of five minutes before a text pinged, causing her to storm back upstairs again, trouble in the paradise of her youth, and Will is at the kitchen table drawing in his book, intense and quiet, after a very lackluster morning cuddle. He's curled over his picture and won't let me see it.

"You okay, monkey?" He doesn't look up. Something's definitely off. "Did Ben scare you yesterday?" Have there been more incidents like that with Ben at school maybe? Pushing a little kid off a trampoline is pretty extreme behavior. What if it's only one link in a long chain of bullying?

"Don't put thoughts into his head." Robert comes in from the garden and puts his toast plate and dirty mug on the side. "He's probably forgotten about it." He's still in his dressing gown and mussy from a good night's sleep. Right now I could divorce him out of sheer envy. After my cold chamomile tea, I'd gone back to bed but I still couldn't drop off, not until the birds started singing when I dozed for an hour or so. All the while he was blissfully kitten-snoring next to me. Oblivious.

I'm not going to go on like this. I need some kind of sleeping tablets. There's a pharmacy at Asda. They must sell NightNight.

"Do we need anything from the supermarket? I've got to get a cake for work. Jade's birthday." Jade is one of my trainees, a sweet girl who's worked hard against the odds of her background to get to where she is, and if I was going to believably buy a cake myself rather than ask Rosemary to pop out and do it, it would be for her.

"Oh, brilliant." Robert rummages around on the counter behind the kettle, a space jammed full of receipts and notes and other bits of paper. He hands me the list. "I was going to go later, but if you're happy to do it then . . ."

"You're kidding me." I stare at the paper, instantly annoyed. This is not a couple of things. This is half of a weekly shop and pretty much everything that's needed for Will's lunches next week.

"Don't start, Emma. It's Sunday, just chill."

"How am I starting?" I ask, clearly now starting, but what does he really expect? I let him off so many times and as much as I'm grateful that he was up for taking on the stay-at-home role, I find I still end up doing so much of it. "I didn't say anything."

"You're saying something now." He refills his coffee. Has a couple ever murdered each other from caffeine overload? "I'm not a bloody housewife," he says. "Stuff came up on Friday. And I would have gone later but you volunteered." He opens the fridge door and I try not to think about eggs.

"You could have gone after dropping Will at school. Asda's on the way home."

"Don't talk to me as if I'm a child. I'm a grown man. I lost track of time and I forgot. It's not the end of the bloody world. And if you think my life is going to be cooking and cleaning and homework then you should know that's not what I want. Will's at school now. I've been thinking about working full-time. Getting a career of my own."

"Is this about what I said yesterday at the barbecue? I was trying to support your friend, not having a go."

"*Our* friend, Emma. Michelle's our friend."

Will looks up from his drawing, dark eyes studying us both. Our conversation is innocuous but we sound like we're itching to row. "Let's talk about it later," I say grabbing the car keys.

"It can't be about you forever," Robert says quietly, and there's almost a growl of menace there. "I need a life too."

I'm in a haze as I go round the supermarket, which is surprisingly busy given that it's only been open ten minutes, but I get some One-A-Night Night-Night from the pharmacist—*yes, they are for me; no, I'm not pregnant; just hand them over*—and then work my way through the rest of Robert's list. It's only my irritation and upset that's keeping me going. I don't think Robert realizes how hard I work to keep our life on track. Yes, I love my job, but the pressures of being a mother *and* the breadwinner can get on top of me, and now he's resenting me for that too. I feel like I can't win. I'm on automatic pilot as I fill the bags and pay and then I'm wheeling it all back to the car.

The sun is bright and directly in my sightline, blinding me, and I hear, "*Out of the way you stupid bitch!*" and then an empty cart is bashing into mine, hard, as if intentional. No one's holding it and, startled, I look up to see three young men, *youths*, the news would call them, in baseball caps and hoodies, laughing unpleasantly as they come toward me. Two still have carts and they launch them my way, laughing as they do so.

"Grow up." I push the shopping carts out of the way. The boys are only about fifteen and although my heart has sped up a little, I refuse to be intimidated by kids in broad daylight. My car is a few feet away, and I don't stop moving as they circle me.

"Keep your granny pants on, just having a laugh."

"Boo!" I didn't know there was another boy behind me and this time I do jump, his breath stale warm tobacco on my neck.

I spin around. "Just piss off!" I snap. He's tall, maybe slightly older than the others, and he backs away a few steps, grabbing at his crotch, laughing at me. "Dried up old cow."

I'm so tired and irritable my fists clench and I want to launch myself at him, but then the others join him and, whooping, they head off at a half-run, the carts abandoned, toward the McDonald's next to the petrol station past the car park. I take a couple of deep breaths, watching them go, and then turn back to my cart. Dickheads. My boy won't grow up to be like that. Not in a million years.

I throw the shopping onto the back seat, before getting in and closing the door, exhausted again. I feel awful. How do people go without sleep? How long until bedtime? Too long.

It's a warm day and with the teenagers off to harangue the poor burger servers, the heat through the windshield is relaxing. It's eleven thirty. I actually did the shopping pretty fast. There's nothing for the freezer in the bags. Maybe I'll sit here for ten minutes or so. Close my eyes. Kill this first hint of a headache before it really starts. Some me time before family takes over again. I need it. I open the windows a crack for the warm breeze and lean back against the headrest. That feels good. Ten minutes. That's all.

I startle awake—*who am I, where am I*—as a screaming baby in a cart goes past, and my head throbs and I'm thirsty. It's hot in here. Did I fall asleep? I wipe drying dribble from my chin and look at my watch, expecting only a few minutes to have passed, but it's twelve fifteen. Forty-five minutes. Bloody hell.

I straighten up in my seat and smooth the back of my hair, my ponytail mussed up with static, and try to shake myself awake. In the side door I find a half-drunk bottle of water and although it tastes of warm plastic, I sip some and it brightens me. Forty-five minutes of rest is like a gift from god, and the sleep must have been deep because it felt like only a moment. I've got half a chance of getting through the day with my marriage intact now. I feel almost human.

"**Where's the** cake?"

"What cake?" We're putting the shopping away and I have no idea what Robert's talking about. He must have felt guilty about our row because he's been to the dump with the cardboard box collection in the garage while I've been out.

"*The* cake. For Jade? The reason you went out in the first place."

"Oh god." Lies breed lies. The reason I went out—the NightNight—is hidden away in my handbag like a lover's letter, and my face must have fallen at being caught out in my little white lie because Robert smiles.

"Don't worry, I'll go back and grab one. I should have gone anyway. It was my job. I'll take Will for the ride. We can stop at the play park for a bit too." He wraps his arm around my neck and kisses my forehead. "We do need to talk about me working though, Em. It's my turn now, surely?"

Stray hairs of my ponytail are caught tight under his arm, so rather than leaning into his chest willingly, I feel trapped there. *His turn.* That sounds more serious than just getting something part-time. I don't want a nanny or for Will to be trapped in afterschool clubs every day, but I can't work shorter days. What he if expects me to step down from my job? There's no way he could ever cover our monthly expenses and there's no way I'm giving up my career. I'm catastrophizing, I know, but with the way he's been recently, I can't help but wonder if this is part of something bigger.

"I get that you're not happy," I say. "And sorry if I was snappy." All I want to do is find a a show to binge-watch on TV and sink into the sofa. "We can talk about it later." I take a breath and reset. He may *want* to work but he's not likely to go into something at an executive level and starting at the bottom at forty will put him off, so why argue about something that probably won't happen?

10

I'm an episode into some tacky but fun thriller and sunk into the sofa with a cup of tea when the doorbell rings. I almost shout up to Chloe to get it, but she'll have her headphones in no doubt, blocking the world of her family life out of her teenage one. If it's the Jehovah's Witnesses again, the language they're about to hear is not going to be very godly.

In fact, it's a woman about my age, maybe a couple of years older, long hair efficiently back in a ponytail, in a nurse's uniform, looking awkward and as tired as I feel. "Um, are you Emma Averell?" she asks. Her badge reads "Caroline."

"Yes?" Is she a nurse from the hospital? Or the Unit? Is she here about *her*? How the hell would she get my address?

"I found this," she says. "At the big Asda? In the car park?" She holds up a wallet. *My* wallet. "By McDonald's? I was going to hand it in, but your driver's license had your address on it and I had to come past this way so . . ." She shrugs, almost apologetically, and my brain finally kicks into gear.

"Oh god, thank you so much." *Those bloody kids.* I take it from her and immediately look inside to check my cards. I glance up. "There was forty pounds in here." My irritation seethes. *Those bloody kids indeed.*

"I didn't take it." Her tone hardens slightly. "Nursing may not pay much, but we don't tend to top it up by stealing."

Robert pulls into the drive and I see this woman—Caroline—looking at his car and then mine and our house and I must seem like such a snooty cow.

"Oh, I wasn't suggesting—" My face burns with embarrassment. A stranger brings my wallet back and I'm basically saying to her face that she's stolen something. "There were these teenagers and—I meant *they* must have taken it. My bag was in my cart and they distracted me. Honestly, I—"

"It's fine," she says. "I understand. Anyway, I should go."

"Let me get you something. As a thank you—I've got some money inside. For your trouble." *For your trouble.* I sound like a granny. But I don't want her to go away thinking I'm awful.

"It's fine. I was coming this way anyway," she says. She turns quickly, almost colliding with a smiling Robert carrying a cake I don't need, before apologizing and walking away, *hurrying* away, probably wondering why she even bothered.

"Thank you so much!" I call after her and she half-raises a hand as she rounds the corner, but in her head I bet she's calling me all sorts of names. Still, I think, as I follow Robert and Will inside and close the door, at least I got my wallet back.

The day passes as Sundays tend to, in a drift of active inactivity, Robert watching TV while I got out the pruning shears and clipped back the overgrown roses at the front, and by early evening the catnap I had in the car won't sustain me anymore and I claim a headache—only a half lie because there's definitely one brewing—and go upstairs for a lie-down. I take the pile of clean towels in the utility room with me—another job Robert hasn't done for days—and go to one of the spare room cupboards and stack them with the rest. The room's stuffy, even though dusk is falling, so I open a window. My breath catches.

Phoebe is standing in the driveway near my car,

staring at the house. At her sides her fists are clenched. Her hair is blocking her face, but the way she's standing, so still and taut, disturbs me. After a long moment, she turns and strides away. I could call out the window to stop her but I don't. She'd come back and what then? One of my own hands automatically makes a fist. *How did we come to this, my big sister and I?*

11

So much for NightNight.

I check the back door handle, rattling it once again to make sure it's locked. I've checked the children, both sleeping. Robert, *of course*, sleeping. The spare room's empty. Only me awake.

My reflection glares at me from the window, my face half-obscured by my long hair. I look tired. Desperate. I was determined to leave the lights on this time, to fight the ridiculous feeling that someone is watching me—*who would be out in the garden at one in the morning?*—but I can't, and I rush to the light switch and turn it off, squeezing my eyes tight against the suffocating darkness until it fades.

Suffocating.

I go back to the window, my reflection there now

barely a ghost, and peer out. I can't see any lights outside and the clouds are thick and low-lying, making the
night a mystery. There is no one there, I tell myself,
as my brain simultaneously whispers that there could
be anyone there. Although probably not Phoebe. She
wouldn't even come to the front door. What was she
doing here earlier? Was she trying to say she was sorry
but couldn't bring herself to? It didn't look that way.
But maybe. Maybe that's why I can't sleep.

Why didn't the NightNight work? Why can't I
sleep?

Very nearly forty. How long *before* did she stop
sleeping?

I put the kettle on and make a chamomile tea. Maybe
I should put vodka in it, like Michelle suggested. I stare
at the booze cupboard for a moment too long, more
tempted than I should be, before turning away.

She drank when she didn't sleep.

The kettle clicks off and I pour and then glance at
the back door once more as the tea steeps. It is locked,
isn't it? Yes. Yes. I check again. This is ridiculous. This
is—I stop myself before the word *crazy*. This is not
crazy. This is a blip. Too much on my mind. Maybe it's
even hormonal. The start of the run-up to *the change*.
I roll my head around on my shoulders and then sip the

hot drink. I look at the clock. Five past two. Creeping closer to Monday morning already.

In the hallway, I pause again by the under-stairs cupboard and crouch, staring at the door. *Here there be tygers,* I think, although I'm not even sure what that means. I put the mug—still hot against my palm—down, unlock the bolt, and open the door.

Nothing. Just the usual junk. Wellies. A couple of old golf clubs that Robert borrowed from someone and never gave back. Henry hoover shoved in at an awkward angle. I reach in and tidy him away, but then the space I've created makes me uncomfortable. It looks like a void that could suck you in and never let you go. It looks like *that* cupboard. I go to close the door but pause and my fingers run lightly down the wood on the inside. Rough but undamaged. Nothing scratched into it. A relief.

This is not then. I am not her.

It's a second relief that when I stand up my drink is still hot. I haven't crouched there forever this time. I go to my study and close the blinds—*nothing to see here*—before putting the desk light on. I quickly type Phoebe a text saying sorry for our harsh words and press send on the olive branch before I can change my mind, then open my bag and get out my notes, my laptop, and my Dictaphone. I've got some letters that need sending out, so I may as well dictate them now and get ahead of myself for tomorrow.

Work is my anchor and within half an hour I'm much calmer, all thoughts of *her* if not entirely out of mind, then pushed back into a dusty corner. I lose myself in the minutiae of case notes and then quietly dictate the letters I need Rosemary to send. When I'm done, it's nearly four and my eyes are burning. I was sure it was only three a few moments ago. Time flies when you're ending marriages.

I wash my mug and check that I've left everything as it was when we went to bed—*no one needs to know*—and then head quietly upstairs as the birds start singing in the nearly dawn blue sky. I slide in quietly next to Robert and pray for at least an hour's rest. I close my eyes and sink into oblivion.

12

EIGHT DAYS UNTIL MY BIRTHDAY

I spot the flat tire as I open the driver's door, no longer obscured by overgrowing roses. Robert's not best pleased about coming outside at six to help fit the inflatable spare, but he does, and I watch and pretend to be learning how to do it myself, although I know that everything mechanical-related will forever leave me baffled and a disgrace to the feminist cause.

"Someone's done that on purpose," he says. "Look." I see the cut. He's right. It's too clean.

"But why? Who would do that?"

"I bet it's those kids always hanging around at the cricket pitch. Michelle says most of them have antisocial behavior orders. At least it went flat while you were here. No real harm done."

No real harm done. He's not the one who was going to be driving it. "I thought you were going to sort security cameras for outside the house?"

"I will." He dusts down his hands. "I just haven't got around to it."

"Like everything else," I mutter before I can stop myself. It seems this Monday is not getting off to the best start in our domestic world. *Thank god for work,* I think as I get in the car, neither of us giving the other more than a cursory goodbye. *Thank god for that.*

As I drive, taking it slowly, I wonder if the kids from the supermarket could have done it. When I slept in the car? Or in the night. My address was in my wallet. Did they come back and want to screw me over one more time? That in turn makes me think of the nurse who brought my wallet back. Her face keeps coming back to me. She looked as tired and fed up as I do. A kindred spirit. Maybe lonely too. I cringe at the memory of how rude I was to her. That's probably the last good deed she'll do for a while.

The road bumps a little under the inflatable and I slow down even more, my thoughts once again on the vandalized tire. Another thought strikes me. Could it have been Miranda Stockwell? I'm pretty sure she scratched my car and left the note under the windshield. Does she know where I live? She isn't stable, that's clear in all the incidents Parker logged and we presented in court. Hundreds of phone calls, abusive messages, telling the police her children had been abducted, breaking into her husband's house and wrecking it. Has she turned her anger on me now? How far is she capable of going? I need to find out.

Alison is already in, her door left open to make sure I can see she's working, but I smile and say good morning as I pass and then put my Dictaphone on Rosemary's desk, and leave a note for her to call someone to come and put a new tire on my car, before grabbing a coffee. I leave the cake in the kitchen with a note for people to help themselves, and then go into my office and slump into my chair, wishing every bone in my body didn't ache so much.

Resigned, I do what needs to be done and call Parker Stockwell. It's only seven thirty, but I know his routines. Up at four thirty latest, as a mark of honor, then straight into the gym, and then working by seven. So he was probably waking up when I was crawling, exhausted, into bed for my pitiful hour.

"Emma, hello. This is a pleasant way to start a Monday." He's smooth in my ear.

"I just wanted to say thank you for the flowers. You shouldn't have, but thank you, they're beautiful."

"Beautiful flowers for a beautiful woman."

Did he really say that? So gross. And then I realize how this must seem to him. That I've been waiting to call him all weekend because I didn't want to in front of my husband.

"I was wondering, have you had any problems with Miranda?" I ask. "Any kind of comeback since the court's decision?"

"Miranda? No. She's gone to her parents in London. I'm pretty sure they came up and got her on Saturday. That's what the boys told me she said. Some time with her family might make her get help."

"Good. That's good." It *is* good. If she was out of Leeds on Saturday then she wasn't slashing my tire on Sunday night. Maybe it *was* those supermarket kids. "If anything does happen, then report it to the police rather than reacting. That's what she'll be looking for."

"It's very sweet to hear you looking out for me still. Look, about that dinner—"

"I have to go, sorry, Parker. I've got a call coming in that I need to take." As it is, my phone *does* ping, and however great it may be proving for my pelvic floor, I really don't want to prolong this conversation now that

I have the information I need. I've already given him the wrong impression.

I hang up and check my mobile. A text from Phoebe. An essay. *"Sorry I didn't answer, I was asleep. Sorry I got pissy too—we're both stressed. Also, were you up early or late??? I know you say you don't care but Mum is apparently slightly worse this morning. I'm going to the hospital for a bit. Sorry I didn't tell you I was back."*

Were you up early or late??? I stare at those question marks. The weight of them. I can read the subtext. She doesn't mention being outside the house last night, but judging from the content of this text maybe she was going to apologize. Who knows with Phoebe? Still, it's good we're not fighting. For today at least.

By lunchtime, between coffee, tiredness, and the stink of the roses, mild nausea has morphed into a headache and I really need some fresh air. I open the window, drinking in the first few gasps of almost-fresh city air, and lean out as far as the glass will let me. I feel better almost instantly and rest against the frame, enjoying the moment, looking down at the passing world. I pause and frown.

I don't even know why the figure standing just inside the alleyway opposite catches my eye, but she does. Maybe it's the stillness of her as others go by. Is she waiting for someone? Such an odd place to meet when around the corner are several cafés and bars. The alleyway isn't exactly classy. She's an older woman, with steel gray hair, in a checkered coat, perhaps too funky for a woman of her age, her face half-covered by enormous sunglasses. She's looking up at the building. As my eyes meet her glasses, she takes a quick step back into the shadows. As if she doesn't want to be seen.

Was she watching me? Or just embarrassed?

I make a big deal of looking the other way and then she darts out of the alleyway and hurries along the road. She doesn't look back. I stare after her.

"A friend of yours is here. Michelle? Wonders if you've got ten minutes." I spin around to see Rosemary at my office door. "I did say it was your lunch hour. Oh, and the garage will be bringing your car back by two."

Michelle's here? What could she want? I'm surprised she knows what company I work for, let alone where to find it. I glance back out the window, but there's no sign of the old lady. Of course she wasn't watching me. It's a ridiculous thought. It does prompt another thought though. Someone else I've seen from a window. Phoebe standing out in the drive yesterday evening. Could she have slashed my tire? Her clenched fist. Her quiet anger. Would she go that far? No, I tell myself. It was the kids.

It had to be them. I close the window, push the negative thoughts out of my head, and tell Rosemary to bring Michelle in.

"What we talk about here is confidential, right, Emma? You can't tell anyone?"

It's strange to have her here, in my domain, but she takes a seat, limited pleasantries done, no coffee required, and looks around. She's fully made up of course, but her skin looks dry and her eyes slightly bloodshot. Maybe she's not sleeping either.

"Yes, that's right. We'll call this a free consultation. It's confidential."

She nods and then fires me a sharp glance before speaking. "I want to know where I stand if Julian and I were to get a divorce."

I'm a bit stunned. There was some tension between them at the barbecue but nothing that would have hinted at this.

"And I haven't mentioned this to any of our friends— including Robert—so please don't."

"Of course." I'm not quite sure what to say. It's not as if we're close. "Are you okay?"

She stares at me, a brittle hardness in her expression. "Julian's having an affair. I'm pretty sure of it. Has been for a while, I suspect. Works late. Stays away more."

"He's probably busy. He always has a lot on, doesn't he? So many projects to manage." I'm trying to soothe her, but experience has taught me that a woman's gut instinct is normally bang on about these things. It's also true, however, that a fling doesn't always have to mean the end of a marriage. "Have you talked to him about what you're thinking?"

"He said I was being stupid. But he's hardly going to just come straight out and tell me, is he?" She looks at me, defiant. "He's played away before, when we were younger. Occasional one-night stands at work events, but nothing that mattered. To him anyway. And although of course they mattered to me, I could always see he regretted it. His remorse. This one is different. He's distant. I irritate him. He hides his phone. It's all so fucking cliché."

I leave a long pause.

"Do you know who the woman is?"

She looks around the room again. "Roses. They don't strike me as a very Robert gift."

It's strange how well this woman knows my husband. "You're right. They're not from Robert. A client." I say it dismissively, embarrassed, although I have no reason to be. Maybe because even though she's come here for my help, she's being so snippy.

"An admirer. Clever Emma." She smirks. "*A toast to Emma.*"

I'm so tired it takes a moment for her meaning to sink in, and when it does, I'm almost too shocked to speak. "Me? You think it's me?"

"You both work late all the time. Neither of you is that interested in sex . . ."—*Oh, okay Robert, that's one for us to talk about,* I think as she powers on—"and before he turned his Find my iPhone off he was always parked around here when he was telling me he was still at work."

"It's the center of town, Michelle! He could have been seeing anyone. It could even have been work meetings. But whatever he was doing, he wasn't doing me. And since it's something you and Robert have clearly talked about, we have less sex because we've got a small child and I've got a job that makes me work twelve hours a day, and then I still have to supervise stuff at home because men are generally shit at clothes and homework and paying attention to the details, and so basically I'm bloody knackered all the time. And for the record, he's not exactly trying to jump me every night either."

She doesn't look convinced, but at least there's a hint of doubt in her expression. "So why is Julian always singing your praises?"

"I don't know. But honest to god, Michelle, I don't have the energy to shag my own husband, I'm certainly not making time to shag yours."

The fight goes out of both of us, and she's on the verge of tears. "Look," I say. "Maybe he's got work worries or money worries you don't know about. Or he could be having a mid-life crisis. You *have* to get him to talk. I can recommend a lot of great marriage therapists and counselors."

"He'd never see one of those."

"You'd be surprised how many times I've heard that before, and then people have changed their minds." I glance at the clock. "I'm really sorry, but I've got a client call to do and then a conference. But what you've said is absolutely confidential, and if you need to come back and discuss your options, then do. Okay?"

"Thank you." She gets up. She's still prickly and I'm not sure she's entirely let go of her suspicions, or maybe, and more likely, she's embarrassed she's raised them with me.

"Oh, and I'm sorry," I add, as she reaches the door. "About the weekend. Snapping at Ben. I get so little time with Will, I get protective."

She goes without saying anything more, and I'm irritated that I tried to smooth things over. She could at least have apologized in return for snapping back.

"Emma?" Rosemary comes in. "There's some potential client call backs for you." She puts four phone notes on my desk, and then lingers, hesitant.

"Anything else?" I ask.

"Yes. It's . . . I'm having a problem with the letters you wanted doing. I'm not sure . . . well, it's a bit odd."

I frown. "Which one?"

She closes the door behind her. "All of them."

"I don't understand." What's she talking about? "There should be three on the tape. For the Marshall, Smith, and Michaels cases? I dictated them last night."

She doesn't move for a moment and I've never seen her look so uncomfortable. Eventually she says, "Something must have gone wrong," before handing me the Dictaphone as if it were made of hot coals, and confused, I press play. There's a moment of static and then a harsh, urgent whispering fills the quiet room. Rapid and angry.

". . . *two hundred and twenty-two one hundred and thirteen one hundred and fifty-five two hundred and eighteen two hundred and twenty-two one hundred and thirteen one hundred and fifty-five two hundred and eighteen two hundred and twenty-two one hundred and thirteen one hundred and fifty-five two hundred and . . .*"

I almost drop the small machine as I gasp. The

whispering continues and I'm sure the temperature in the room drops slightly with each word.

". . . *eighteen two hundred and twenty-two one hundred and thirteen one hundred and fifty-five two hundred and eighteen two hundred and twenty-two one hundred and thirteen one . . .*"

It's her, is my immediate thought. I'm back in my childhood with my mother pacing and muttering, the sequence of numbers an agitated harshly whispered mantra spewing from her mouth. It takes almost thirty seconds before the awful truth dawns on me.

It's not her. It's *me.* Barely recognizable, but me.

I click the Dictaphone off and tighten my fingers to stop the shaking in my hands showing. How can that be me? I don't remember that. It was *letters.* I dictated letters. Not that. Not *her* numbers.

"It's the same all the way through," Rosemary says, nervous. "An hour of it."

I force a laugh. *Her numbers from my mouth.* "Oh, I think I know what's happened." My throat is so dry I think I'm going to be sick. "It's a meditation trick. I was doing it last night to get to sleep and I must have accidentally recorded over the letters."

Did I even dictate the letters at all? Did I just think I did? How can I not know?

"Oh, that's all right then." Despite the several

massive holes in my story—why would I have my Dictaphone near me when I was trying to get to sleep for one—Rosemary smiles with relief. "But how annoying."

"I'll get them done again before Mr. Wither's conference this afternoon. Okay?" My grin is fixed, rictuslike, on my face.

"I'll bring you in some biscuits and a coffee. You missed your lunch."

"Lovely."

I wait until she's left the room and then I retch slightly, my head spinning.

Those are my mother's numbers.

How long before her fortieth birthday did she stop sleeping?

How long before that night did she start going mad?

13

I am not going mad, I tell myself for the thousandth time this afternoon as I get out of the car—new expensive tire attached—and lean on it for a moment before heading inside. I have to think logically. I must have drifted into a half-sleep when I was dictating the letters and started thinking about *her*. That's all. Despite having pushed the joys of therapy onto Michelle in my office, I can't sum up the will to make a call on my own behalf. I just need to sleep. Tonight I'll sleep. Tonight is another night and it's going to be an early one.

"What do you think?"

I'm eating one of the fajitas they've left for me when Chloe appears and does a spin in the doorway. I frown. "Isn't that—"

"Auntie Phoebe's dress. She came around with it earlier. Looks good, doesn't it?"

Whereas my seventeen-year-old daughter wouldn't be seen dead in anything from *my* wardrobe, she's wearing the tie-dye minidress exactly as Phoebe did, over a pair of black leggings. It's almost like Phoebe chose it knowing that Chloe would want it. Gold star brownie points for Auntie Phoebe. She's been here. Again. And once again she didn't let me know.

"You look great."

"I'm going to Amy's. I'm probably going to stay over?"

"Okay. Text when you get there and let me know for definite though." When did things shift from her asking us if she could go out to telling us?

"Cool." She's already racing to the front door, and out to freedom.

"Phoebe came round?" I look over at Robert. It shouldn't unsettle me. Not after our texts today. But why, after last time, didn't she tell me she was coming over?

"Yeah." He's scraped enough leftovers for an extra fajita for himself and takes the seat opposite. "She brought the dress and played with Will for five minutes and that was it. Barely popped in really." There are two mugs upside down on the drainer. She stayed long enough for a cup of tea, which to my mind is slightly more than *barely popped in.*

"There was a situation at school today," he says. "Will wet himself."

"What?" All thought of Phoebe vanishes. "Why? He hasn't done that for ages." Will got dry fast—faster than Chloe and definitely fast for a boy. There haven't even been any accidents since he was about three and a half.

"Not sure. It was at lunchbreak apparently." Robert seems unconcerned as he opens a beer. "He won't answer any questions about it. Phoebe couldn't get anything out of him either."

"I should go and talk to him." A sharp pang of career guilt hits hard. Even my absentee sister was here trying to help my child when I was working.

"He's asleep, Emma. He'll be fine."

"He didn't say anything at all?"

"No, not really. Said he had a fuzzy head but that was it."

"He said that the other night too." All the worst outcomes run through my brain. Those things you never expect to happen to your own child. "Maybe he's sick."

"He said it's gone now." He gives me *that* look, the one he saves for when I'm overthinking and worrying too much. "He's fine. And this stuff happens when kids go to school."

"Speaking of which, what did his teacher say?"

"She's not concerned. She said he was playing with Ben when it happened."

Now it's starting to make sense. My worry is replaced with swift anger, my exhaustion brooking no middle ground. "Ben who pushed him off the trampoline at the weekend?"

"Come on, that was an accident. Ben's okay."

"You don't think it's a bit coincidental? You should speak to the teacher again tomorrow. Make them talk to Ben."

"I know how to do the school stuff, Emma." He's irritated now. "That's what I *do*, remember?"

"Oh, like you're going to complain about your best friend Michelle's kid." I'm still annoyed at him for bitching with her about our sex life and even more annoyed that I can't raise it with him.

"What's the matter with you?" He's on his feet. "I'll speak to the school tomorrow. There's no need to be so shitty with me. And I'll speak to Michelle too, if you want me to."

"I want *you* to want to. I don't know why you're not angry about this."

"I don't know why you're *so* angry about this."

I stare at my unfinished dinner and bite back more argument. I can't be bothered with another spat. "It's been a long day," I say. *My mother's numbers.* "And Will's been off for a couple days and that worries me." Men can be so blinkered, and Robert may well talk to the school about it, but I know him, he'll accept whatever they say as gospel and it will be a case of *boys will be boys.* It will blow over and that will be that. Will's five. Bad things can happen when you're five.

"Don't take it out on me," he says, quietly. "I'm doing my best here." He takes his beer and heads off to his den. His dirty plate sits in front of me and the frying pan is still on the stove. *Are you though?* I find myself thinking. *Are you really?*

I hate messy kitchen sides. I always have. Another echo from her. I grit my teeth and start to clear it all away.

14

Once again, it's night. Once again, I'm still awake. I'm staring into the under-stairs cupboard. *It is not a void. It will not swallow me up.* Dark yes, but just a cupboard. I'm getting pins and needles in my calves from where I'm crouching, looking into it. Henry hoover is there to one side by the golf clubs. Just a cupboard. I close the door and get back to my feet, my legs tingling with the rush of blood. I took two NightNights this time and yet here I am. Wide awake.

I go back into the kitchen to rinse out my mug. The back door is locked. I know because I checked it when I came downstairs just after ten past one. New routines, new anxiety tics. As I put the mug away, I look at the white backsplash, stylish and expensive, which also doubles as a wipe-clean board where Robert writes all the daily reminders we need. Dentists. Doctors. Humdrum. At the bottom I see "EMMA'S BIRTHDAY PARTY PREP." Ugh. I go and rub it off. I find I'm wiping away all the other reminders with it and just stare at the blankness left behind. It's soothing. I'm so shattered. Nothing is working right. After a moment I take a long breath. I may as well go back to bed and try to sleep again. Must. Try. Harder.

I feel like an echo as I drift up to the grainy darker upstairs corridor. Am I passing through ghosts of myself going the other way? The me of last night and the me of tomorrow night maybe. *Yesterday upon the stair, I met a man who wasn't there.* I shiver. I'm so tired.

I get a sharp urge to check on Will again. I don't need to. Will is fine. But still, I stand outside his door for a moment and check my watch: 2:21 A.M. I have to go into his room. I *have* to. It's a compulsion. Nothing can have happened since I went downstairs, but still I *need* to be in his room. I give in and sneak through his door. I don't know what I'm looking for. He's fast asleep, just as he was earlier. I stand by his bed and watch him. He's growing up so fast.

I go to my own bed and lie down on my cool pillow. I want to cry. I want to sleep.

"You okay?" Robert mutters, shifting slightly.

"Just went to the loo," I say.

"Go back to sleep," he mutters.

If only it were that easy. I roll onto my stomach, and I grip the sides of my pillow, squeezing hard to stop myself from screaming with the frustration.

After an hour of just lying there, my heart racing, I give up and go back downstairs again. Maybe I'll be able to doze on the sofa more easily. In the kitchen I peer out at the garden as the kettle boils but can't see any threat. *Paranoid much, Emma? Who does that remind you of?*

I make the chamomile tea and find myself reaching for the vodka bottle. *Fuck it,* I think, adding just a dash. Vodka at three thirty in the morning is not a good idea. I know that, but I'm all out of good ideas— the NightNight is useless and anything that might help me relax is worth a shot. I want the first hint of dawn to come. My tiny, life-saving sleep window.

As I turn to go to the sitting room, I freeze. I thought I'd wiped the backsplash clean. And I did. And I thought that I'd left it blank. I was *sure.* But the backsplash isn't blank. Something else has been written there. I stare at the jaggedly scrawled numbers. *Oh no.*

1 5 5 2 1 8 2 2 2 1 1 3 1 5 5 2 1 8 2 2 2 1 1 3

No, no, no.

15

SEVEN DAYS UNTIL MY BIRTHDAY

I did fall asleep at dawn for an hour or two, surprised that it was possible through my fear—*I am going mad*—but I still feel like death. I'm nauseous and my nose is running. A whole day looms long, endless, ahead of me. I need a lot of coffee and maybe a cake or a bacon roll or both for an energy injection on the way to work.

With the radio on and Robert sorting breakfast and last-minute packed lunches, everything seems too loud. Everything but Will, who is still unnaturally quiet. My little boy is definitely not himself. I should be enjoying this rare later morning—I don't have court today and no clients to see until eleven—but I'm wound tight with anxiety and tiredness.

"You okay, monkey face?" I ruffle Will's dark hair. My boy, not blond like Chloe and Robert.

He nods but stays hunched over his notebook. He's drawing with a red pen and his hand moves fast. I don't try to peek, despite my curiosity. Robert tried a couple of minutes ago and Will had slammed the book shut, turning his shoulder angrily to his daddy. Robert still looks hurt, so I bite my tongue instead of reminding him to speak to the teacher at school about Ben as he pours Will's cornflakes out. I put some toast on, claiming a small parenting task. I don't know their routines, not really. Being here for breakfast is a once-a-month thing if I'm lucky. I sometimes feel guilty about not feeling guilty enough.

"Can you pass the milk?"

There's only dregs in the bottle I hand over as I grab the butter and jam. "That's it for in here," I say. "It's milkman day, isn't it?" Robert must know I'm worrying about what happened at school, especially given Will's mood. Why can't he say he's not forgotten and he's going to speak to them? And then it dawns on me and I get an actual rush of—*halleflippinglujah*—energy that pings me awake. *I've* got time to do the school run this morning. Problem solved. I'm not a fan of confrontation, but someone messing with my kid on top of no sleep and I'll either get to the bottom of it or at least make sure that Will is safe for the day.

There's a refreshing morning breeze as Robert opens the back door to get the milk in and I'm wondering how best to broach the subject with my husband when there's a yell of surprised pain from outside, followed by "*Shit, fuck!*"

"Stay there." Will has looked up, alarm distracting him from whatever he's drawing, but by the time I get to the back door, Robert is already hobbling back into the house.

"What happened?" His jaw is clenched and I help him to a stool. He's gone out barefoot as usual and he leaves a trail of blood from where his foot is bleeding. I crouch and pull out a large chunk of glass as he swears some more.

"Daddy?"

"I'm fine." He wheezes. "Why don't you go and watch some cartoons on the iPad for a minute?"

Will may be in a funny mood, but he doesn't need telling twice when it comes to extra screen time, and he give us one last concerned look before taking his notebook and scurrying off to the sitting room.

"Hang on." I scrabble around in a cupboard for the first aid kit. The cut looks worse than it is, but it's still not pretty.

"The bloody milk," he says between gritted teeth. "One of the bottles was broken. The glass was all spread on the other side of the gate. Like it had been put there."

"What do you mean *put there?*" I hold his foot tight and he flinches as I dab antiseptic on it. It's going to be sore, but it won't need stitches.

"I mean it was fucking put there."

"You think it was those kids again?" If he'd got the cameras sorted, then we'd know for sure. And I'd know who slashed my tire. Maybe now it's affected *him* he'll sort it out.

"Probably. Little shits."

"You stay here and rest." I carefully wrap a bandage over the pad and plaster and then lean forward and kiss my husband's hurt foot as if he were a child. "I don't have to be in till after ten. I'll take Will to school."

He's right, though, the broken milk bottle had been laid out right by the gate. My mother's ghost shifts in my head, unfurling a little to get a closer look.

So many milk bottles in our house then, weren't there? Piled high from when the milkman used to come. Remember what I used to say? We wouldn't want to break them. You might get glass in your feet. And then you wouldn't be able to go to school.

Coincidence. That's all it is. Drunk teenagers and coincidence.

16

"Don't worry about Daddy." Will's quiet in the back seat. "He's fine. Sometimes cuts look much worse than they are." He nods, but he's looking out the window. This is not my bouncy, chatty boy. How can his teacher not have noticed? He does get quiet moods, that's true—an *old soul* Phoebe once called him when he was two—but this one has lasted a couple days now. *Fuzzy head.*

"Are you feeling poorly? You're very quiet."

"I'm okay." He's still not looking at me.

"No fuzzy head?" He doesn't answer. "Will?"

"No."

"If you're not sick, what's the matter? You know you can tell me. That's what mummies are for." I wait but get no response. "So what happened yesterday? At lunchtime?"

"I had an accident."

He still won't look at me, but at least he's speaking. "That's not like you." We're nearly at the school. Thankfully we're early, so we'll avoid the scrum. "Was Ben there? He's your friend, isn't he?" My tone is light as I try to con information out of my reluctant son.

"He shook me."

I feel a sudden rage. I knew there had been something. I *knew* it. I park. "He shook you? Why?"

He shrugs again but I don't need to push him anymore. I've got enough. I hold his hand tight as I stride through the playground gate, past the woman there who jokes to Will that Daddy must have a day off. *Daddy has every bloody day off*, I think as I give her a tight smile.

Will has to remind me where his classroom is—another stab of absent career-loving mother guilt—and the sight of the small tables and chairs makes my heart squeeze. Sometimes it feels like he's growing up too fast, but in this space I'm reminded of what a little fragile person he still is.

His teacher, Miss Russell, looks like she's not long out of the classroom herself as she glances up from her worksheets and smiles.

"Mrs. Averell. Good morning."

"My husband told me what happened yesterday," I say. "I'm very concerned."

"Oh, don't worry, it was an accident. These things happen." She looks at Will. "Why don't you go and hang your coat on your peg? Then you can help me sort out the colors, if you like?"

I crouch and kiss his face before he heads off and he gives me a half-squeeze back. "He said that Ben Simpson shook him. We've had problems with Ben before." That's an exaggeration, but I'm going with it. "There was an incident between them on Saturday."

"Oh, really?" She looks confused. "Ben can be a handful but not normally a bully."

"Or perhaps you haven't noticed because you're in here while they're out there?"

"The children are always supervised and—"

"I'd like Will to stay in the classroom for break and lunch today until you get to the bottom of it. He's clearly not himself, and while I obviously don't expect you to know the children as well as we parents do, I can't believe you haven't noticed."

"He has been quieter, yes." She concedes as she stands. She's very tall. Even in my heels, I'm having to look up at her. "And I will look into it of course. But please don't worry, Mrs. Averell. I'm sure it was—"

"Just find out what happened and make sure it doesn't happen again." I'm small but formidable. "I don't want to have to file a complaint."

"Of course." She's cowed, and as I turn to leave, I feel bad. A bitchy, demanding spoiled school gate mum is how I'm coming across—just how I did to poor Caroline, who brought back my purse—and I've never wanted to be that.

"I'm sorry for being so snappy," I say, more gently. "I'm hectic at work, and didn't need this on top of everything else. I'm having one of those days." *And several of those nights.*

She smiles, happy for a truce. "I can tell."

I must look confused, because she nods at my thin sweater. "I think that's on inside out?"

I see the label at the side and force a light laugh. "Oh. Thank you."

Another memory whispers inside me, the misty rotten breath of it filling my head. *Coming down the stairs with Phoebe on that last day, clutching my mother's fortieth birthday card. Looking down, my school sweater on inside out.*

I give Will another quick kiss on his return and then I'm in the corridor yanking the sweater off and putting it on right. Something is wrong with me today. Not just tiredness. *The numbers.* Not just Will. *The broken milk bottles.* Something else. *Bitch. Slashed tire.* I'm tired and my patience is gone, but it's more than that. *Inside out.* I'm filling with a quiet dread. She's in the hospital. My birthday is ticking closer. Phoebe was right. I am afraid. I don't want to be like her. I don't want to do what she did. I don't want to go mad like her. I don't want to have the bad blood.

I'm out of the playground and heading back to the car when I hear a familiar voice behind me.

"Hurry up, Matthew, don't dawdle. I'll be late for hot yoga. And for god's sake, tuck your shirt in, Ben."

I dart behind a tree and watch as Michelle, flustered, ushers the two boys into the school, before glancing at her watch and rushing back to her own car, up on the curb. I stay where I am for a second. Matthew has run straight inside, but Ben is loitering, wandering down between the building entrances that a century ago divided the girls and the boys.

"Sorry," I say to the cheerful woman at the gate. "Left my car keys in there."

She doesn't turn to check that I'm going back into the building. Which is good. Because that's not where I'm going.

17

I startle awake with no idea where I am or even *who* I am. Bright light. Hard chair. Blank computer screen. *Shit.* I sit up suddenly straighter. Work. I'm at work. When am I at work? What day is it? What time? Is this a dream? Before I have time to gather my thoughts—my twelve thirty canceled and I was using the time to catch up on billing, it's all coming back to me now—and peel my dry tongue from the roof of my mouth, a voice cuts through my haziness.

"Emma?" Angus Buckley is standing in my office doorway, looking confused. "Are you okay?"

"Yes. Yes, sorry, yes. Was caught up in my own thoughts."

"For a minute there I thought you were asleep." His little laugh implies that he's still not sure I wasn't.

"I was stretching my neck. Trying to fend off a headache. What can I do for you?" I smile brightly, although I'm still in that awful, vague no-man's-land between asleep and properly awake.

"Parker Stockwell. He wants to bring us more business on the commercial side. He suggested we have dinner on Thursday. The three of us. He's booked The Elderflower Garden."

"I'll have to check with Robert and . . ." I see his expression harden. "But I'm sure it will be fine," I finish.

"Good."

Great. An evening with Parker Stockwell. As Buckley closes the door I slump back in my chair and realize that is the least of my problems. *I fell asleep at work.* My heart thumps hard as that sinks in. This is worse than the car—at least then I'd made a conscious decision to close my eyes. This time I'd been working. And then, just like that, gone. Out like a light. How long had I been asleep? It's one twenty. I figure I was out for maybe thirty minutes and I'm lucky no one else came into my office. I'm not sure what Rosemary would have thought after the Dictaphone incident.

My brief sleep has brought me some clarity. It's been only five nights of insomnia but it feels like a lifetime. A long tortuous nightmare of a lifetime. I remember, suddenly, how I snapped at Will's teacher, and then how I . . . Well, enough is enough. I can't go on like this. I'll end up getting fired. And divorced.

In the ladies' I splash water on my face, getting too much of my hair wet as I do, and then touch up my makeup. I have only an old mascara in my bag and it clumps in my lashes. There are dark rings around my eyes and dry patches of skin on my forehead that have made my foundation flake. I look a mess, crumbling on the outside as I crumble on the inside.

You are not like her, I tell my tired reflection.

My reflection stares back at me, unconvinced, and I'm not liking what I read in her expression. *There's only one way to get past this. You have to go and see her. While you can. Phoebe was right. Make your peace. Before you do actually drive yourself mad.*

I collide with Alison, coming in as I'm leaving. "You look awful," she says bluntly as I try to get past her.

"Migraine."

"I've never known you to have those." Her face is a mask of sympathy, while her eyes are calling bullshit on my headache. "Maybe you're working too hard."

"I'm fine," I snap back. "But thank you." I keep walking, heading straight to Buckley's office. I need to go now before I change my mind.

18

My hand trembles as I sign in and then I hurry along the corridor to where Phoebe's waiting for me outside the room. *Her* room.

"Well, that text was a surprise," she says, but for once without her droll tone. She sounds genuinely pleased. "But I didn't believe it until just now. You're actually here."

"I won't come again." I feel sick but I'm wide awake thanks to the adrenaline pumping through me. "Only this once." I glare at her as if she's physically dragged me here rather than its being my idea.

"Shall I wait?" she says. "Or do you want me to come in with you?"

"Can you go somewhere else? You didn't need to

come at all. I'll feel weird with you standing out here. I need privacy." My fingers are ferociously picking at the skin around the edges of my nails, and there's a sharp sting as some tears away. I haven't done that since I was a kid.

"If that's what you want." She shrugs. "I thought you might need the support. I'll go home for an hour or so."

"Where are you living anyway?" I ask. She's wearing a pub polo shirt: THE HAND AND RACQUET. I can't imagine Phoebe working in a bar, putting up with all the bullshit from drunks. She's too high and mighty for that. But if she's here for only a few months, maybe it's all she could get.

"Not too far from here." She leans in and nearly, but not quite, kisses my cheek. "Just go in and see for yourself that there's nothing to be afraid of anymore."

That's easy for you to say, I think as I watch her stride down the corridor, smiling at the nurse who gets up from behind her desk and walks out with my big sister, who can't relax with me but can chat away easily with strangers. I feel a pang of envy. Phoebe no longer has forty looming. And she was never afraid of *it* being in her blood. Not like I've always been. She wasn't marked by our mother as the one who'd go mad. I feel completely alone and afraid and as if I'm five years old again, but this time no one is holding my hand as I get ready to see Mummy.

I take a deep breath. I'm not five. I'm a successful career woman with a beautiful family, and I can do this. I grip the handle, twist it, and go inside.

The blinds are closed, the lighting soft in the warm room, and a machine by the bed lets out a soft *whoosh* and then *click* in a steady rhythm.

I look at the figure in the bed. There *she* is.

Her hair is still long but now it's steel gray against the pillows instead of matted dark brown. Her face is sunken below her closed eyes—*finally got to sleep then*—concave under her cheekbones, and her arms are sticks over the blanket, veins blue and angry under her pale, papery skin. Her hands are clenched in fists and that's how I know the bundle of twigs bound by loose skin is my mother. Somewhere deep inside, she's still raging.

I'm surprisingly calm, as if I left all my anxieties *out there* in the real world when I stepped across the threshold into this window in time. Maybe it's because it's so surreal to be actually seeing her, this decrepit stranger, that I can't quite process that it's *her*.

There's a vase of fresh flowers on the side table, a

medley of cheerful blooms that stand bright and out of place against the magnolia wall. There are more flowers on the card beside them. "Get Well Soon!" Inside it reads, "*Dear Mum, lots of love, Phoebe xx.*" I look at those kisses. How could she? I remember drawing kisses on *that* card on that day. Before school. Before she . . .

. . . I grip the banister and start to climb, forcing one foot in front of the other, my legs numb from being cramped so long. Another flash of cold lightning makes me jump. I'm only five and I'm so scared, but the upstairs hallway is empty. There are noises though, strange sounds I don't quite understand, coming from down where mine and Phoebe's bedroom is.

"*Mummy?*" *I say, quietly.*

My hand is trembling as I put the card down. I'm shaking, not with fear, but with rage. *Mummy.* She was everything a mother shouldn't be, and even though she's now just this husk in a bed, I can still feel the embers of the fear I felt that night.

Her medical notes hang on a clipboard above her bed and I lean forward to look at them. There are mainly just a lot of medical expressions I don't understand, but then at the top I see *Hartwell House in-room CCTV recorded the initial injury at 1:13 on 06/24. The patient was found at 2:00 on a routine check and immediately transferred to Leeds General.*

I stare, frowning.

1:13 on 06/24.

The twenty-fourth of June. That was last Friday. She did this late Thursday night. Last Thursday. That was the day of the *Stockwell v. Stockwell* custody judgment. The first night of my insomnia. I woke in the night and couldn't get back to sleep. It's coming back to me with perfect clarity. I remember being in a panic—*there's someone in the house*—and looking at the clock.

It had showed 1:13 A.M.

My heart races as I look back at the clipboard and notes: *1:13 on 06/24.* I woke up terrified at exactly the time my mother was bashing her own brain in against a mirror.

How can that be? It's a coincidence, I try to tell myself. But the dread I've felt since waking that night coils in the pit of my stomach. *What is happening to me?*

Icy fingers clamp around my wrist, the hand coming up from the bed fast. I shriek—a quiet airless panicked sound—and stumble backward in disbelief, but she holds tight, knuckles straining white against cold skin, even as the rest of her body lies so still and deathly and unmoved.

No, Mummy, no! Memories crowd in and it feels like she's dragging me to the under-stairs cupboard again, grip like a vise as I cry out pleading with her, and in my panic the past and the present become a jumbled mess and I'm sure I'll pass out. *No, Mummy, please no!*

Her eyes flash open wide, jaundice-yellow and bloodshot, and her gaze fixes on mine. I try to pull myself free and I can hear my wheezing breath as my face burns, and I'm sure—sure—that this time she'll drag me into the darkness, the void in which she's trapped and I can feel a scream building and then—

As fast as they grabbed me, her fingers let go. Her arm drops to her side, as if it's never moved at all. Her eyes are closed again.

I crumple into the visitor's chair, almost breathless. The machine continues its *whoosh* and *click*, keeping her alive. I look around the room in disbelief. No one is here. I glance up—there are no cameras watching this room. No one saw it. I rub my wrist and can still feel her cold fingers there. I stare at her, so peaceful, as if nothing has happened. Maybe it hasn't. Maybe this is the start of my going mad. Turning into her.

1:13 A.M. The moment my insomnia started she was smashing her head apart.

I was wrong. She can still scare me. And her fingers might have fallen away, but she refuses to let me go.

There's no nurse at the desk when I stumble past a short while later, desperate for fresh air and desperate to get away, not stopping to sign out. I hurry out of the building, knocking into an older woman coming the other way, not pausing to apologize, and then I reach my car just before my legs give way. A rush of heat floods my body, black spots forming at the corners of my vision, and I'm sure, for a minute, that I'm going to pass out. I get the air-conditioning blasting and suck in deep breaths, the cold sweat on my skin slowly fading.

I shouldn't have come. I should have stayed at work. No good could come from seeing her. I should have known that. The buzz in my ears fades, and it's only then that I realize that somewhere deep in my bag, my phone is ringing. It stops and then starts again.

I dig it out. It's the school. They want to see me. Of course they do. I hang up and want to cry as exhaustion settles heavily back in my bones.

19

I've been waiting outside the headteacher's office for fifteen minutes by the time Robert turns up, hurried and flustered.

"Where have you been?" I ask, annoyed. The school secretary told me they'd called and got his voice mail, and no answer on the landline, but that they really wanted us both here if possible. I'd got his voice mail too, and then I went from worrying about what the school was going to say to worrying that Robert had driven into another tree.

"Sorry, I must have had a bad signal. What's this all about?"

I don't have time to answer—*thankfully*—before the door opens and we're ushered inside amid polite greetings. God, I wish he wasn't here for this. What's he going to think? He's going to be mad, and I can't really blame him.

"Mrs. Fincham," I say as we take our seats. I need to face this head-on. "If this is about what happened this morning . . ."

"What happened this morning?" Robert looks at me sideways, surprised.

"Ah, that. Yes, actually we had a phone call from a member of the public." The headteacher leans forward on her desk, looking at me over her glasses, as if I'm a naughty schoolchild. "They were very concerned about what they saw."

My face is burning again. "Honestly, I'm so sorry, I—"

"They said they saw you shaking one of our students. You were leaning in close to his face and it looked like you were very angry and saying some very unpleasant things to him. They said he was trying to pull away."

I frown. No, that can't be right. I held his arms, yes. Maybe shook him a little. But I wasn't mean. I wasn't.

"It wasn't like that," I say, but the little voice in my head that won't shut up about numbers and Dictaphones and broken glass is already whispering, *Are you sure?*

"They knew you weren't his mother because they'd just seen her dropping her children off. They said you shook the boy hard enough to make him cry." She pauses. "The only child anyone saw crying at that time this morning was Ben Simpson."

"Jesus, Emma." Robert looks both annoyed and embarrassed, and I feel a stab of anger at him for being so quickly against me. I don't really have a leg to stand on but he could at least have given me the benefit of the doubt.

"I feel awful," I say, and it's true. "And of course I'll apologize to Ben. But I wasn't horrible to him and I certainly didn't scare him. All I did was say that he mustn't be mean to Will and if he didn't play nicely in future there would be repercussions."

"You threatened a child?" Robert's eyes widen. "I told you that I would speak to Michelle. We had this conversation. We agreed."

"I didn't threaten him and—"

"While I understand your concerns for your own child, Mrs. Averell, this sort of behavior is absolutely unacceptable." She gives me a sharp look and I'm horrified to find that tears are pricking the edges of my eyes. Shame. Guilt. I know I shouldn't have gone back in to speak to Ben and the thought of some busybody passerby thinking I was threatening him is awful.

"I know. I'm sorry."

"However," she continues, "we spoke to Ben and he

says you didn't frighten him, you just told him off. We will have to tell his mother though."

Oh, thank you, Ben, thank you.

I'm not worried about Michelle's reaction. She sat in my office and accused me of sleeping with her husband and this is nothing next to that.

"But that's not why we called you here."

I look up, surprised, and then glance over at my husband, who looks equally baffled.

"This is more delicate. It's about Will. It may go some way to explaining his subdued mood of late." She slides Will's blue notebook across the desk, its battered edges curling up from being carried everywhere with him. "His teacher saw this today."

"His sketchbook?" Robert says, and we both lean forward. "What about it?"

"Please look inside."

We glance at each other and I open it, seeing what I expect. Various attempts and dinosaurs, or squashed dogs, and animals. I look up.

"Further along. The more recent drawings."

I turn some more pages. And then I freeze.

This can't be right.

I think of my little boy, all quiet moodiness, hunched over his notebook and not letting us see, and my blood chills. *This* is what he was drawing? *How can that be?*

The picture is very childlike but drawn with concentration and care. A woman, with long hair hanging loose, and a big angry frown on her face, is leaning over a bed with a dinosaur duvet on it, *just like Will's*, with a little boy beneath it. Where the boy's eyes should be are X's, drawn hard into the page, indenting the paper.

As my middle finger scrapes at my cuticles and my thumb bleeds again, I look back at the hunched madwoman drawn in red pen on the page.

She's holding a pillow. Gripping it.

As if she is about to put it over his face.

"He says it's the scary lady who's in his room at night," Mrs. Fincham speaks quietly. "He won't say any more than that."

No, no, no. No.

I flick the pages forward, my heart racing. Five and then ten, maybe more. Every page holds the same crudely drawn picture. In some, the scary, frowny face is like a huge balloon looming over the bed, but in each the scenario is exact. A terrifying madwoman about to suffocate him.

How can he know? How can he know what she did?

"What is this?" Robert mutters, clearly disturbed. He looks at me. I realize they're both looking at me, wary and cautious.

"You think this is *me*?" I half laugh, shocked and appalled. "This isn't me." *It does look like me.* But it's not me. I know it's not. *But how could he know?*

"I know you haven't been sleeping, Em. You're never in bed when I wake up. Could you have done something that might have scared him? Accidentally? That he might have messed up in a nightmare?"

"This isn't me!" I say again, hearing the slight hysteria in my raised voice.

"His teacher presumed it was something from a bad dream," Mrs. Fincham says, and then pauses and reaches forward. "But then she saw this." She turns to the next page. There's no drawing on this one, but one word is printed large.

MUMMY

20

"Phoebe," I say, for what feels like the millionth time. "It has to be."

The sketchbook is open on the island between us, Robert having thrown it down as soon as Will, surprisingly almost his normal perky self, had scuttled off with some juice and an iPad.

"If you'd let me speak to him properly—"

"Like you did with Ben? What the hell is wrong with you?"

"I didn't shake Ben." I take the sketchbook and hold it up, refusing to be shamed by it or afraid of it. "This is not me. This is Phoebe's doing. She's put this image into his head."

"I have no bloody idea what you're talking about." He stares at me.

"My mother," I say. I'm not giving him more than that. He can swing for it. "Phoebe must have been telling him about her."

"What's your mother got to do with this?"

"Nothing." I rub my wrist. I can still feel those bony fingers gripping me. "Well, not quite nothing. Something from when we were little, before she died, something only me and Phoebe—well, it's private." I know I'm rambling but it *is* private. I've spent my whole life *not* being defined by it. "But *Phoebe* has everything to do with this. There's no other explanation. She's back. She's been here. She put Will to bed. Must have said something then."

"It doesn't feel very like Phoebe," he says, and I want to laugh.

"Oh, but you think this could be me? What did that teacher say? The scary lady who's in his room at night? You think that's me? Seriously?"

He wavers then, no longer so sure of his own narrative. "No, of course not. But I don't think it sounds like Phoebe either."

"Thanks for the vote of confidence." It niggles me when he defends Phoebe. As if maybe he sometimes feels like he chose the wrong sister all those years ago.

"Look, Em . . . ," he starts, and then the doorbell rings, three sharp demanding bursts, and we both know who's going to be on the other side. Michelle. Whatever softening of mood toward me Robert was entertaining vanishes. This one really is my mess.

"**I'm so** sorry, Michelle." She hasn't come in farther than the hall and she's angry, but not as livid as Robert was expecting. My theory was right. She's frying bigger fish in her emotional life and this is just one more thing she could have done without, rather than a serious concern. "But I don't care what that passerby said, I didn't shake Ben."

"I know. He told me." She glares at me. "But you shouldn't have been telling him off at all. And certainly not without me there."

"You're right. I should have come to you. It's just that Will hasn't wet himself for years, so it was a shock. I'm sure it was all just a playground prank gone wrong or something but—"

"Ben didn't make Will wet himself by shaking him," she cuts in. "Ben shook Will *because* he was wetting himself."

I stare at her, momentarily confused.

"What?" Robert says. He's been loitering behind me, out of the firing line, but now he steps forward.

"Ben said Will was staring into space on the playground when the others were calling to him to play.

He didn't move. Wouldn't look up. Matthew and the others in Will's class got a bit freaked out and ran away. Ben called over to him but Will didn't respond and then he saw—well, that Will was wetting himself. He shook him to make him snap out of it. And he did."

She looks at me and then at Robert and then back at me. "Whatever scared him, it wasn't Ben."

As Robert swoops in, apologizing some more and ushering Michelle toward the door, I think back to what Will said in the car. *I had an accident.* And then *Ben shook me.* He'd actually told me the truth and I'd drawn a line between the two statements and made up a truth of my own. Oh god.

"So if it wasn't Ben," Robert says when we've said our apologetic goodbyes to a mollified Michelle, "then what *did* make him wet himself?" That suspicion is back in his face.

"It wasn't me." I'm cold this time, tired of trying to explain myself. "Maybe we should take him to a doctor. He had a bad head and then was just staring into space, isn't that what Michelle said? Maybe he's got an inner ear infection."

"That doesn't explain the drawings."

"And I'm going to deal with that right now." Phoebe. Bloody Phoebe. I get my mobile from my handbag and go to my study, closing the door. There's no place for

Robert in this conversation.

"**What the** hell do you think you're playing at?" I snap as soon as she answers. "What have you told Will? About *her*? He's having nightmares—and he wet himself at school. None of that shit back then was my fault, Phoebe, it never was, and I won't have you bringing it into Will's life. I'm sorry you're still so resentful, I'm sorry you think I somehow had it all better than you afterward, and I'm sorry you're on your own, but I don't want you near us for a while. Do you understand?"

I'm shaking when I finally stop my rant, and then there's a long silence at the other end.

"Are you still there?"

"She's dead," Phoebe says, eventually.

"What?"

"Mum. She's dead."

Air *whoomphs* from my lungs, a sudden sharp exhale, and for a moment I forget to breathe back in.

"I came back to her room and she was dead." Her voice is quiet. Controlled. "I should have stayed." She lets out a long breath and in its raggedy sound I can hear all her contained emotion.

"What happened, Emma? She was fine when I left her with you. *What did you do?*"

21

I lie awake all night, itching to get up, to check on the kids, to go downstairs, to complete all my new nighttime routines that are becoming more obsessive compulsive than habit. I can't risk it though. Our bed is full of tension. Robert's got his back to me, but I know that I'm not alone in struggling to sleep.

Ding dong, the witch is dead.

There should be some relief with that knowledge. The door finally closing on my childhood. Freedom. And yet I don't feel any. Not yet. Phoebe's words echo in my head.

What happened, Emma?

I'd hung up after that, pacing around the kitchen while Robert gave Will a bath and put him to bed, and then, when he asked me what Phoebe had said, I told him I couldn't get hold of her and then I'd had a very long bath of my own, emotionally exhausted.

The ceiling is a grainy universe above me. What was Phoebe implying? Is this a circle of accusation? I accuse her of filling my son's head with nightmarish glimpses into our past, and so she accuses me of something worse? The hours tick by. I think about madness. About how I woke up at 1:13 A.M., the exact time my mad mother was bashing her brains out against the mirror, and how I haven't slept properly since. Just a coincidence. It has to be.

As Robert drifts in and out of half sleep, I open my mouth to talk to him at least a dozen times but no words come out. I can't tell him about *her*. Not now. Not after today. So I lie there in silence, desperate to flee my bed and wander the house, until the night cracks black to midnight blue and then gray, and I finally catch an hour's sleep myself.

22

SIX DAYS UNTIL MY BIRTHDAY

"I thought I was going to see one of the normal counselors." My palms sweat as I take the seat Dr. Andrea Morris is offering. She smiles, friendly and open. She's a bit older than me, maybe mid to late forties, and glamorous in an unintentional way, and after becoming almost friends from the amount of clients I've sent to her, it's strange to be here talking to her in her professional capacity.

"From what you discussed on the phone I thought you might need someone with a broader remit."

"So you think I'm crazy?" I'm trying to joke but I don't think it lands. She laughs though.

"No. But you might need a prescription for some

better sleeping pills than over the counter can give you."

"Oh god, yes please. NightNight isn't even making me drowsy."

"I can—and will—give you something that will get you some rest, but we need to deal with what's causing your insomnia. You weren't overly clear on the phone."

I'd called her on the way into work, not giving myself time to change my mind, and she's politely saying that I was very garbled. But where do I start?

"I'm nearly forty," I say, and she smiles.

"I'm nearly fifty. Perspective is a great thing. But seriously. Why is that troubling you?"

"It's nothing to do with the getting older." I take a sip of water. "I'll be very happy when forty is behind me. I've been afraid of turning forty all my life. It's not the age, it's because of my mother."

She leans back in her chair and waits for me to elaborate.

"My childhood wasn't great. Not the early years anyway. My dad—well, I have no idea who he was, really. My sister, Phoebe, claims to remember him vaguely, but I don't. He left not long after I was born and then he died a little while after. Apparently a lot went wrong after I was born. My mum? She could have filled up your appointments until retirement and I don't think you'd have scratched the surface of fixing her. She's—she *was*—a very broken woman. Before I came along my sister claims our mother was almost normal, not that Phoebe could possibly remember that. I think she just says it so she can have something that I can't. Anyway, what *is* clear is that if she was a little cracked before I was born, my mother properly broke afterward. By the time I was five, and in the last few days as Mum got close to her fortieth birthday, she was—"

I hesitate and then decide to go with the blunt truth. "She was insane. Muttering to herself. Not sleeping. Phoebe would help me dress for school, make sure I got fed, try to shelter me a little." I'm appalled to feel tears stinging the backs of my eyes thinking about me and Phoebe back then, when all we had was each other. "But there was no hiding place for either of us." I take a breath and continue. "I think the court's verdict was that on the night of her fortieth birthday she was in the grip of a complete psychotic break."

If Dr. Morris is surprised, she doesn't show it. "My mother used to tell me that I would go mad," I continue. "Like her. She said it over and over. She never said it about Phoebe. Only me. Happened to my great-aunt, then to her, and it was going to happen to me. And maybe she was right. I'm nearly forty and now I'm not sleeping either."

"Where is your mother now?" she asks.

"Dead. She's spent the past thirty years or so in a secure unit. But she died yesterday. Right after I'd seen her for the first time since the night of her fortieth birthday." I hiccup a laugh that sounds like a sob.

"How did she die?"

"Self-inflicted brain bleed."

"I'm sorry." She pauses. "And how do you and your sister feel about that?"

When I answer, I'm like a tap that's been too tightly wound for years and now that it's loosened everything is pouring out. I talk about Phoebe's visiting our mother and not telling me, I stumble my way through what actually happened on the day and night of our mother's fortieth birthday, and how I think Phoebe has always resented me for it, and how whatever closeness we had back then was lost years ago when we went into different foster homes.

I say how that memory of my mother telling me I'd go mad like her coats me like grease on the inside of an oven, dirty and hidden. I tell her about when Phoebe and I shared a flat briefly when I was at university, and how one night, drunk, she brought a boy home from a bar, and how when Phoebe fell asleep, me and the boy stayed up talking and by morning we were halfway in love and now we have two children, and are in the main happy, but recently I've felt as if he's started to resent me too and maybe I feel the same about him.

She listens patiently as the clock ticks round and she spots how I pick at the skin around my fingernail as I talk about my insomnia and the dread it fills me with and the need to check on my children. I even end up telling her about my mother's numbers and the Dictaphone and my scrawling them on the backsplash. If she didn't think I was crazy at the start, she must now.

"No wonder you're stressed," she says at last. "That's an awful lot to be dealing with. All things considered, I think you're coping admirably."

"You do?" I was half-expecting her to be calling Hartwell House and telling them she had another Bournett to replace the one they just lost.

"I do. And you're also dealing with the loss of a mother with whom you had a complicated relationship—"

"That's one way of putting it."

"But it's still a loss. Even if you didn't love her, which is also perfectly fine—there's no obligation to love someone, even a relative—you can still be experiencing grief. She has been a weight on you for a long time and now she's gone and you're not sure how to be without that. I think we should book some more sessions in. This isn't a quick fix. This is a massive childhood trauma that you're dealing with."

"Sure. Of course. I'll call by the end of the week and sort something out." I pause. "And the sleeping pills?"

She scribbles out a prescription. "This is for two weeks and we'll review after that. Take one, an hour before you go to bed. And don't drink alcohol with them. If you start sleeping better, then cut down to a half and see how you go. You want to take these for the shortest amount of time possible, okay? It's easy to get too attached to them. Give me a call later when you've checked your work diary and we can fit in another session for next week. Hopefully by then a few good nights' sleep will have cracked the nighttime anxiety."

She smiles at me as if there really *isn't* anything to worry about, and I'm giddy with relief.

"Thanks so much. I actually feel a bit better already. Aside from the shattering tiredness."

She leads me out and as we go down the corridor to the lift, nods toward another door. "I may have a client for *you* as it goes. One of my colleagues is heading toward divorce and asked me if I'd recommend someone. I'll send him to you as and when."

"Great." The lift pings. "And thank you. For everything. It's been so good to be able to talk about this.

Sometimes I feel, well, that I have to hold everything together for everyone and it gets overwhelming, and I wouldn't know where to start talking to Robert about my mother. I can't even remember the last time I *did* really talk about her."

"I'm glad to have helped."

23

I go straight to the pharmacy and get my prescription. Dr. Morris is right. I *will* feel better about everything after a good night's sleep. Then I'll tackle Phoebe and find out why she scared Will with tales of madwomen in bedrooms. And maybe I can persuade her to see a shrink too. We're both damaged, it doesn't take a doctorate in psychiatry for anyone who knows our history to know that.

I'm heading out when I see a woman I'm sure I know standing by the vitamins and sleep aid counter. I stare, wondering for a moment if she's a client, then I remember, just as she looks up to see me staring at her. It's *her*. The woman who brought my wallet back.

"Caroline?"

She's not in her nurse's uniform today, but in paint-splattered jeans and a top, hair pulled back in an untidy ponytail, and she looks as fed up as I've been feeling.

"Emma Averell." My face is flushing. "You brought my wallet back and I was horribly rude. I'm so sorry, I was having a crap day and everything I said came out wrong."

"Yes, I remember." She looks back down at the shelves, awkward, and I should probably walk away, but I don't.

"You're not sleeping either?" I nod at the stand she's at and hold up my prescription bag. "Avoid the Night-Night. It's useless. I've had to get some stronger stuff."

"Vitamin D." She holds up a bottle. There's a large plaster along one side of her hand, a little red at the center.

"What happened to your hand?"

"Oh, nothing. I'm doing some decorating. A pane of glass broke."

I look down and see she's got two cans of paint at her feet. No wonder her cut is bleeding again if she's been carrying those. "Look," I say, reaching for them. "You pay for the vitamins and I'll help you to the car with these."

"I got the bus," she says. "Honestly I'm fine."

"Don't be silly." I pick up the two cans, heavier than I thought, one in each hand, and quietly hope the bus stop isn't too far. "I owe you a favor." I give her my biggest smile. "I *insist*."

"Okay," she says, and I sense she'd rather I didn't but can't really say no. I only want to make it up to her for being rude and she can hardly manage with the cut hand.

She pays and then we leave the pharmacy, awkward strangers, and I think that out of her nurse's uniform she looks younger, less severe, but she does look really tired. "Is this your day off?" I say, making conversation.

"Supposedly. But the house needs painting among other things before I can sell it—it was my mother's— and I can't afford to get people in and it's a bigger job than I was expecting, but I really need to get it done, so no day off for me." She gives me a small smile then, a genuine one. "Sorry. Just been one of those days."

"I know how you feel." I get a flush of warmth that she's relaxing a bit. Something about her really appeals to me and I can't put my finger on it. Maybe this is someone I can help. Maybe she'll be a new friend. Someone unconnected to the bloody school gates. My stomach rumbles and as we go past a Wetherspoons I hear myself saying, "Brexit burger? I think it's two for one."

"Honestly, I should get on."

"Don't make me insist again," I say, trying to sound jovial. "I hate eating alone. I have to spend the whole time scrolling through my phone pretending to be busy."

She glances toward the bus stop but doesn't say no yet.

"Come on. Half an hour. Give that injured hand a rest. It's a thank-you for bringing my wallet back. And my social conscience hates me for it, but I'm a slave to their blue-cheese burger. Share my shame. And then I'll drop you home afterward. My car's parked only a couple minutes away." I sound like I'm trying to drag her out on a date.

"Okay," she says, after studying me for a moment. "I could use a break."

When we're settled in a booth with burgers ordered and a small wine each, she nods at my prescription packet. "Not sleeping well?"

"Not really." There's a massive understatement. She's looking at me quietly, and I do what I always do in awkward situations—fill the silence. "My son's having problems at school and my mother died yesterday." Her face falls and I quickly add, "She was old and we weren't close—it's a long, complicated and boring story—but it's causing some friction with my sister. Family stuff, you know how it is."

"I'm an only child, so no. Sometimes I'm happy

about that, but then, also, when you're an only child it all falls on you."

"Oh god," I say as the burgers arrive efficiently quickly. "You said you're decorating your mother's house to sell. Is she—has she passed away too?"

"No, worse, she's in a home." She's relaxing now she's had a few sips of wine and she reaches for a chip. "That sounds terrible, I know, but those places drain money. If you want an at least half-decent one. Still, once the house is sold it'll be fine. Will pay for her home and leave enough for me to get a place. I've lived with her to care for her. Long story."

"Well, good luck with it," I say, reaching for my own food. "Husbands and children can be a money drain too."

"I guess especially if you're starting a new business. Or at least your husband is."

I'm so distracted by eating that I take a moment to register that she means *my* husband. "What new business?"

I have to wait for her to finish chewing a large bite before I get an answer. She swallows fast. "The bar? Aren't you—I must have the wrong end of the stick. Ignore me."

"What bar?"

"Oh, it's nothing. It's just—it's been a weird day

where you're concerned. I've not only seen *you*, but I thought I saw your husband too. There's an empty bar on Albion Street. I saw him come out of it earlier when I was on the way to the paint shop. I couldn't figure out why his face was familiar; then I saw his car and remembered him."

Why would Robert be looking at an empty bar?

"Maybe it wasn't him, though. I only saw him for a couple seconds outside your house." I can see her questioning herself just as I'm mentally questioning him. It's too much of a coincidence, surely? Robert's been talking about going back to work, wanting something of his own, and then Caroline spots him outside a vacant business premises?

"Oh, it could have been him." I keep my tone light. "He gets pipe dreams and does stuff like that. Sometimes he's just being nosy and wants to see inside. He must have driven past at some point and the whim to know more gripped him."

"How nice to have pipe dreams," she says softly, and then we both let quiet settle as we eat. I'm already having an argument with Robert in my head. I should probably say nothing. He *does* have pipe dream moments, he always has, and this could all come to naught. But how the hell would he even start thinking about running a bar? That's a 24/7 commitment.

Unless he's thinking about divorce. The voice is quiet in the back of my head. *Then he'd have the free time.* I dismiss that quickly. First, we may have the odd problem but we're nowhere near in divorce territory, and second, and more practically, without me paying all the bills he wouldn't be able to take a financial risk like that.

After we've finished, our conversation more about our own work than anything else, I carry the paint to the car and then drive her home, which thankfully isn't too far away. Buckley will be wondering where I've got to, and, after telling Alison off about her billable hours, I'd better not let my own slip.

The house is a small Victorian terrace, like so many others in the city, and although there are a couple of pretty hanging baskets, the paint on the windowsills is chipped. It might be well-loved, but Caroline's right, it does need some work.

"Good luck," I say as she gets out, taking her paint from the back seat. "Sorry if that was a bit odd. I just—I don't know, I guess I just didn't want to have lunch on my own."

"I get it, Emma." She looks back at me from the pavement. "Sometimes life is hard, isn't it?"

I nod and almost feel like crying suddenly, so I do my best to smile it away. She starts walking up the tiny path to the front door and I call her back.

"We should swap numbers," I say. "Maybe I could come over when you're finished," she says. "For a wine or a takeaway or something." I grab my phone from the well. "What's your number? I'll text you mine."

She gives me the digits and I send her a message. I feel better for it. I've been calmer in the past hour or so than I have since all the shit with my sleep started. There's something gentle about her, I think. Not harsh like Michelle or cold like Phoebe, or so busy with their own lives like all the other women I know. Like me. Maybe I can be the friend *she* needs?

24

I'd had music on driving home—Radio 6 for a change—and I'd hummed along to something folk-rocky that I hadn't heard before and probably never would on my normal Radio 2. With the windows open to let in the summer evening breeze, I'd realized I was in a good mood for the first time in ages.

Now I'm back to earth with a thump. I'd decided to come straight out and ask Robert what he was doing looking around a bar. I'd tried not to make it confrontational, more just curious, but now he's acting as if I've caught him in an affair.

"Are you spying on me?"

"Don't be ridiculous." I try to laugh. "I bumped into that woman who brought my wallet back and we got talking. She'd seen you and she mentioned it. Nothing sinister."

"I told Alan I'd go with him, that's all it was. He's looking for some new investments. He knows I'm looking to do something more with my future. I've had five years of being a stay-at-home dad for the second time and I'm done with it."

"It was the deal we made," I say.

"Yes, nearly twenty years ago! I want more than this. I'm tired of being emasculated by you."

"What is this, the 1980s?"

"It's not a joke."

"I can see that." I take a deep breath. This is getting us nowhere and I may hate the idea of our status quo changing, but it's clearly more than a passing fad for Robert. And maybe it won't be so disruptive, especially if it makes him happier. And I do want him to be happy. I want *us* to be happy. "So, what is it exactly Alan wants you to do? Design the marketing?"

"No, not quite."

"What then?"

"He wants me to be a partner. It'll be our bar. Not just his." He looks at me defiantly. "Julian, him, and me. My share is fifteen grand and I would put in more of the hours to make up the difference."

"Fifteen thousand pounds? We don't have—"

"Yes, we do. We have savings. And Chloe keeps saying she doesn't want to go to uni for at least a year. So we can take the money out of that pot. If she goes, she can get loans and we can sort them later."

I can't believe what I'm hearing. "A bar? I know you're due a mid-life crisis around now but this is ridiculous. And you'll put in more of the hours? Does that mean you'll be out every evening?"

"Well, *you* are."

"How long were you going to keep this a secret from me?" I get a bottle of wine from the fridge and pour myself a glass and he reaches for a beer.

"It's not a secret, I hadn't even seen the place until today. I didn't tell you before because I was still thinking about it." He swigs his beer. "And we've had other problems. Maybe we should talk about the more pressing matter of Will's drawings. I tried to talk to him about them but he clammed up. Not like him at all."

Outside, night is slowly falling, and as the light fades, tension seeps back into me. "I know exactly what happened. Phoebe spooked him with a story. Our mother used to—" I look for words that aren't exactly a lie but aren't the truth either. "Come into our room and scare us when we were in bed. Especially Phoebe."

"Why would Phoebe say something like that to him?"

"I don't know, Robert." My irritation is rising now. "But why are you finding it easy to think that it might be me, but not that it could be her? And since I—your wife—am telling you I haven't been scaring my child in the night, can we get back to this bar business?"

"But you aren't sleeping, are you?" he says.

"If you must know, I saw a doctor about that today—she says I'm fine. She's not concerned at all. So now I'm going to go and check on my son."

"Emma—"

"What's going on?" Chloe says, closing the front door and being welcomed by her father's annoyed tone and my angry stomp up the stairs.

"Your father wants to spend your uni money, that's what."

"For God's sake, Emma." Robert glares at me from the kitchen doorway. Chloe drops her bag and shrugs. "If he needs it, he can have it. I'm still thinking of a year out. Maybe longer."

I stare down at them, two peas in a pod, the blond half of our family, and I bite back the words that I know will make this simmering pan of tension boil over. *Well, it's not his bloody money.*

I was hoping Will would be awake and we could snuggle and maybe he'd open up about the drawings, but he's curled up on his side and he doesn't even twitch as the soft hallway light comes in like a tide across the carpet. My dark-haired angel. I love them both but it's a case of Mummy's boy and Daddy's girl in our family. I leave him to sleep in peace, but just as the door is almost closed behind me, I take a quick final glance back, and for a moment I think that his eyes are open, watching me. If so, he closes them quickly again. Are his eyelids fluttering? No, I decide. That can't be the case. Why would he pretend to be asleep? The thought disturbs me, echoes of my own childhood.

He can't be afraid of me. Surely?

Robert and I are still barely talking at ten—I've hidden in work and he's watched some *Fast and Furious* film in his den—when we go to bed. I took one of the sleeping pills at nine thirty and with the wine added into the mix, at least I fall asleep as soon as my head hits the pillow.

But not for long.

I wake, with a gasp, a song playing loud in my head, music that fades the instant my eyes open to an almost tune I can't quite grasp. I sit up, heart racing, and look at the alarm clock. It clicks to 1:13 A.M. *That number again. Of course it is.* I curse myself for closing the blinds so tightly because the room is on the cusp of pitch-black as I listen out for any sign of something bad in the house.

Did I check the back door before I came to bed? I should have checked the back door. I lie back down, and under the sheets my forefingers pick at the skin around my thumbnails. I have to stay in bed. I have to go back to sleep. This is all ridiculous. If I give it a chance the sleeping pill will kick in again, I just need to try to relax. I manage fifteen minutes, but despite my best efforts at yoga breathing, the tension keeps rising until it's almost constricting my chest. I push back the covers. I need to at least check on the children.

"Where are you going?"

I pause, caught out. Robert's awake. "I need a glass of water," I say.

"There's water by your bed."

He's just a shadow in the darkness, a disconnected voice. "It's stale," I say, getting up and taking the glass. "I'll get a fresh one. Do you want anything?"

"No." His voice is cool, discontented maybe, disgruntled definitely, as I head out of the room. My skin prickles even though it's a hot night, and somewhere in the back of my head the song is still playing loud, but the words are irritatingly out of reach as I come down the stairs.

I almost race to check the back door, my new tics all out of sync—*it's the wrong time I should do this at 1:13*—but still I feel better as I rattle the handle. Locked. I pour a glass of water and drink, staring out at the black night, half expecting to see someone on the other side of the glass staring in.

I look at the under-stairs cupboard as I come past, but resist the urge to open it. I can't afford to have one of those weird lost-time moments. Not with Robert awake. I go straight past and head back to bed. When I reach the landing I glance over to my left, and for a moment the shadows by the window look like a figure just out of sight round toward the children's rooms. I turn, I have to check, but there's no one there. The corridor is quiet.

I go to our beautiful arched window and peer out to the dark landscape beyond. My free hand touches the glass, palm flat against the cold, and I shiver, my toes curling into the thick pile carpet.

I open my mouth wide in an O, and breathe out a silent scream that fogs up the pane. If anyone is watching me, what will they think? Will I look like a woman in trouble? Or a crazy lady, wandering her house in the night like a ghost?

Look, look, a candle, a book and a bell . . . I put them behind me . . .

A lyric bubbles up in my head, the tune haunting. The song I heard on the radio. I should go back to bed, but I'm so close to the kids' rooms I'll check on them anyway. There's no harm in that.

I look in on Chloe first, lost beneath her duvet. Her phone is just under her pillow—she must have been texting her friends as she was falling asleep—and I carefully pull it out and put it on the side. The screen lights up—two messages that came in at midnight that she hasn't opened. I have no idea who they're from. Instead of a name there are just emojis. A heart and kissing lips. A boy? Maybe but maybe not. It could be Amy for all I know. I don't understand the language of teenage friendships anymore.

I leave her alone and head to Will's room. One quick look, that's all. I'll never get back to sleep again if I don't, sleeping pill or no sleeping pill.

Oh look, look a candle, a book and a bell, there to remind me . . .

I open the door, and look to where my little boy is sleeping. Warmth floods through me. He's fine. Of course he's fine.

"Jesus Christ, Emma." A shadow breaks away from the dark corner of the wall, a menacing beast hidden in the gloom, and I almost cry out, one hand covering my mouth.

"What the hell are you doing?" the monster finishes, angry eyes glaring at me. I almost scream, but then I realize it's not a monster at all. It's Robert.

"I knew you'd come in here. I knew it."

He makes it sound so terrible, as if I've done something wrong.

"No wonder he's having bad dreams." He takes my arm and pulls me out of the room. "You can't disturb his sleep every night. You can't."

"You're hurting me," I say. His fingers are tight, hurting me, but once we're back in the corridor he lets go. "All I did was look in on him. You're the one who was hiding in here!"

"What is wrong with you, Emma?" he hisses at me, as we climb back into our bed. "What the bloody hell is wrong with you?"

25

FIVE DAYS UNTIL MY BIRTHDAY

I was at work by six forty-five A.M., my head thumping with a sleeping pill hangover without the benefit of a good night's rest. I'd laid awake half the night, and although I could have stayed in bed longer without any real work repercussions, I wanted to get out of the house and avoid any cold shoulder from Robert over breakfast.

Now, more than twelve exhausted hours later, I'm doing my best to appear semi-human as the waiter tops up our sparkling water and wine between dinner courses that are delicious but barely filling. As I nod a thank-you, I smile and pretend to care about some posh boys' school anecdote Stockwell and Buckley are recalling.

"Poor Johnson," Buckley says, chuckling. "I think he must still hold the record for the receiver of most wedgies during one school year."

"Didn't do him any harm. He's foreign office now. But as far as I know he never had kids."

They laugh again.

"How are your boys?" I ask.

"Fine," Stockwell says. "They're getting on with the new nanny. Miranda was never keen on nannies and the one I managed to persuade her to have was an old battle-ax. This one is at least young and pretty."

"Key requirements in a nanny." The words are out before I can stop them and Buckley gives me a sharp look, so I laugh and try to make a joke out of it.

"Miranda's rung a few times wanting to speak to them," Stockwell continues. "Always bloody crying, that woman, as if she didn't bring all this on herself."

"Women are very emotional creatures," Buckley says, and I take a long swallow of wine to try to ease my irritation at their casual misogyny.

"Still," Parker says. "It makes them easy to predict." He turns his smile to me. "Unless they're as smart as Emma. Beauty and brains are quite a breathtaking combination." His teeth are too white and he's only one step away from a Simon Cowell over-tan, both of which mar any natural good looks he might have. He makes me cringe. Rich men who are used to getting what they want don't really float my boat.

"My husband thinks so." *Or at least he used to.* "What can I do for you though, Mr. Stockwell? Your divorce is done."

"Thanks to you."

"But if you're looking for more corporate representation," I continue, "then I'm not sure I can contribute much to this dinner. I haven't practiced outside of family law for a while now. There are far more experienced lawyers than me for what you might be needing."

"I wanted you here to thank you and to make sure Buckley knows your worth." He reaches across the table and squeezes my hand. "Especially as I hear there might be a partnership in the works." His palm is dry and too hot against my skin. Is he really trying to claim some credit for my potential partnership?

"Well, I hope so." I glance sideways at Buckley, who gives me a tight smile. Is there a warning in it? *Play nice.* "So maybe," I say with a bright smile, "I should refresh some of my corporate law skills. In fact, I already know someone who's done some work for you, I think. Julian Simpson? In construction."

My phone buzzes on the table. Robert. I cancel the call. If he's forgotten that I'm out for dinner tonight, that's not my fault. It rings again, and I cancel it fast, tucking it into my bag.

"Julian, yes. Clever man. I'm amazed anything is getting built by him at the moment." He flashes Buckley an amused, *boys together* look. "From what I hear he's got blue balls for that young thing he's running around with. Can't think of anything else apparently." He winks at me. "Too young for me." *Oh god, so Michelle is right. There is another woman.* My face must be a picture because he laughs. "Ah, I see you didn't know about that. Don't worry. His wife has a reputation for turning a blind eye." He drains his wineglass. "So many marriages would be saved if all the ladies were better at that."

Buckley laughs in agreement, as if he too has had to navigate mistresses and one-night stands, although I know he's absolutely devoted to Belinda, his wife of thirty years. Suddenly I can see them at school, Parker Stockwell, a loud, good-looking, over-cocky bully and Buckley doing his essays for him in exchange for his friendship.

"Excuse me a moment." I get up. "I just need to powder my nose." I changed into a black dinner dress at the office and I can feel Stockwell's eyes on me as I slide through the narrow gap between the tables. He doesn't move his chair, forcing me to brush my body past his arm, and for a moment I imagine picking up the water bottle and smashing it across the side of his skull and not stopping until his brains are all over the table, and then doing the same to Buckley for being so weak. Men. God.

I find my way to the ladies' room, away from the somewhat sedate restaurant area and past the busy cocktail bar. I'm annoyed at how I've let the two men get under my skin. I've dealt with Stockwell for months, throughout the whole mess of his divorce, and although I've never liked him, that's also never bothered me. I don't have to like people to do my job.

The stylish restrooms are empty and as I pee I reset myself. It's one dinner, and when Buckley's got Stockwell's business I can fade into the background. Some pretty thing will turn his head before long, I'm sure. Maybe even the poor nanny. That's what's irritating me. He's gone to all these lengths to get custody of his kids and now someone else is raising them. Still, it's not my business. I've got my own shit to sort out.

"I wondered how long it would be before he made a move on you."

Miranda.

I'm washing my hands when she emerges from the next cubicle, and although I know straightaway from that shrill, not entirely sober voice that it's Miranda

Stockwell, the scorned wife, she looks different. Her long hair is now dark, hanging free around her shoulders, and her makeup is heavier, vampy. I wouldn't have recognized her.

"Miranda, what are you doing?" I'm exasperated and also concerned. "You shouldn't be here."

"I can be wherever I want."

"Did you follow him?" My heart beats faster as another thought dawns on me. "Did you follow me?" Her mouth twists in a bitter smile, but she doesn't say anything.

"Look." I use my most sensible, unfazed solicitor's voice. "I can deal with the note on my windshield, but slashing my tire was dangerous."

"I hear my boys have a new nanny." She sways slightly, looking at her own reflection as if at a stranger. "I thought I might confront him. I came here to confront him. To embarrass him. But I can't, can I? Anything I say or do—however fucking reasonable—will be one more year without my kids."

"You should go home." She's standing between me and the door, and I'm willing someone to come in. "I don't think it will go well if you speak to him."

"It doesn't matter. I'm invisible." She smiles. It's a bitter, angry expression. "I don't exist. I probably didn't even need to change my hair."

"Look, Miranda, I'm worried about you."

"No, you're not." For a moment I think she's going to cry. "You're worried about what I might do." She leans forward. "And you know what, Mrs. High-and-Mighty Emma Averell? Maybe you should be. Maybe I'll do something crazy. Maybe I'll make *you* feel invisible."

"You need to stop drinking," I snap. "And you need to leave me alone. And I am not sleeping with—" She's already out the door before I can finish the sentence, passing three women coming the other way, bustling into the narrow space and stopping me from going straight out after her. *Fuck fuck fuck.*

I can't see her anywhere on my way back to the table. Has she left? Is she waiting for me outside? Should I speak to the police? And say what? She's made some drunken mild threats but hasn't actually touched me? I think she slashed my tire last weekend? It's not exactly going to leap to the top of their priority list. I should at least tell Buckley and maybe Stockwell. I don't need this shit on top of everything that's going on at home.

The maître d' is waiting by my table, and all three of them stare at me as I approach. Buckley looks embarrassed.

"Is everything okay?"

"Your husband rang the restaurant. He said he's been calling your mobile."

I thought he'd just forgotten I was out, but what if there's been an accident? The terrible dread that comes at night roils in my gut and I feel nauseous. "The children—"

"Your husband said your children are fine, madam." The maître d' looks apologetic. "But you have to go home." I feel like every diner is turned my way, and I see one face clearly, the solitary woman standing between the bar area and the restaurant, her eyes on me. *Miranda*.

The maître d' continues to speak, louder than I'm sure is necessary. "The police are there." He pauses, giving me and everyone else time to hang on his final words. "They want to speak to you."

26

There's a police car outside the house—the neighbors will love that—and I park quickly, and, feeling queasy, hurry inside. Chloe is wide-eyed, peering out from the sitting room. "They're in the kitchen," she says quietly as I go by. "What the fuck, Mum?"

What the fuck, indeed, Chloe, I want to answer, but instead I mutter something about whatever it is being just a mistake and that she should stay in there or go and look after Will, and then I see Phoebe coming down the stairs as if she owns the place. She looks at me like I'm poison and I'm pretty sure I'm looking at her the same way. My spine stiffens. "What are you doing upstairs?" I say. "In fact, what are you doing—"

"Emma." Robert comes out from the kitchen, face like thunder. "They're in here."

"It's about our mother." Phoebe's behind me, and between her and Robert ahead I feel like they're guards escorting me to the executioner's block rather than family.

There are two police officers, a man and a woman, both in their thirties, sipping coffee from our best mugs. They introduce themselves and show me their badges, as if I think they might be liars.

"What's going on?" My face is burning and I feel guilty, even though I've done nothing wrong. "I was at an important work dinner." My first lie given that I was basically at the restaurant as eye candy for Parker Stockwell.

"So your husband said. Sorry to have disturbed your evening." It's the woman speaking, Hildreth, I think she said her name was. Hildreth and Caine. That's it. "But we need to ask you a few questions about the circumstances of your mother's death."

I stare at them, fully aware of Robert's eyes boring into me, and my stomach lurches as I figure that whatever they're about to tell me, he must now know she didn't die all those years ago. My age-old lie is getting called out. "She was in hospital," I say. "I presume the doctors there can tell you in more detail what was wrong with her."

"You saw your mother on Tuesday?"

"Briefly. And later on in the evening my sister told me she'd died. What's the issue here, Sergeant?"

"You were the last person to see your mother alive."

"I don't know if I was or not but I'll take your word for it." Where are they going with this? I study them for a clue but their faces are impassive.

"Talk us through your visit."

"Certainly. But first tell me why you need to know. She was an old woman with a head injury and she died. What has that got to do with the police?"

Caine looks up from his coffee. "You don't seem very upset."

"I'm not. I've considered her dead since I was five." I dread to think what Robert's reaction was when they turned up. *Her mother? But she died when they were children. That's what she's always told me.*

"But you still went to see her?"

"And now I very much wish I hadn't," I snap. "For god's sake, what is going on?"

"There was a pillow on the floor." The words come from Phoebe, watching from the sidelines. "Beside her bed. They think maybe someone . . . well . . . I don't need to spell it out." In the silence I stare at her, and then at the two officers as the implication dawns on me.

"You think I smothered her?" I slump onto a stool at

the island. "Why would I do that? She was dying. And she was alive when I left."

"We've sent away swabs from her nostrils for analysis." Hildreth's tone is terrifyingly neutral. "If there are cotton fibers that she's inhaled, we'll have a better idea of what's going on." She looks at me thoughtfully. "But someone saw you running out of the hospital wing clearly distressed. Which seems at odds with your reaction now."

"While I was in her room, my mother grabbed my wrist for a moment. It frightened me."

"But that's not possible." Phoebe frowns. "Not with her brain injury."

"It *was* possible." Why can't she be on my side for once? "Because it happened. I was looking at her notes above the bed and then her eyes opened and she grabbed my wrist. It lasted a moment and then she let go and that was that. I presume I don't need to explain what my mother was locked up for? That's why I was upset. I ran out of the ward, got back to my car, and then the school rang and I went there."

"What time was that?"

"I don't know exactly." I rummage around in my bag. "But the call time will be in my phone."

"I'm not sure what you hope that will prove."

"Oh, this is ridiculous." I scroll back through my call log and thrust the phone into Hildreth's hand. "Look there. Three oh five P.M. they rang. What time did she die?"

"Three oh nine. But we can't know that you answered that call in your car."

"So maybe I was chatting to the school while I shoved a pillow over my mother's face, is that what you think?"

Hildreth puts the phone carefully down on the island. "That call only lasted two minutes. So you could have used both hands."

I stare at her. She can't be serious.

"But I'm sure this will all be cleared up when the lab results come back." Hildreth's face is a closed book, but I doubt she's imagining the results coming back in my favor. "You can understand why we needed to speak to you, though. According to your sister you didn't want anything to do with your mother. You wished she were dead. And then you go and visit her." She pauses. "And then she's dead."

"I went to see her *because* she was dying. I would have thought that was obvious to anyone." Tiredness washes over me. "And now I'd like you to leave. Unless there's anything else?"

"Not tonight."

"I'll see you out." Robert ushers them toward the corridor. I wait until they've gone and turn to face my sister.

"Emma, if you did anything—" she starts, but I cut across her.

"What did you say to Will, Phoebe?" I take a half step toward her. "Why would you scare him like that? Why would you tell him about what our mother did? And why now? Just before my birthday? What is wrong with you?"

"I don't know what you're talking about." Her voice is low and cold. "And don't make this about me." She glances over her shoulder, checking we're alone. "You're not sleeping, are you? That's what Robert says. And you're paranoid. Why would I tell Will anything about that? I'm not insane." The word hangs between us. "But what is wrong with *you*, Emma?" she asks. "I think maybe you need help. I worry about your family."

My face burns hot with anger. She's one breath away from calling me crazy. "This is *my* family," I hiss at her. "Not yours. They'll *never* be yours, however much you think they should be." I take another step forward. "You think everything is easy for me. That it's not fair that I have this and you have nothing, but that's just your excuse to yourself. Nothing was easy for me either, Phoebe. It's all been hard work. Relationships are hard work. Children are hard work. Having a bloody career is hard work. But I put the hours in, Phoebe, and that's the difference between you and me. You think the world owes you because of what our mother did. Because of our childhood. Because you were the eldest. The world doesn't owe anyone. I went out and worked hard for what I have. And so you can fuck off, Phoebe. You can fuck right off. Starting now. Get out of my house."

She grabs her jacket from the back of a stool. "You were the last person to see her, Emma," she says. "And the police don't turn up for no reason. And this crap about her grabbing your wrist. Honestly? It. Wasn't. Possible. Only in your head maybe. I don't know what's going on with you but good luck, Mrs. Get-what-you-want-whatever-the-cost, Mrs. Never-to-blame. Maybe our mother was right to worry. Maybe you are going mad like her."

I slap her face so hard that my hand stings and her cheek goes instantly blotchy in the fraction of a second I can see it before her own hand protects it.

Neither of us speaks, the slap ringing between us, and before I can bring myself to say something, she's gone. I see Chloe in the doorway, staring at me like I'm a stranger, as Phoebe disappears toward the front door.

"This is so fucked up," Chloe says before running

up the stairs to the sanctuary of her bedroom. I don't blame her. I don't blame her at all.

Robert comes back into the kitchen and we look at each other for a long moment. I wait for him to start shouting, but when he speaks, he's calm, and that disturbs me more.

"Haven't you got anything to say?" He looks exhausted—*as if he knows anything about exhaustion*—lost, and warily suspicious.

"I didn't kill her." It's such a ludicrous sentence to have to say out loud. *I did not murder my mother.*

"That's not what I'm talking about. You told me she was dead. All those years ago, you said she died when you were little."

"Well, she's dead now." My flippancy is brittle.

"It's not bloody funny, Emma. Why didn't you tell me she was alive?" He's looking at me as if maybe I've been a stranger all these years. I fill the kettle to make us some tea. A nice cup of tea, the great savior of every emotional trauma in the English nation. I'm not sure it's likely to cure anything today but at least I can turn away from him while making it. I shrug. Where to start? *It was none of your fucking business?* "It was a long time ago. It was easier that way. It was private."

"I would have understood your never wanting to talk

about her," he says, sounding far from understanding. "If you'd told me what she'd done."

"How do you know what she did?" I look back at him and suddenly the answer is obvious. "Oh, Phoebe told you."

"Not much. Only how your mother was suffocating her when you found them. The police spoke to her first today and she figured it would probably look better for you if I knew what really happened before they got here."

"I'm sure." Always thinking of me, that's Phoebe. It obviously hasn't occurred to him that she could have called *me* first and then I could have told him myself.

"I didn't tell you because she didn't deserve to be part of us. She wasn't even really part of me. I was so young." I'm appalled to feel hot tears welling up as my breath hitches. "And honestly, I don't even know why I went to see her. Phoebe told me it would make me feel better and then I couldn't get it out of my head, so I did, and now I have all this shit to deal with."

He finally gets up and puts his arms around me, my face pressing into the familiarity of his chest. "It's a mistake, that's all. The swab results will come back fine." His words are comforting but he doesn't sound that convinced. "I'll cancel your birthday drinks in the morning. Let's just get through this." He gives me a half-hearted squeeze and then I'm alone again. "Time for bed," he says, still not quite able to meet my eyes. "Get a good night's sleep so we can face tomorrow head-on."

"Maybe we can watch something funny on your iPad while we fall asleep?" I don't want to talk anymore, but I do want to be close to him, to feel like there's somebody on my side in this.

"Good idea. I'll go and talk to Chloe. Let her know that it's nothing to get in a stress over."

"I'll bring the tea up."

"Thanks." He gives me a wan smile. "We're just having a weird week."

That's one way of putting it, I think as he heads upstairs. I look down and my hands are shaking. Can the police seriously think I killed my mother? Does Phoebe? I take a deep breath. How am I going to explain this to Buckley at work tomorrow?

As the tea brews I get my phone out and see all the missed calls from Robert and notice a text way back from Phoebe telling me to call her, which *did* come in before Robert's and now I feel even worse about slapping her. My hand tingles as I think about it. I really slapped her. Now she probably *does* think I did away with our mother.

There's also a text from Parker Stockwell hoping

everything is okay. That's another situation I'm going to have to deal with. Miranda drunk in the restroom seems like a lifetime ago. She'd love this twist of events. The realization that my life is far from perfect right now too.

I look out through the kitchen window. The summer night is finally falling and my nerves are stretched too tight, guitar strings about to snap. It'll be fine. The police just doing their job, and I guess a pillow on the floor is going to be suspicious given our family history. But she must have had a little fit or something before she died and it fell out from behind her head. I can't even remember how the pillows were when I left. I don't remember much of it at all after she grabbed me. A blank space in my head I don't want to think about.

I go to the back door and check that it's locked, making a mental note that it is, so that if I wake in the night, I won't have any doubts. Maybe that will stop my compulsion to come downstairs. Maybe I'll be able to go back to sleep. What about Robert? Will he sleep after this? We've had the police here basically accusing me of murdering the mother he thought was dead years ago. And then there's Will's drawings, and him waiting for me in Will's room last night. Despite me saying Phoebe's been scaring him, he must have doubts. His face last night said it all. *Stop scaring our boy by stand-ing over him at night.*

I think about the pillow that the woman in Will's drawings is holding and then about our mother and what she did and then the pillow found beside her bed. The police would have a field day with all that if he'd told them, and Robert must be going over and over it all in his head.

I pour the tea and add milk and then two sugars to Robert's and my phone buzzes again. I almost don't look, dreading what might be coming next, but it's Caroline. It reads: *Sure. Sounds great.* What sounds great? I scroll up to see a text from me suggesting drinks again at some point. When did I send that? I look at the time. Three-thirty in the morning last night? I remember scrolling my emails trapped in my bed, I must have sent it then. My head is throbbing. It doesn't matter and doesn't really come as any surprise. The nights get fuzzy.

I turn the phone off. It makes me feel a hint of warmth in the awfulness of the evening. Maybe she wants to be friends too. Time to go upstairs to face Robert and hope he doesn't implode on me. I'm sure we still have arguments to come when he's "processed it all" as Dr. Morris would say. I remember the way he gripped me last night, dragging me out of Will's room. That anger and distrust. I look again to the back door as my sense of threat increases. It's locked. I know it's locked. But I give it one last check before I go to bed.

I do it when Robert goes to the bathroom to brush his teeth. I take my own prescription sleeping pill and then, before I can change my mind, I crumble a NightNight into his tea and give it a quick stir with the end of a pen from my bedside table drawer. I sit back, heart racing, and hope he won't taste anything odd under all the sugar.

I know it's wrong, *of course it's wrong,* but I've read the leaflet and it can't hurt him, and I can't stand the thought of him staying awake to watch me in the night. Hopefully we'll both sleep well and then in the morning the police will ring and this whole business with my mother will all be a stupid mistake. Then I'll get Will to admit that the drawings are Phoebe's fault and then there'll just be the business of the bar between us, and my looming fortieth to get past.

But first, dear god, please let me sleep.

27

I'm not asleep.

I'm in the under-stairs cupboard, pressed against the wall, my knees tucked under my chin. It's dark and musty and dust tickles my nose as memories rage in my head.

No, Mummy no!

Time folds in on itself and I'm back in that night, in a different under-stairs cupboard, locked in by my mother, the blackness a terrifying void gobbling me up, almost as terrifying as the noises on the other side. Her pacing, opening the back door, closing it, going upstairs, coming back down. Pacing, pacing, pacing.

There was a storm, I remember that. And now the storm is inside me.

Look, look, a candle, a book and a bell, I put them behind me.

Oh look, look, a candle, a book and a bell, there to remind me.

The song is too loud in my head and I can't think. I'm so tired. Why did I crawl in here? What can this possibly achieve? My finger, a ghostly grainy shape, reaches sideways and touches the door. On *that* last day Phoebe and I came home from school and found her crouched low in the hallway and scratching away with a compass on the inside of the under-stairs door, muttering to herself. "*One hundred and thirteen one hundred and fifty-five two hundred and eighteen two hundred and twenty-two.*" I draw the numbers with my finger against the smooth wood: **113155218222**.

Look, look, a candle, a book and a bell, I put them behind me.

Why is this happening to me every night? My mouth is dry from the sleeping pill that didn't work. I won't take another one. No point. It's making me feel sick but giving me no rest. Not like Robert. He's dead to the world on his one NightNight.

Oh look, look, a candle, a book and a bell, there to remind me . . .

I draw the invisible numbers against the wood again, and they're soothing. I feel like I've been in here forever rather than a few minutes. Although maybe I have. Maybe I've had one of those little black spots when I lose time.

At 1:13 A.M. I checked the back door. *Rattle, rattle.* It was locked, of course. I knew before I checked that it was locked. I remembered locking it. But as the minutes crept around in my battleground of a bed, I couldn't stop the urge to go and check again. More than an urge. Something primal. Something I couldn't fight.

At 1:55 A.M. I went upstairs and stared out the hall window, my hands pressed against the glass, my heart racing. And now? Now I'm here. Back in the understairs cupboard, like I was all those years ago in a different house, but this time I've put myself in here.

Turning forty. Turning into my mother.

Everything feels wrong at night. Pieces out of place in my head. No straight edges in the jigsaw to anchor me. I thought I would be better when my mother died, but I'm worse. Tonight feels distorted, thoughts fragmented and yet so loud, filled with dread and worry and unease. How did my mother die? *Was* it me? Can I trust myself? In daylight I'd say yes, no question, but now, in the dead of night, I'm not so sure. Am I my own unreliable narrator?

No, I decide, my finger sketching numbers fast against the wood. I'm exhausted. Maybe I'm even having some kind of breakdown. But I didn't kill her. I couldn't have. I'd *know* if I had.

Are you so sure? It's my mother's voice, hissing in my ear. *You're hiding in a cupboard under the stairs for no reason. The past is repeating itself. Mad like me. Like mother, like daughter. Bad blood.*

The door opens, my finger left drawing on air, and I gasp, clutching my hands over my mouth, pressing myself into the corner, trying to make myself smaller. I'm so terrified that for a moment I'm convinced that the figure crouching there is *her*.

But this is not *then*, and the shadow is not my mother as she was on the night of her fortieth birthday, long hair hanging straggly and unkempt across her face, tilting her head. *"Ah, there you are."* Surprised to see me, even though she was the one who'd locked me in.

The shadow now in front of me is smaller, much as I was back then.

"Mummy?" His whisper is quiet, but the sound of his voice shatters the confusion in my head, like cold water on my face, and I feel like myself again. *Will.* It's Will. He's giving me that funny look, like when I squeezed him too hard reading *Paddington,* as if he can't rely on me for safety anymore. It breaks my heart.

I scramble out and see what made him find me. A

mug of chamomile tea, cold, sitting on the floor by the door.

"It's okay." I kiss his face, my hands freezing against his hot skin. "Don't be scared." He looks past me to the cupboard beyond. I force myself to smile. "Don't tell anyone, but that's Mummy's secret hiding place." His eyes come back to me. "It can be your secret hiding place too, if you like," I say. I sit cross-legged on the floor and pull him onto my lap. His little body is so warm, and I wrap my arms around him, holding him like I used to when he was a toddler, a happy lively boy. I rock us backward and forward.

"But the thing about secrets," I whisper, "is that you can't tell anyone about them. Not even Daddy. Okay? It has to be just us. Our safe space. Our special place." He nods, so serious, like an old man, and I want to shake this quietness out of him, to get my funny little boy back.

"Are you okay, monkey?" I push his hair out of his eyes. "I'm so worried about you. You can't sleep either? Did Auntie Phoebe scare you?" He doesn't say anything, but licks his lips. He always does that when he's thinking hard about something. "Is that why you did those drawings in your book? Did she say something to you?"

He chews the side of his bottom lip. I know that tell

too—he's feeling awkward. He doesn't know what to say. His body has stiffened and he's picking at the skin around his fingers, just like I do.

"It's okay, baby. I just need to know. What were you drawing?"

He wriggles away from me, knocking over my mug of cold chamomile tea and vodka as he gets to his feet.

"Will, wait!"

He gets to the bottom step and then stops dead, one hand on the banister, and looks at me.

"You, Mummy," he says eventually. "It's you." And then he's gone, running up the stairs as if a monster is chasing him.

Me.

I'm half up on my feet but now I crumple back to the floor. How can he be drawing me? Yes, I check on him at night. But that's all. I want to keep him safe. *Safe from what?* My mother is whispering in my head again. *They think you killed me. You're not even entirely sure you didn't yourself, are you? You don't remember whispering my numbers into your Dictaphone. You don't remember much of the hospital after I grabbed you, not until you were running. Maybe you don't remember scaring him either?*

I stay on the floor for a long time after that.

28

FOUR DAYS UNTIL MY BIRTHDAY

I've spent the night worrying about Will and what he might say to Robert about finding me in the cupboard—*why the hell was I in the cupboard?*—but it's Chloe who finally lets rip over breakfast. I'm making a second double espresso in the coffee machine we rarely use and Robert is doing something on his iPad—avoiding me basically. The atmosphere is unbearably tense and probably not helped by all of us trying to act as if everything is normal.

"I'm the teenager," she says as she gathers her stuff together, ready to leave for school on time for once. "I'm supposed to be the dysfunctional one."

I haven't gone in to work early. I finally fell asleep at nearly five and didn't wake until Robert got up at 6:45, and anyway, I wanted to see Will, to make sure he was okay, but it's as if he's forgotten that last night ever happened. He's playing with a toy truck on the breakfast bar, making *brrmmm brrmmm* sounds while eating his cereal and spraying quite a lot of milk down his chin. He's so much closer to normal than he's been for a few days that neither Robert nor I have asked him to stop.

"What's wrong with this family at the moment?" Chloe continues. "It's like everyone's gone mad."

Mad. There's that word again. My mother in among us.

"Everything's fine," I say.

"Fine?" She half laughs. "You've got these secrets you've been keeping from us—I had a grandmother who was alive all these years for one—and you've been acting weird and looking like complete shit for about a week, and now the police have been here clearly thinking you've done something wrong, and we're all acting as if that's perfectly normal."

"Chloe, listen—"

"On top of that, Will has totally shut down and no one seems to be doing anything about that, and you, Dad." She glares at Robert. "You're not normal either.

As soon as I get home and can look after Will, you go out. Neither you nor Mum are ever in the house these days. Will's my brother, not my child. It's not my job to look after him. And maybe if you were both here more, you'd see that something is really bothering him."

"I'm not out all the time. Don't exaggerate."

Robert looks pissed off. Guilty. Caught out. Is this why he's been so shit at doing things around the house recently? He's been out. Has he been skating in just in time to feed Will and get him to bed and make it look like he's been home all day? I don't care if he's out doing stuff, but I care that he's not telling me. Is this all part of this buying a bar midlife crisis plan? Or is it something else?

Chloe looks at us, from one to the other. "Are you getting a divorce? Because if you are, just say so."

"God no," I say, when she finally pauses for breath.

"Of course not," Robert adds, a few seconds after me, as if hesitant. "We're just working through a few things."

"Are we?" I look at him, surprised. "I wasn't aware that we were."

"Freddie's mummy and daddy got divorced." Will looks up from his truck. "Freddie's dad lives with a lady called Jane now. Freddie's mummy says Jane's a bitch."

Chloe barks a laugh, as I look on shocked. *Bitch.*

I kiss his head. "You shouldn't use that word, it's not nice."

"Freddie's mummy does."

"We're not getting divorced," I tell him. "And as for the police"—I turn my attention back to Chloe—"that is all a mistake. And I'm sorry I kept—" start to apologize and then pause, feeling a sudden heat in my belly. What the hell am I apologizing for?

"No, actually, I'm *not* sorry I kept my mother a secret." My tone is sharper. "It was *my* business. *My* past. From long before you were born. And just because you are my child does not mean I have to tell you everything—or even tell your father everything—that went before. I'm sure I don't know all your secrets." I see her falter a little then. She's a teenager—her life must be one big tangle of secrets. "And trust me, life is complicated, Chloe. We don't all have the advantage of being cocky teenagers who know everything."

She glares at me for a long moment. "God, I can't wait to get out of here," she mutters before turning and flouncing out to the hallway and leaving us with a slam of the front door.

"What is a bitch anyway?" Will asks, and all the questions I have for my husband about where he's been going and what he's been doing are going to have to wait.

"I'm so sorry, Angus." I'm in his office, giving him my most disarming smile, looking neat and professional, and I've put some expensive highlighter under my eyes to battle the dark shadows. "But someone tried to break into the house. Left a mess." I'm still feeling bullish after my spat with Chloe and I don't see why I should tell Buckley what's really happened given that I haven't done anything wrong.

"Whoever it was—they think perhaps some teenagers who've been seen hanging around the cricket pitch at night—tried Robert's car too. They needed me to come home to make sure nothing of mine was missing. And calm Will down, of course. I think the broken glass scared him. Well, it would, wouldn't it?"

I've got caffeine jitters but my mind is thankfully clear. The mornings have become like crisp clear water after the muddy mental bogs of the night. Can you just go mad at night? Is that possible? Things are always worse at night, that's what my foster mother, Rachel, used to say when she'd comfort me before I woke her own kids with my screaming. Maybe she had a point.

"To be honest it stressed me too," I add. "We need to get some CCTV cameras."

Angus Buckley's expression doesn't change, not even a murmur of sympathy, which is very much out of character, and I feel a prickle of sweat under my blouse when he finally meets my eyes. He looks very awkward and uncomfortable.

"The police were here early this morning," he says. "They've just left. They were asking some questions about you. When you've been in the office, what time you left, that kind of thing." He pauses. "Not the sort of questions one would ask regarding a burglary."

Oh, those bastards. My face flushes. "I see. Well, I haven't done anything wrong."

"I'm sure you haven't." Now that I'm on the back foot, he's regaining his usual confidence. "But until whatever it is has been cleared up, perhaps you should take a couple of days off."

"I'm fine to be at work."

"It wasn't a request, Emma." He pauses. Is that wariness in his expression? "At the very least," he says, "consider it bereavement leave. For the loss of your mother." The words land anvil heavy in the room.

"They told you about her?"

"They mentioned the nature of their inquiries, yes. Look, your family life is not my business, Emma—"

"Well, it seems to me like you're making it your business—"

"*Until* it impacts on our practice. And last night I was left highly embarrassed at dinner with a client who could bring a lot of business to us."

I stare at him. All the shit I've got going on, and his nose is out of joint because of dinner? "Oh, come on," I say, all apology gone from my tone. "You only had me at that dinner because Stockwell wants to shag me. *You* were embarrassed? I felt like a slab of steak being held out as an offering. Which, now I'm thinking about it, I should probably make some sort of complaint about."

His gaze turns to stone. The company prides itself on its equality policies even if we all know that Friday nights can get a bit *touchy,* at worst, and mansplainy at best after one too many in the bar.

"Go home, Emma." His voice is low and cold. "I'll call you in a couple of days. Let's not make this worse than it should be."

"Wow, Angus. You haven't even asked me how I am or what happened. But fine. I'll go home." I turn on my heel and try to keep my back straight, even though my legs are shaking. "Thanks for the support."

Home? The last place I want to be right now is at home. Not with Robert there, probably compiling a list of questions about my past and going through my clothes, picking my best prison wardrobe. And what if Will said something to him on the way to school about finding me in the cupboard last night?

In my office I gather what I need—a few case file notes I need to catch up on, a notepad, paper, and my spare laptop charger—and am cramming it all into my bag when Rosemary comes in.

"Are you okay?" she asks. "We don't normally have that kind of excitement here so early. I'm presuming that whatever it is, it's all some misunderstanding." She gives me a smile but it doesn't quite reach her eyes. Not really surprised, given that I asked her to type up a Dictaphone tape full of whispered numbers only days ago.

"Family stuff." I grab my desk diary too.

"Yes, that's what they said. To do with your mother?"

"I'm sure you told us your mother was dead." Alison casts a dark shadow across my office doorway, almost elbowing Rosemary out of the way to get inside. "Didn't she die when you were a child?"

"Yes, that's what I told you." I glare at her. "And as far as I'm concerned, she did. I'm sorry if the police have been asking you questions, but my childhood was complicated to say the least and they're just doing their jobs, even if they're barking up the wrong tree."

Rosemary looks down at her shoes, but Alison holds my gaze for a second longer. I'm just about to tell her in no uncertain terms to fuck off, when she shrugs. "Your family isn't any of our business anyway. I certainly wouldn't share any of my private history with people if I didn't want to. It was bad enough when Jim left me and everyone was talking about that. I hope it's sorted out soon."

She disappears off down the corridor and I'm glad, because I'm suddenly biting back tears. Alison being relatively supportive. Who would have thought?

"Anyway, I'd better get on," I mutter, letting my hair fall over my face so Rosemary can't see how affected I am by Alison. "Just call me if anything comes up you need me for."

"Yes, of course," she says. "I'm sure it will all be back to normal by next week."

Her spine is stiffer as she walks away, and I realize that whatever *easiness* our relationship has had is gone. She might say that it's not her business to know but she's taken my omission of my past as a deception.

I close my bag and sling it over my shoulder. Sod her, I think, as I stride out of the office, my face straight ahead and chin high. It really *isn't* any of her business.

29

I'm so angry and humiliated when I leave the office that I get in the car and drive with no thought whatsoever, lost in a haze of arguments in my head and worrying about the police and thinking about Will's drawing, and only when I turn onto a final street do I realize what I've done. I've driven to Caroline's house.

I stare at her front door, wanting to go and knock, to see what she's doing, to be in her company. Now that I'm here the urge is like a terrible itch. It reminds me of my nighttime routines. Something *compulsive*. I sent her a text I don't even remember. Why am I so keen to be her friend? I've never been a person who needs a lot of friends, but I *felt something* when we had lunch. Like she was a kindred spirit. Like we're bonded. It was a definite spark, and now that I'm here I realize that it's been quietly bubbling under the skin, through all the shit of last night, a longing to see her again. My palm is sweating as I reach for the car door handle. I pause. I can't go and knock on her door without texting back. It's too weird. She'll think I'm a stalker. She'll probably think this is sexual after the way I dragged her to lunch. She'll maybe even think I'm crazy.

That's the thought that stops me, *I'm not crazy*, and then moments later her front door opens and in a panic, I duck down into the seat, my heart racing. I lift my head slightly so I can just about see, and I catch a glimpse of her, dressed for work, hair back in a tight bun, getting into her car.

Thankfully, she doesn't look my way. I wait until she's driven off and then sit up straight. What am I doing? It's tiredness and trauma, that's all. I wanted to see a friendly face. I check my emails on my phone, taking my time, and I tell myself it's because I'm professional, but really, I'm giving her a head start. I'm a little bit scared I'll follow her and then I really *would* be crazy.

After a few minutes, I'm laughing at myself for hiding in my car rather than saying hello, and my sense that I'd done something *wrong* has gone, but I don't want to go home yet, so I decide that I might as well find somewhere to hole up and have some lunch. I consider calling Dr. Morris and telling her that I still can't sleep but decide against it. *Oh, the police think you may have killed your mother? No wonder the pills aren't working.* I head back into town and park, choosing a trendy hippy cafe that I know no one I work with would ever go into. It's near the college and I'm about fifteen years older than the staff let alone the clientele, but the woman behind the counter is friendly and it's the kind of place where you can nurse a coffee for an hour without anyone giving you filthy looks or telling you to get out.

I take a table in the corner by the window and wait for my soy milk cappuccino and organic carrot cake to arrive. I'm not even hungry, but I need some energy if I'm going to get anything done. There's a gnawing in my stomach that won't go away, and I keep checking my phone every few seconds in case I've missed a call from the police telling me that the swabs came back fine and my mother's death was brought on entirely by her head injury. But I'm disappointed every time.

An hour passes and I pick at the cake and most of my coffee grows cold. I can't relax. My insomnia is making me question everything, even my own guilt or innocence. My brain is constantly foggy and time's been slipping away from me, I know that. I've fallen asleep at work. When I stare at something for too long it's like I drift into somewhere between sleep and wakefulness, I zone out. Could I have done it and forgotten about it? But surely I'd remember doing *that*? And why would I kill her? I didn't even know her. *Because you hated her. Because you're afraid you're going mad like her? Because you don't want to have a head full of her numbers.*

My phone stays silent. Robert doesn't call, the police don't call, Phoebe doesn't call, and neither does work. As I stare at my case notes for the Marshall divorce—I need to follow up on their mediation—the flash of a familiar red jacket through the window distracts me and I frown, confused. The red-jacketed girl takes a seat at a table outside the urban-chic-looking bar opposite and lights a cigarette.

It's Chloe.

I stare at my daughter as she takes a deep lungful and exhales. When the hell did she start smoking? I thought the whole point of that vape that she carries around like a fashion accessory was that she wouldn't smoke the real thing. That cigarettes were *so last century.*

I'm also sure she didn't leave the house in those clothes. Not a dress. She never wears dresses. She looks sophisticated. Older. What is she doing? I know the school timetable is pretty relaxed at the moment with some revision sessions in place of lectures, but I'm sure she's supposed to be in a class right now. Has she snuck away to meet a boy?

I pull away from the glass in case she sees me. I don't wave or go out and call over to her, because every mother's instinct in my body is screaming at me that I'm watching something secret. Something that my daughter would rather cut an arm off than talk to me about. She looks nervous as she checks her phone. Nervous or excited? Maybe both.

And then she's on her feet as the person she's obviously been waiting for approaches, stubbing the cigarette out, and arm in arm they go inside. My stomach drops, lead-heavy, as the truth sinks in.

Oh, bloody hell, Chloe. Oh, bloody, bloody hell.

I order another coffee and drink it slowly, checking Chloe's timetable on my laptop, now wide awake despite my burning eyes and racing heart telling me that under this adrenaline rush I'm really fucking exhausted. I force myself to be patient, and then once she's left and headed back in the direction of the school I send her a text.

"Hey Chlo, I'm finishing early today. Don't worry about getting the bus, I'll pick you up. Give us time to

have a chat before we get home. See you at two thirty. Love you, Mum."

And then I wait.

"I told you that you didn't need to bother." She throws her bag on the back seat, takes a last puff on her vape—no cigarettes in front of her mother—and gets in, phone clutched tight in one hand as she drops the vape in the side door.

"I know I didn't need to," I say as I pull away. "But I wanted to. And we never seem to get time to ourselves anymore."

She shrugs. "That's because you're always at work."

"And you're always out. But that's okay. Because that's how life is." I don't want this to be any more confrontational than it has to be. She's my daughter and I love her and my anger isn't for her. She's in her jeans now, hair pulled back in a ponytail, and she's still wearing makeup, but it's muted. A lot of work has gone into this transformation back into teenager from young gorgeous woman. "But sometimes I just want to know how you're doing in more than a five-minute conversation while passing in the corridor."

She gives me a sideways derisory glance. "I'm sure we can get really deep and meaningful on a fifteen-minute car ride though."

All her defenses are up, but I give her a bright smile. "I'll take the scenic route. Go through the villages. We know how to have quality time, right?"

She doesn't laugh at my lame joke and we're both quiet as I negotiate my way through the traffic and try to think of the best way to start this. All the planned openings I'd thought up in the café have evaporated and I realize that I'm very out of practice at having difficult conversations with my daughter. In general, she's a really great kid. But now there's this. She certainly saved it all up for one big hit.

"What's going on with you, Mum?" She breaks the moment first. "What do the police think you did?"

"I haven't done anything. That's a misunderstanding."

"That's not what I asked. I asked what they thought you did. Auntie Phoebe was really upset. And Dad was weird."

"I don't want to talk about that. I told you. It's not worth your worrying." I need to get this questioning going in the other direction.

"I hear you moving around at night," she continues. "Going downstairs. I'm not always asleep. I heard Auntie Phoebe talking to Dad. Something about you turning forty." She looks out the window. "I mean, Jesus, Mum, if that's why you're being so weird, it's just a number. Nothing to get so stressed about. You should be feeling empowered. I can't wait to be older."

I let out a laugh that she thinks all my erratic behavior basically stems from vanity. "Thanks, Chloe. I'll bear that in mind. And speaking of my birthday, how's the party looking?"

"The party's canceled. That's what Dad said. After that stuff with Ben. And whatever's going on with you."

"It'll be fine if it's just our gang. They're not such a bad crowd, Dad's friends from school. You like them, don't you?"

"They're okay." She shrugs, looking down, hands fiddling with her phone. "But it's still canceled. Auntie Phoebe and Dad think—" She pauses, half-committed to saying something that she's obviously wishing she hadn't started.

"Phoebe and Dad think what?" I sit up straighter behind the wheel. Robert and Phoebe. Since when did they start getting so close again?

She shrugs. "That you've got some kind of paranoia thing going on. Because of your mum. Well, that's what Dad said anyway."

My foot presses slightly on the accelerator, speeding up in my anger. He'd told me he was going up to tell Chloe there was nothing to worry about and instead he does the opposite.

"Your dad's got secrets of his own, it turns out," I say. "That bar for one. I think he's having a midlife crisis." My tone sharpens. "Or maybe I am just paranoid." Sunlight glints off the windshield and I go a little faster. Paranoia. How dare he? And how dare he talk to Phoebe about me like that? Why don't they talk to *me* about it?

"But tell me, Chloe," I start, my tone conversationally light. "Is it paranoia that makes me think you're sleeping with Michelle's husband, Julian, or the fact that I saw you in a bar with him today?"

Her eyes widen, her mouth falling open, and I grip the steering wheel. "Don't even think about denying it. I'm not stupid. Although how could *you* be so stupid? What about all your talk of feminism? The sisterhood?"

She says nothing but her face is like thunder.

"He's nearly twenty years older than you," I continue. "You were their babysitter. Jesus Christ, Chloe, you're a walking bloody sexual cliché. It's disgusting."

"It's not disgusting! Only you making it sound that way is disgusting!" Pink blotches have risen up on her neck. She glares at me, defiant. "I'm not going to deny it. I'm eighteen in a couple of months. I'm not a child. I'm basically a grown woman and I love him." She looks out the window at the winding road. "And slow down or stop. You're going too fast."

"Love? You only *think* you love him." I can't stop with the car behind me, and anyway, I'm barely hearing her. My head is in a white rage. *Paranoid. My husband who's supposed to love and support me thinks I'm paranoid.* And how could Chloe add this to everything else that's going on? "You don't know what love is. This isn't love—it's just a stupid mistake. He's using you. You're flattery to an old man's ego."

"He's thirty-six, he's not that old."

That old. And in that phrase is the reveal of just how young she really is. I look at her. "Michelle knows. She doesn't know *who,* but she knows. She came to see me to find out where she'd stand in a divorce. She knows he's seeing someone. For god's sake, she thought it was me!"

"You?" Chloe barks out an unpleasant laugh, as if that's the most ridiculous suggestion in the world, as if the idea of anyone actually wanting to fuck me is highly comical. "He wouldn't go near you." There's a twinge of jealousy there too, I realize, and remember all the energy of youthful all-consuming love. I had it with Robert once. I'd get green-eyed if he laughed with Phoebe too long or anything else that reminded me that he'd come home with her on that first night. Phoebe and I are a tangled-up sack of old resentments and jealousies and love. *Paranoia.*

"And a good job too, because if he did, I'd send him home with his tail between his legs." Another thought strikes me. "He wants your father to go into business with him in this bar. Was that your idea?"

She gives me that dismissive shrug again. "I know Dad was fed up of being stuck at home. I thought it would be good for him. And Jules likes him and—"

"And what did you think your father was going to do once he found out about this?" *Jules?* I've never even heard Michelle abbreviate his name. "Your dad wants to invest all your university money in this stupid bar plan. Money I worked hard to put aside for you. What would have happened to that when all this eventually came out? God, I wish I hadn't seen you together. Now I have to deal with it."

"I'm glad you know." She glares at me. "He loves me. He's going to leave her and we're going to live together. He's just waiting for me to finish my exams."

It's my turn to laugh. "Yes, of course he is. I'm sure Julian has your absolute best interests at heart and I'm sure he's going to turn his back on his big house and his lovely family just to shack up with some selfish seventeen-year-old who's too stupid to see him for what he really is." I turn the corner and feel the car pull from my speed. "He's going to fuck you till he's bored and then he'll forget all about you."

"I hate you," she says, quiet and cold, staring down at her hands. My heart is racing. I'm the bad guy again. Never Robert. Always me.

"I love you, Chloe. But end it now and I won't tell your dad. No one has to know."

"I hate you." She says it louder this time, and as I glance across, for a moment I can see her as she was at two, simmering, all contained rage as a tantrum approached, brow furrowed so tight that her eyes were hooded, jaw clenched, and mouth pursed.

"No you don't. You just think you do." I'm even using the tone I used with her then, but she's not a toddler anymore, she's a near adult, and suddenly she's lashing out at me.

"Yes I do. I really hate you." She snarls it louder and then twists away, grabbing at the door handle. What's she trying to do, jump out of the bloody car to get away from me?

"Chloe, for god's sake!" I reach out and grab at her, frantically pulling her back.

"Let go of me!" She pulls herself free, shoving me away, then we're pushing at each other as I try to keep my eyes on the road. "What's wrong with you?" She lashes out again, hands whipping at me, the car swerving under us. I push her hard, protecting myself, and she bangs her head on the passenger-seat window.

"Chloe, calm down!"

There's nothing ahead but bends in the country road. I look behind and the driver has pulled back, no doubt concerned by my erratic driving.

"Mum, look out!"

The loud blare of a horn fills the car, and as my heart almost stops, I realize I've veered into the other narrow lane. Seeing the truck bearing down on us, I pull the wheel hard to the left, my whole body in a panic. Chloe cringes back into her seat, her head turned away, eyes closed, arms up to protect herself, and only then do I see the vape that she must have been reaching for, not the door at all, and my feet feel like they're slamming on all the pedals as the car spins and all I see is the tree coming at us so fast, and then I'm closing my eyes too.

30

We are lucky all things considered. My new car is, however, a write off. The front on the driver's side buckled on impact and the chassis is rippled like corrugated iron underneath. At least, at the last second, I'd managed to turn the wheel so the crash was more on my side than Chloe's. She has a split lip and a nosebleed from her airbag, but other than that is thankfully only shaken. My airbag didn't deploy and my right arm and shoulder are jarred, my knee is bruised, and I can already feel whiplash kicking in by the time the police and ambulance arrive, but my overwhelming emotion is relief that Chloe is okay.

In the quiet aftermath, my whole body shaking, I'd been afraid to look across at her. When I finally did, the shock of seeing so much blood on her face and down her top had me shrieking and fussing at her to find where the injury was, and in the end, she had to shout at me to stop, lifting up her T-shirt to show me her unharmed midriff and to point out the blood was all from her lip and nose. Even then it took a few seconds before I calmed down. All this nightly fear that something was going to hurt my children, and then I nearly kill my precious girl.

"What were you doing, Mum?" She'd been close to tears as she stared at me. "Why did you attack me?"

"I didn't, I didn't," I'd said. "I thought you were trying to get out of the car. Reaching for the door. That's all."

The fright of the crash doesn't ease the tension between us; if anything it makes it worse, and she's still distant, wary, like a wounded animal, when the police and an ambulance turn up a few minutes later. We don't tell them we were fighting; instead I say I was distracted by an animal running across the road and then lost control. It's more than an hour later that the police car drives us home and by then the adrenaline has worn off and I'm so tired I could throw up and my whole body feels broken.

"It can't go on, Chloe," I say quietly to her. "You know it can't."

She doesn't answer but looks out the window, chewing on her thumb. I look out mine and see my wan reflection staring back at me, my bloodshot eyes and messed up hair. I've lost weight and my skin is dry and uneven. No wonder my family thinks I'm losing it.

"What the hell happened?"

Chloe and I are in the hallway looking like the last survivors from some horror film after the policeman who drove us home leaves. Robert's face is aghast. "Are you hurt?" He comes forward to hug Chloe, but she puts her hands up to stop him.

"I'm fine."

"I'll put that top in to soak," I say to her quietly as she heads to the stairs. She doesn't look back.

"Mum lost her shit, that's what the hell happened," she calls over her shoulder.

"That's not fair and you know it," I snap back. It's also not true.

Robert looks at me. "What's she talking about?"

"You know how you drove into a tree once?" He stares at me nonplussed, so I spell it out for him. "Well, now I have too."

"Fuck's sake, Emma. How?"

"The same way you did. Accidents happen. I need

a shower before my neck totally seizes up." He hasn't even asked if I'm okay. "I'll call the insurance people after."

"What did Chloe mean, you lost your shit?"

My intention had been to tell Robert straightaway, but now I find the whole sorry mess of Julian and Chloe gets tangled and stuck in my throat. I've got to tell him, of course I have, but god knows what he'll do. Go around there? Fight Julian? Try to kill him maybe. Chloe's his little girl and always will be. Maybe once Julian knows I know he'll want to end it anyway. The fear of getting caught will outweigh anything else.

"I'm okay, thanks for asking." I glare at him. He looks almost apologetic and is about to say something when the doorbell rings again. "Just leave it," I say. "The world can wait, there's something we need to—"

"It might be the police again," he says. "Did you leave anything in their car?" He pulls the door open and we both freeze where we are.

It *is* the police, but not the ones from the accident. It's Hildreth and Caine. Behind them is a car, the light turning silently on top and a uniformed officer standing beside it. My heart starts to race again as Robert regains his composure and lets them in. The door closes and we stand in silence for a moment as they all stare at me.

"What is it?" I say, an alert frightened rabbit.

"We've had the swabs back from your mother's mouth and nasal cavities." Hildreth's tone is impassive but her expression is cool. Cold. "Fibers that match the hospital pillowcase were found in both."

The ocean rushes in my ears. "But that can't be right. That means someone . . ." I look up at Robert. "I didn't—it wasn't me—"

"She's been in a car accident." Robert steps forward, blocking the space between them and me. "Can't this wait until the morning?"

This time it's Robert who's the focus of Hildreth's withering look. "No, it can't wait until morning." She looks at me again. "We need you to come down to the station, Mrs. Averell. I'd rather not arrest you, but I will if I have to."

I'm aware of Chloe peering over the banister, wide-eyed, and Robert's mouth is moving, but all I can hear is my own heart pounding. I think I might faint. Caine comes forward and touches my arm, and the world falls back around me. This is actually happening.

"I'll call Buckley." Robert looks terrified, as if it's him being dragged off to the cells. "He'll know some-one."

"No. Not him." My brain whirrs. The last thing I want is Angus Buckley being dragged into this. But who will help? A name comes to me. "Darcy Jones. In my address book in my study. Call him." And then they're efficiently whisking me away from my family and out of my house. Oh, please god, I hope Darcy hasn't changed his number.

31

"And that's it?" Darcy leans forward and, as I sit, palms sweating and body aching in the seat beside him, I would swear that he sounds almost amused. "That's all you have?" he continues. "A few fibers from a pillowcase, which, let's face it, could have come from an overtired or too busy nurse being slightly too rough when adjusting the patient, or indeed caused by the patient herself in the moments before her death. Since no one was present to witness what happened."

Detective Sergeant Hildreth must have been expecting me to get a solicitor with some clout, but I doubt even she thought I could go as high as Darcy Jones, QC, criminal barrister extraordinaire. Even back at uni, we all knew Darcy was going to be the kind of lawyer who struck fear into others—charming, witty, sharp as a tack, and with a shark's prey drive when he has the opposition's arguments in his sights. The one thing I've learned from watching his career unfold from a distance is that *If I'd lived another life I might be Mrs. Jones now, I wonder what that would be like* kind of way, is that no one fucks with Darcy Jones, QC.

Darcy doesn't lose, and if there's the slightest crack in your case, he will come barreling through it, just as he's doing now with Hildreth and Caine. Hildreth leans forward.

"Mrs. Averell has, according to both family and colleagues, claimed that her mother has been dead for her entire adult life."

"There's no crime in that," Darcy counters. "My client had no relationship with her mother, and had no desire for one, and so it's natural that she took the option of telling people her mother was deceased. Her past is her private business."

"Emma." She looks at me. "Your sister, Phoebe, says that you're not sleeping."

"Everyone goes through phases of poor sleep." I speak after a nod from Darcy. I've said very little throughout the interview thus far, with Darcy like a growling tiger barring the door, allowing me just an answer here or there so I don't appear uncooperative.

"Your mother's mental health went into steep decline when she started suffering from insomnia, didn't it? In the weeks leading up to her fortieth birthday."

"I was five, so it's hard to say," I snap. "But given how things turned out, I guess you could say so."

Darcy's hand touches mine, quieting me, and I'm surprised at how much I like the feel of it. Safe. Protective. Totally on my side.

"Get to your point, Detective. We all know the history here."

"Phoebe also told us that you've always been worried that, like your mother, you too will have some form of psychotic break on your fortieth birthday, which is, what, a few days away now?"

"You can't arrest someone for their worries," Darcy says.

"And now you're not sleeping." She looks at me as if Darcy hasn't spoken. If Darcy's a tiger, she's a terrier. "Just like your mother didn't sleep. I imagine it would be very hard not to be afraid that you might do the things she did. She always said you were like her, didn't she? You've worked very hard to prove her otherwise. A high-flying career. A family to support—I believe your husband doesn't work. It's all a huge amount of pressure, isn't it? And then your mother comes back into your life when she's transferred to the hospital."

I could throttle Phoebe right now. I can just see her,

so full of faux concern, efficiently blabbing our entire history, even the parts that aren't in those clinical legal records from the past, and making me look like a potential monster.

"You visit her in that hospital only once, leaving visibly shaken and upset, and immediately afterward, Mrs. Bournett is found dead and there is a pillow on the floor by the bed and subsequently evidence is found that suggests she may have been suffocated. Tell me, what would you think in my position?"

"Why would I leave the pillow there like that?" I'm so angry and frustrated that I ignore Darcy's signals to stop speaking. "I'm not stupid, why wouldn't I put it back? Why leave it like some big neon sign declaring that I've just murdered my mother?"

"Perhaps you panicked," Caine says. "People do."

"We're not here to talk about what other people might do." Darcy rustles the papers in front of him. "From what I can see from this initial report, there's no bruising on the alleged victim's face or neck and no evidence whatsoever of a struggle or force used. There are no defensive marks on her hands or skin scrapings under her nails from scratching at an attacker."

"Patricia Bournett was sedated and unable to move at the time of her death—"

Darcy refuses to let Caine finish. "Not according to

my client's statement, in which her mother reached up, gripped her wrist tightly, and opened her eyes."

"We have only your client's word for that." Hildreth has leaned back in her chair, arms folded, and looks thoroughly pissed off. Whatever she thought she could intimidate me into confessing, Darcy's not given her a chance, and I may have been terrified when they brought me here, but I know the law and I knew better than to say *anything* in the couple of hours we had to wait for Darcy to get here.

"Actually, not so," Darcy says. "I spoke with the hospital staff on my way here, and Patricia Bournett's heart rate and blood pressure had a spike that lasted approximately thirty seconds at two forty-eight P.M. Not the kind of spike they would expect to see in someone fully sedated, and which supports my client's statement that her mother was active at that moment. The next time Ms. Bournett's heart rate increased–very rapidly–was at the point of her death." He pauses. "When my client was in her car after taking a call from her son's school."

"Where she was when she took that call is up for debate."

"For now, yes." He smiles again. "Although I will be requesting permission to view the security camera footage of the hospital car park where Mrs. Averell's car was parked. I'm surprised you hadn't already checked it before threatening my client with arrest."

Hildreth glares sideways at Caine, who looks down at his coffee cup, awkward, and it's clear that was a job the detective constable was supposed to have in hand.

"And as for the rest of your very circumstantial evidence, I'd like to remind you that of Patricia Bournett's two daughters, my client is the one who completed higher education, has a very good career in law, and has a family that she has been with for nearly twenty years. The *other* daughter—the one whom Patricia actually tried to kill by suffocating her with a pillow back on the night of her fortieth birthday—is a loner who has never achieved her full potential, and is certainly not without familial resentments herself, and was also at the hospital that day."

I look across at him, shocked. Surely he doesn't think that—

"I'm not suggesting, of course, that Phoebe Bournett killed her mother. That's ridiculous. Almost as ridiculous as suggesting that my client would throw her very impressive life and career away to kill a woman who was basically a stranger to her and who was in all probability dying anyway. And her concerns about her personal history repeating itself? Ask anyone who had a parent die young of a heart attack, and trust me they worry about the same thing happening to them at the same age. It's human nature." He leans back in his chair. "And that, Detective Sergeant Hildreth, is me destroying your case without even trying. I'm presuming my client is free to leave now?"

32

I t's past eight by the time we get out of the station and the heat of the day has cooled to a pleasantly warm evening, and as Darcy drives through the center of the city, the outdoor bars are full of people relaxing and enjoying themselves. I feel a pang of envy. How wonderful to be so carefree.

"I would rather you billed me," I repeat for about the third time. He's acting like it was no bother to come out and that he wasn't busy, but I know that's not true.

"It's fine. Honestly. What are friends for? If I ever get married and then need a divorce, I'll come and reclaim the time."

"Deal." I accept defeat.

"How are you?" He looks over at me. "I mean, you look great. Well, great for a woman who's not slept, crashed her car, and then been taken in for questioning by the police."

"It's my best look." I grin at him. He, on the other hand, really *does* look great. He's not all that different from when we were barely twenty. Probably the only man I know who can make that claim. He hasn't got a middle-aged spread, his hair is still as thick as it ever was, with a sprinkling of gray that seems to add to his charm, weirdly. Still gorgeous, basically.

I look out the window. It's funny how life turns out. If I hadn't got pregnant so young with Chloe, who knows what would have happened. Robert and I had been getting snippier with each other. I was studying hard, spending a lot of time with Darcy, and we were definitely both feeling the attraction and having *wouldn't it be nice if* thoughts. One drunken kiss was all we had and then I found out I was pregnant and that was that. I never told Robert. I didn't see the point. He and Phoebe had grown closer then too, alone in the flat together so much while I studied. I remember wondering if anything had happened between them, but never asked. I felt guilty enough about my own crush on Darcy. And then when we decided to keep the baby, the future with me and Robert was decided and in the main, I had no regrets. I did love Robert. I *do* love Robert.

"So come on," he says. "How are you? Aside from all this crap. How's married life? Still disgustingly happy?"

How to answer that? "Pretty much, I guess," I say, damning my marriage with faint praise. "Twenty years is a long time, and we're very different people. But don't get me wrong, Robert's great. I could never have focused on my career if he hadn't agreed to do all the stay-at-home stuff with Chloe and then Will. I owe him a lot for that."

"I think it probably suited him too. He barely made it to his lectures I remember you saying. What did he get? A third? You had to not work pretty hard to get a third back then. A third took a lot of work-avoiding effort."

"Harsh!" I can't help but laugh. "But maybe fair."

"Definitely fair. He only worked in that bar for the free beer and cigarettes. No one could figure out what the two of you were doing together."

"Really?"

"You were so driven. So determined to succeed. He was just cruising."

"That's what I liked about him. He was happy in himself." That part is true. Robert was so *normal* and I had wanted normal more than anything. "Now he wants to open a bar of his own. I think he's having a midlife crisis." We both snort a laugh and I feel disloyal, but it's so nice to be with someone who's helping me rather than looking at me like I'm barking mad.

"What about you? How come you're not married? I'd have thought they'd be lining up to drag you down the aisle."

"Oh, there have been a few close calls along the way, but you know what the law is like. Long hours. And when I'm in a case, I'm properly *in* it. I love the buzz of the game. That's hard for someone to compete with."

"I remember that about you. Even back then, we all knew you'd be *the one.* The superstar barrister."

"How the hell are we forty, Baby Spice?" he asks and I laugh out loud at the old nickname. Emma Bournett. Emma B. Baby Spice.

"I know. More like Granny Spice these days."

"Still looking good." He winks. "For an old bird. And I'm glad you called me, because I'd have been very annoyed to find you up for murder and someone else getting the gig."

I like that he finds the idea so ridiculous that he can joke about it, but my smile still falters and he sees it.

"Hey, I'm sorry. I know it's not funny. I can be a dick sometimes."

"No, it's nice to have someone on my side." We're just coming into the village, and I gaze out at the peaceful quiet as I speak. "I didn't love my mother, that's for sure. She scared me as a child, and the memory of her scares me as an adult. But I didn't kill her." A thought that's been niggling at me comes to the fore. "Why did you say that stuff about Phoebe?"

"Just making the point that they were being lazy." He looks up at the road. "You'll have to direct me from here."

I point at the crossroads. "There's fine. The fresh air will do me good and I need to move or my whole body is going to seize up."

"Are you sure?"

I nod and he pulls up to the curb. "When I've seen the footage from the car park, I'll let you know. And call me whenever." He pauses. "It's good to see you again. It really is."

"Although next time," I say, "let's catch up in a bar, not a police station. Deal?"

"Deal," he answers, and then his hands-free kicks in and the name *Veronique* comes up on the dash. I can tell from his awkward expression that this isn't a work call, and I'm surprised by the pang in the pit of my stomach. Of course he has someone. No doubt a gorgeous, stylish intelligent thirty-year-old.

I get out of the car feeling foolish for having a nanosecond flutter of longing for a life I could have had. I close the door, waving goodbye, and I keep my smile fixed on until he's driven off, and then my shoulders slump as much as they can with the whiplash and bruising as I start the walk home.

33

I let myself in quietly, slipping off my shoes as soon as I'm inside. There's post on the hall table, bills mainly, I think. They can wait. Underneath those envelopes I see some photocopied paper is poking out. The details of the bar Robert wants to invest in. That can wait too. He can't use any of our savings without both our signatures, so he can't invest in it without my agreement. And I can't see that happening with the way things stand.

I head to the kitchen, my feet silent on the wooden floors, and then come to a sudden standstill. My husband and my sister are hugging each other tightly by the breakfast bar. They obviously haven't heard me come in.

"This is cozy," I say. Phoebe breaks away and immediately comes to hug me, so out of character for her, and I yelp in pain from my bruises.

"I'm sorry for the things I said. I was . . . I don't know. Concerned."

"I'm sorry I slapped you," I answer, awkward. "It was a terrible thing to do." And I *am* sorry. I'm too tired to be anything but sorry and it was an awful thing to do.

"Robert called me," she says. "He was worried. We're both worried."

We. I stiffen and pull back. Is her rare hug a distraction from the two of them?

"Where's Chloe?" I ask, and the atmosphere shifts again among us three, the two adults who are supposed to love me most now uncomfortable, and my irritation at their closeness too obvious.

"Upstairs asleep." Robert steps forward. "The shock of the accident."

I get one of his beers from the fridge, open it, and take a long slug. "Don't worry, Darcy's dealing with the police. He can prove that I didn't do it." Will that give Robert a pang of jealousy? Or has he forgotten that time when our relationship was so fractured that we nearly broke off in different directions?

As I turn back, I catch a glance between him and Phoebe. Something furtive that makes my skin prickle. It seems they have discussed the potential for my guilt and aren't as sure as Darcy that I didn't do it.

"I should go." Phoebe grabs her bag. "Let you get some rest."

I say nothing and Robert goes to see her off. There's paper and poster paints on the kitchen table, Will's efforts spread across it to dry. Art. That will be Phoebe's doing. Maybe if she learned to be less uptight her own paintings would have more soul. I look at the pictures. A boat on the sea. Better than I could get out of Will. For someone who's spent so long away, Phoebe's certainly worming her way into our family life again.

"You and Phoebe are getting on well." We're drinking beers at the island as I wait for the Nurofen to kick in on my aches and pains.

"I guess so," Robert says, picking at the label of his beer. "She's great with Will. She's worried about you." He glances up at me. "I'm worried."

"So you both keep saying."

"I need you to talk to me, Emma. Tell me about your mum and why it freaks you out so much. What happened to you?"

I stare into my own bottle. I wanted to tell him about

Chloe, but that can wait until tomorrow now. He wants answers, even though I'm exhausted, battered from the accident, and don't want to talk anymore. "I thought Phoebe told you already."

"She said she can't speak for you."

"Big of her." *She didn't hold back so much with the police,* I want to add.

"I'm trying to connect with you on this," he says wearily. "And it may make you feel better to actually talk to me. Get it all out."

I already *got it all out* to Dr. Morris and any relief at that was short-lived, so I can't see it making me feel better, but if I keep shutting Robert out then whatever happens in our marriage will be my fault too.

My sheer exhaustion and the events of the day have left me almost numb emotionally and my palms don't sweat like they did in Dr. Morris's office. I'm being carried on a wave of *what will be, will be.* I take a deep breath.

"I know that I'm not like her," I start. "I know that she was a sick woman. I know that it's all in the past, and it's only a small percentage of my life that gets smaller with every year. I *know* all these things, but what I *feel* is entirely different." I pause. How can I explain my early childhood?

"The oddness back then was normal for us, even if

we knew it wasn't normal for everyone else. No friends after school because at their houses the curtains were always open, and in ours the curtains were always shut." I pick at the beer label, the skin around my thumbs too raw. "Phoebe says that sometimes before *then* there'd be times, weeks even, that Mum would come up for air and the house would be clean and she'd be full of love and entirely present. Hugs and promises that things would be better. I don't remember those times. Sometimes I think Phoebe just made them up but maybe not. Social services would have eventually noticed if Mum hadn't pulled it together often enough. But in the run-up to her fortieth birthday there was no respite." My throat dries. "She stopped sleeping. She would mutter to herself constantly. Stuff we didn't understand." I take another drink of the beer that's almost down to the dregs as I remember. Those numbers whispered over and over. The same numbers that now fill my head.

"It got worse. *She* got worse. On the day of her birthday, we got up early and made her a card out of some colored paper Phoebe brought back from school. Phoebe made it really, I just wrote my name inside."

Sitting here in my beautiful kitchen I can still smell the musty air and feel the cheap carpet under my knees. "When we went downstairs"—*hand in hand, Phoebe first, our bellies a mixture of fear and excite-*

ment, *wanting to make her happy, see Mummy see, we do love you, please love us back*—"we found her in the kitchen. She was holding a box of eggs. God knows how old they were. She was smashing them, one by one." *I can see her as if it were yesterday. Her back to us. Hair unkempt and dirty, straggling down it. Her arm straight out to the side.*

Crack. Crack. Crack.

"We knew then—even me—that something was very wrong. Phoebe wanted to go back upstairs, but I didn't. I was so proud of our card, I wanted to give to it her. So I tried." *Taking one step forward as Phoebe tried to pull me back. My heart racing. "Mummy?"*

"She grabbed me fast, pulling me right up close and shaking me. She scared me. She said I was keeping her awake at night." *I glance at Robert. Are his eyes narrowing a little at the shaking? Is he thinking of what I did to Ben?*

"After school, well, that's when—" I break off. How much to tell in this violation of my privacy? "I remember the heavy thunderclouds, the tiny swarms of flies on our skin as we walked home along the river route. Phoebe wanted to go to Mummy's friend's house, but I just wanted to go home. I thought there might be a cake. A special tea. I thought she might be all right." I take a breath. "She wasn't all right. She was worse.

Drinking wine. Scratching numbers into the under-stairs cupboard door. When she saw us, she grabbed me and locked me inside it. I was there for hours. All through the afternoon and into the night. It was end-less. And then the storm came.

"It was a trauma for Phoebe, yes, undoubtably. But it was a trauma for me too." My mouth is sour and I'm regretting the beer and resenting Robert. "The storm was raging when she finally unlocked the cup-board door. I'm not sure she even meant to let me out. She opened the door, spoke to me, and then closed it again before wandering off. She didn't lock it that time though. I pushed it open." My heart races. No amount of telling it will ever free me of that night.

"The wine bottle, empty now, was abandoned on the floor. I could hear the creak of the stairs as she went up them. It was the middle of the night and all the lights were off. The back door was open, I re-member that, because even though it was summer, the wind was cold and carrying the rain into the kitchen. I could hear it pattering onto the linoleum. I wanted to run out that door and never come back. Just run and run and run. But I knew Phoebe was upstairs and so was our mother, and I was more afraid than I'd ever been in my life."

I pause, not sure how to tell the next bit. I don't talk about climbing the stairs. The strange sounds I heard that made my heart thrum so hard in my tiny chest as I forced myself along the corridor.

"I can still see her," I say eventually. "Standing over Phoebe's bed, pressing the pillow hard over her face. I was so confused. I didn't understand what she was doing or why. It's Phoebe's legs I remember the most. I used to have nightmares about them. They were drumming against the mattress, bicycling in the air and then kicking out at nothing.

"Anyway." I take a deep breath, my tone firmer as I cut to the end, the main details done. "I don't know what would have happened if she hadn't looked up, seen me there, and then collapsed. A ministroke they thought at first, but there was no medical evidence of that. Whatever exploded in her head, it wasn't veins or capillaries. It was the *essence* of her. Her sanity maybe. Phoebe and I left her there on the floor and ran out of the house. A neighbor called the police and that was that. Phoebe was never the same and neither was I." I look up at him and see he's expecting *more*.

"It didn't help that we went to different foster homes," I continue. "Phoebe still has a chip on her shoulder that all the families wanted me and not her but it's not true. I was younger, that's all. Easier, I imagine. One lovely family came for me and I was so excited about going to live with them, sure they were going to adopt me, that I think I soured Phoebe against me. No one wanted her at that point. But that first family changed their mind, and then we were both in the same boat. A couple of different foster families each until we were old enough to fend for ourselves. Mine were nicer than hers, I think she's right about that, but I wasn't as angry as she was. I *wanted* to be loved. Anyway, you know that stuff. I didn't lie about that."

Robert's looking down at his bottle. "So what your mother did to Phoebe was like Will's drawings," he says finally.

"Yes," I say, getting to my feet. "Which is how I know Phoebe must have said something to him." He's about to protest but I cut him off. "Whether she meant to or not. Because I certainly didn't."

I shuffle past him like an old woman—*hunched over like her*—every joint screaming with aches and tiredness. "I'm going to have a bath. I need to get onto the tow truck people in the morning and sort the car. Will you bring a chamomile tea up with you?" He nods and I wait for him to say something comforting, but he doesn't, instead giving me a wan smile as if he's the one who's had the shittiest day.

While the bath is running, I knock on Chloe's door. She doesn't answer and when I knock again and still get no reply, I let myself in. She's in bed, lying on her side, facing away from me.

"Go away, Mum." She's sullen, very much a teenager and not a grown woman at all. I sit on the side of her bed. I don't want to fight with her. I want to look after her. I wait a moment before I speak, hoping that she might turn to face me, but she doesn't.

"I wasn't much older than you when I met your dad, you know." I put one hand on her shoulder and she stiffens under my touch, but I leave my hand there as I speak softly. "And then, of course, you came along and we were a family. So I do understand love, Chloe. And I'm not so old that I don't remember how powerful it feels when you're so young. When everything is new." Still no response. "I'm sorry for a lot of the things I said in the car. I didn't mean them; I was shocked and angry and worried about you. I'm sure you do love him. And yes, he might love you too. Why wouldn't he? You're beautiful and bright and kind and full of wonderful energy. You're very easy to love."

Parker Stockwell had been laughing at how distracted Julian was these days—*got blue balls, can't think of anything else*—so he's probably infatuated. Maybe he does think he's in love, even though that thought makes my blood boil again when I want to be calm for my baby's sake. I'm trying to reframe Chloe in my mind as a young woman rather than a little girl, but it's so difficult. Where does the time go?

"But the thing you haven't learned yet is that there are so many other men out there who you can love. Some you can probably love *more*. How do you see this panning out, Chlo? Honestly? Even if he does leave Michelle for you? There's a twenty-year gap between you. And I know you're going to say age doesn't matter, but it does. You're going to want to *do* stuff. Have adventures. Go to uni and go partying and all those things that are part of being young and free before real life kicks in. He's already got two children, so he's always going to be tied to Michelle and so will you. A stepmum at eighteen. And the fallout. God Chloe, he's your dad's friend. His wife's your dad's friend. It will be such a mess."

"I said go away." Her tone is cold, but I hope she's at least been listening. She's a clever girl, and despite herself she'll think about what I've said. "I love you, Chloe. I will always be here for you whatever happens." I get up. "I haven't said anything to Dad yet. But I will.

And it would be good if it was over before he knows about it. Okay?"

She may as well be fast asleep for the response I get. When I get to the door I look back. "And I didn't lose my shit, Chloe. I thought you were going to open the passenger door. I was trying to protect you. That's my job. I'm your mother. I will always protect you."

34

It's past two A.M. The window glass is cold under my hands as I press up against it. My mouth open, I breathe a wide O of condensation. How would I seem to someone down in the garden looking up? I press my body closer, until I feel the cold through my shorts and T-shirt, and then turn my face to push one cheek against the window, even though it hurts my whiplashed neck. I want the chill to lift this haze of dread that fuels the tics that fill my nights.

Madness.

During the nights, I'm as concerned about me as Robert and Phoebe are. At least I don't have to worry about Robert waking up. He's fully out thanks to another NightNight. He'd asked me if I wanted Chloe to go to university only so the money would be gone and he couldn't have his bar. What kind of woman does he think I am? What kind of husband is he?

And what kind of wife drugs her husband?

Who am I? Exhausted daytime Emma, crashing cars, shaking kids, paranoid and suspected of murder, and nighttime Emma, carried along on a haze of odd behaviors that somehow reassure me. Is the real me stuck somewhere in between?

I imagine myself in the garden looking up—the me who's always ready to take on the world, the me who knows exactly what she wants and how to get it. The one other people always turn to. *Pull yourself together,* that's what she'd be saying down there, the me I used to be. *Get a grip on this situation. Get to the bottom of it and move on.* I'm fighting the overwhelming urge to go down to where the under-stairs cupboard is calling me to climb in. I have to break this cycle. I have to.

"Two hundred and twenty-two one hundred and thirteen one hundred and fifty-five two hundred and eighteen . . ."

I don't realize I'm whispering the numbers until I'm suddenly not. A shadow shifts at the end of the corridor to my right and I freeze. *An intruder in the house. My children.* No. Too small a shape. Watching me.

"Will?" Speaking aloud jars me back into the moment. The shadow retreats back into his room and my night haze falls away momentarily. It must be him. God, what must I have looked like, smearing myself against the window? I go after him.

His night-light isn't on, and the room, so cheerful in daylight, is soaked in ash-gray gloom, only a little moonlight creeping in from outside. It's unusually tidy, his thick colored pens and coloring pads all in their boxes and his toys in his trunk. Did Phoebe do it? Or Robert? Surely not Will, my little tornado, always leaving a mess in his wake. Not so much this past week, I think sadly. I'm not the only one who's not been myself recently.

He's back in his bed, to all outward appearances fast asleep, but I can see his breathing is fast and his eyes are moving behind their lids. "Can't you sleep, monkey?" I ask quietly. He doesn't answer but his fingers tighten on his duvet. "Do you need a glass of water? Did you have a bad dream?" Nothing. I lean forward and carefully touch his shoulder, and he stirs slightly, sliding onto his back. Now I don't know what to think. Maybe he *is* asleep. Maybe he was sleepwalking. Maybe I just imagined him in the corridor. Maybe I'm actually asleep and this is all a dream. Maybe, maybe, maybe. Who the fuck knows?

I sit there, watching him, for a few minutes, maybe longer, but he doesn't wake.

35

THREE DAYS UNTIL MY BIRTHDAY

I sleep from around four thirty until seven, a rest deep and dark as the grave with no dreams or nightmares, just an empty nothingness that is only broken by Robert getting up. I drag myself to the bathroom and straight into the shower, my body a sack of aches and pains and the bruise on my knee blooming large and bright. A glance in the mirror confirms that I'm looking as bad as I feel. I'm falling apart.

I turn the water up high, until it's nearly burning my skin, and let the power jet pummel my shoulders in a brutal massage until I can't take any more and get out. It's the weekend, so maybe I can spend the whole day in bed after breakfast. Sleeping during the day may be less of a problem than at night. Then when I wake up hopefully, despite its being Saturday, Darcy may have straightened out all the other mess and I'll be able to tackle the Chloe situation with a clear head. Maybe I should ring Julian. No. Chloe will have already told him I know, and I imagine that's probably put the fear of divorce into him and he'll finish it anyway. The end of a tawdry affair and a learning curve for my beautiful girl about older men who seem so charming from the perspective of youth.

Once dried, I'm about to pull on some scruffy joggers and a top when Robert shouts out.

"Emma!" For a second, I think he's calling me down for breakfast, but it sounds like he's upstairs.

"Hang on." I tug on the joggers. They're baggier now. Insomnia burns calories it seems, along with car crashes and accusations of murder.

"Come here." His tone is cold. "Now."

Oh god, what now?

"Jesus."

Chloe is in the doorway to Will's room, her mouth open, an expression of disbelief on her blotchy face, eyes pink from tears. Has Julian broken up with her? Is that one less problem on my plate? She turns to look at me and all thoughts of Julian are ash on the wind.

She's aghast. "This is some messed-up shit," she mutters, turning away to head to her room. "This family is so fucked."

I come forward and then it's me with my mouth open, staring in disbelief. "What happened?" I say, although I can see what's happened. The drawing from Will's sketchbook, the one he'd done over and over, is now all over his bedroom walls, drawn large and small, in every available space in thick marker pens. He must have climbed up onto his chest of drawers to reach some of the spaces. I can't stop looking. The little boy in the bed. The crazy lady with the mad face, her long hair hanging down like some kind of ghoul from one of those terrifying Japanese horror films. Scribbled everywhere around the pictures is the word *Mummy* in uneven letters, over and over, and then, more accusatory, there are two instances of *Emma*.

"What is this?" Robert asks, staring at me from where he's standing in the middle of the room.

"I don't know." I look at Will, sitting on the bed with his knees pulled up under his chin, not looking at either of us. His colored pens—*weren't they tidy in the box last night? Did I make that up? Why are the nights such a haze?*—are all over the floor, lids off and colors soaking into the thick plush cream carpet like pools of multicolored blood at a crime scene.

"What happened, monkey?" I go to sit with him but Robert blocks me.

"Don't touch him."

"What the hell, Robert?" I try to push him out of my way, but he grips my arms, stopping me.

"Did you come in here last night?" His voice is all growl. I say nothing, my mouth opening and closing like a guppy's, trying to find a truth that works or a lie to save me. "Did you?" He shakes me as he shouts.

"Only for a minute! I thought he was awake. I thought—"

"For fuck's sake, Emma, you need help."

"Honestly, I—"

"You what?" He shakes me again. "What? What excuse this time? Look at our boy, Emma! Look at him!" He spins me around so I'm facing away from him, but his hands are still firm on me, making sure I can't break free. Will's pushed his face into his knees and is rocking backward and forward. "Look at what you're doing!"

I break free. "I have never hurt our children! I would never hurt our children!"

We stare at each other, both breathless, and then he runs his hands through his hair as if he's the one who's exhausted. When he looks at me again, his rage has gone but it's been replaced by something worse. Complete mistrust.

"You need to move out for a few days."

"What?" I recoil as if I've been slapped.

"Go somewhere else." His eyes slip away from me. "Until we know what's going on here. With you. With Will. I'm going to take him to see someone and get to the bottom of it. And it's probably best you're not here until we've got to the bottom of the other things too."

"The *other things*?" It's gone from feeling like a slap in the face to a punch in the solar plexus. "You mean my mother?" We stare at each other for a long moment. "Jesus fucking Christ, Robert." I turn and storm away before he can see my tears.

36

It's nearly eleven by the time I collect my courtesy car and check into the Raddison Blu, my hands trembling and my stomach in knots. I drink the strong but awful coffee from the machine as I hang up the few clothes I managed to grab in my fury, and then flop on the bed. I'm so angry at Robert, but I'm also angry at myself for not getting on top of this insomnia, as well as worried about both Will and Chloe. Our family is crumbling in front of my eyes. I check my phone but there's nothing from Darcy yet, and I don't honestly expect to hear from him until later in the day, if at all. The only light ahead is knowing that Robert is going to feel like absolute shit when he realizes that I couldn't have done it.

But someone maybe did.

It's my mother's voice again, a parasitic worm, whispering in my head. I try to squash it. As Darcy said, the fibers probably came from a rough-handed nurse or something my mother did herself. Probably. *What else did he say, though?* The voice probes. *Don't tell me you haven't thought it yourself.* Phoebe. My big sister. I can't shake what Darcy said about her. My mother *did* have two daughters that she royally fucked up. It was Phoebe she was trying to kill that night, so why wouldn't it be Phoebe who did this? She told Robert about our past. And terrified poor Will. That's hardly balanced.

A thought strikes me suddenly, one so obvious I can't believe I didn't think of it before. It's followed by a hot flush of shame. *Maybe Phoebe didn't tell Will?* What if Will overheard Phoebe telling *Robert?* Robert's said twice that she told him some things about our childhood. What if Will heard Phoebe telling him what "Mummy" did to her? That could easily have frightened him, and of course he would hear "Mummy" or "Mum" and think of me. Especially if they were also talking about me. It could have all got messed up in his head. A story of a mummy and a scared child in bed and a pillow.

I'd feel happier about this likelihood if I was less worried about all the other things. *The secret things.*

The things that are definitely about *me*. The numbers. The lost moments. If Phoebe's done nothing wrong, then could *I* have smothered my mother and not remembered? I think of the cold tea on the hallway floor. The numbers recorded on the Dictaphone, time slipping through gaps. How can I expect my family to trust in me if I don't even trust myself fully?

I text Darcy *Anything back on the cameras?* but get no reply. What do I really expect? That he's dropped all his weekend plans to clear me? I'm embarrassed that I thought maybe there was still a spark of attraction there. Old friends is all we are. And I'm married. I have to laugh at that as I take in my surroundings. Married. Yeah right, that's going well. I close my eyes, and as my head starts to pound with the bloom of a migraine, I find song lyrics falling in line with the pulse in my skull.

Look, look a candle, a book and a bell, I put them behind me . . .

My phone rings and I startle, the music falling quiet, and I answer quickly, hoping it's Darcy, but it's only Dr. Morris checking in.

"Sorry to call on a Saturday, but you didn't book in another session," she says. "Are you sleeping better? Is everything okay?"

"No, not really." I half laugh, as if it's all a joke, but tears threaten to spill from nowhere. "The pills are helping a bit, but not much. There's some family stuff going on."

"Is this what's keeping you awake?"

"No." What's the point of lying? I let out a long, shaky breath. "I don't know what's wrong with me. I can't stop thinking about my mother and what she did. I have these new tics too. Things I have to do at night. Check the back door handle. Look out the up-stairs window. Look in the under-stairs cupboard. Go into Will's room." I let out a shaky breath. "It's com-pulsive. I can't stop myself. I'm so afraid." My voice is trembling, as I finally say it out loud. "I'm so afraid I'm going to go mad like she did. What if I hurt my children? I crashed my car yesterday with Chloe in it and I know Robert thinks I did that on purpose. I'm just so tired."

"Slow down," she says. "That's a lot to absorb. Take a few deep breaths." I make a half-hearted attempt but she cuts in.

"Deeper and slower. I want to be able to hear you breathing. In through the nose . . . and now out through the mouth." I do as I'm told, and finally my heart slows and my hands stop trembling. "Sorry," I say. I hate being vulnerable. I'm the one who takes care of everything. I'm never the one who falls apart. *That's what all the ones who fall apart say.* My mother's voice whispers, amused, in my head. *Just before they shoot their children and spouse with a shotgun and then turn it on themselves.*

"Never apologize for your feelings. The point is to try to understand what's driving them. It seems to me that, understandably, you've become fixated on a very short period of time in your mother's life. A traumatic time that massively impacted on you at a young age. Everything you think or know of your mother is from that moment. That short time leading up to the night of her fortieth birthday. But she lived a very long time both before and after that. Perhaps what you could spend some time doing is find out more about those years? Get to know the rest of her life a little bit?"

"I'm trying to forget her," I say defensively. "She's dead."

"As far as I can tell, trying to forget her isn't working that well for you. Perhaps what you need is to try to understand her."

"I don't want to understand her." I'm like a toddler stamping my foot.

"That's not true. You don't want to *forgive* her. But I think you very much want to understand her."

There's a long pause where I say nothing, and then she says she's got to go and she'll check on me in a couple of days. "Think about what I said," she finishes. "What have you got to lose?" And then she's gone.

What *have* I got to lose? Her last words still echo in my head. I have so much to lose. My family. My job. My sanity. But they're falling away from me anyway. And she's right. When I try to think about my mother's life other than that night, there's nothing. A void on either side. Where would I start getting to know her though?

Of course. There's only really one place I can find out anything about my mother. Hartwell House's Secure Unit. She lived there for more than thirty years. She was probably their longest resident. Maybe they can tell me more about her. Phoebe's visited and I'm sure they'll understand my need to lay ghosts to rest.

I find Hartwell's contact details in my phone but can't bring myself to dial. Instead, I send them an email from my work account to appear as professional and sane as possible, asking if I could come to talk to anyone who knew my mother, Patricia Bournett. I press send before I can change my mind and then take my phone and flop on the bed. My head is throbbing and the lyrics from that bloody song fill up my head again.

Finally I give up and search it on the iTunes store. Sweet Billy Pilgrim, "Candle Book and Bell." I download the acoustic version and then hit repeat, the volume on low. Maybe this will help me doze. I close my eyes, and as the first notes kick in, I drift into a haze.

37

The ringing phone wakes me and I'm shocked to see that it's past two. I've slept for over three hours, even with the song playing around and around on an endless loop. My dry mouth tastes of daytime sleep and stale sour coffee, but when I see it's Darcy calling, I sit up fast, my heart immediately racing, my headache gone.

"Hi, Emma? It's me."

"Hi." I can barely get the words out. "Did you get anything from the cameras?"

"Not yet. Believe it or not you parked in a camera blind spot. I can see the edge of the passenger side of your car, but it doesn't show the time you got in, and you pull out a few minutes *after* your mother died. So although it would be very tight timing, the police could still claim it was you."

No no no. I'd been so sure this would be the end of it, and now I feel once again cut adrift. "But don't panic," he adds. "I've spoken to the hospital administrator and they've assured me that all the entrances have cameras covering all angles. So can you remember which exit you came out of? The one nearest your car park?"

"Yes. Yes!" My heart leaps. "The one where the Starbucks kiosk is. I didn't come out of the main entrance that time. This one was closer to the wing."

"Great," he says. "I'll get on it now. Chin up, Baby Spice. We'll get this sorted." And then he's gone before I can even say thank you. *We'll get this sorted.* God, I bloody hope so.

My nerves are still on edge and I need to get out of this hotel room for a while. I should get some food even though I don't feel much like eating. Between work and family, I'm not used to having all this time to myself. I brush my teeth and freshen up and then head out. It's one of Will's football juniors afternoons, and if I go at pick-up time, maybe I can talk to Robert. We can go for a coffee somewhere and I can tell him my theory about Will overhearing. Surely that will make sense to him?

I get to the football field and Michelle is waiting, and I can't avoid her as she makes a beeline for me.

She looks as tired as me. "I'm going crazy," she says. *Join the club.* "Julian won't even speak to me now. And this morning he left early when I was trying to talk to him." Her bottom lip is scabby where she's been biting at it. "I'm so done. I know he's planning to leave, because he's also pulled out of this stupid bar business. Alan rang last night to say—"

"I didn't even *know* about this stupid bar business," I cut in and she looks shocked.

"God, really? Ugh. Men, what is wrong with them? I'm so sorry. I presumed you knew. Oh god, that means you don't know . . ." She trails off.

"Don't know what?" *What now?*

"Alan rang to say that Robert wanted to buy Julian's share. He's going to be the majority owner."

"Robert is?" This day just gets better and better.

"I'm so sorry," she says. "I would have told you, obviously. I'm guessing you're not happy about it?"

"You guessed right." She looks genuinely sorry for me and I get a stab of guilt. I know exactly why her husband is being such a bastard, and I should probably tell her. She deserves to know. But I've got enough problems right now. I look up. One of them is coming right toward me.

"Emma?" My sister doesn't look at all happy to see me. "What are you doing here?"

"Will's my child. I think the question is more what are *you* doing here?"

"Robert asked me to pick him up." Michelle shrinks away to talk to some of the other waiting mums, leaving me and Phoebe alone. "You shouldn't be here. He won't like it," she finishes.

"*I* shouldn't be here? Who the hell are you to say that?" I'm fiery anger to her ice. "And I didn't realize that what Robert liked or didn't like was so important to you." I think of that hug I caught them in. How innocent was it really?

"What do you expect, Emma? After the walls in Will's bedroom? After what the police are saying?" She glances around, checking that no one can hear her hissed accusations. "Robert took Will to a child psychologist this morning. He said he's been through some kind of trauma. He said his behavior and this quietness is in keeping with PTSD. This is you, Emma. You're acting like her, and you know it. So excuse me for trying to protect them."

"I have done nothing to hurt Will. All this stuff with the drawings. Maybe Will could have overheard you telling Robert about our past? Seems like you've been talking to a lot of people."

"He didn't overhear us," she says.

"Then you must have told him!" I snap loudly.

People look over at us but I don't care. "Like you probably slashed my tire and you're probably trying to fuck my husband. Still jealous after all these years. Maybe *you* even suffocated Mum. You're pathetic! There's no other explanation. You! You're doing this to me."

She stares at me, cold, expression unreadable, and then she leans forward. "But it's not the only explanation, is it?" Her voice is soft. Controlled. Terrifying. "And certainly not the obvious one. When are you forty, Emma? Monday? You're not sleeping. You're behaving erratically. Need I go on? What's the obvious explanation here? What would you believe?"

She straightens up, turning to smile as Will comes running up to the gate, waiting for the coach to open it. She looks as if butter wouldn't melt in her mouth and she doesn't glance my way as she says, words like ice, "Now leave before Will comes out and I won't tell Robert I saw you. Don't make this worse than it is."

I stumble back to my car, the wind knocked from my lungs, and my face is burning as I slam the door. I want to ring Robert and scream accusations and hurt at him, but I'll wait. When Darcy gets the camera footage from the hospital exit, then both he and my bitch sister can eat some humble pie. And Robert can fuck off if he thinks he's getting that bar.

My phone rings and when I see it's an unknown

number I can't answer it fast enough, thinking it's Darcy again, but it's not.

"Hey, Emma, it's Parker. I called the office yesterday and they said you were having some problems at home." Oh god. Parker Stockwell.

"Everything's fine, actually." I watch Will head toward Robert's car, hand in hand with Phoebe—*has he already insured her to drive it?*—oblivious to my presence. As she smiles down at him, the urge to run and strangle her is almost overwhelming. I'm like a tigress whose cubs are under threat. *My family, Phoebe. Mine.*

"I like when you act tough," Stockwell continues, smarmy smooth in my ear. "But everyone needs a shoulder to cry on sometimes. Look, the boys are staying at school this weekend. Why don't you come over? I could cook you dinner. Or get the cook to cook you dinner."

In Robert's car I see Phoebe laughing at something as she makes sure Will is strapped in. How easily she's sliding into my place beside my son.

"Emma? Are you still there?"

My rage bubbles over down the phone line. I snap. "Why did you take the children from Miranda if you never have them? And no, I don't want to come for dinner. I have never given you a moment's encouragement that I might want to socialize with you now that your divorce is done—"

"You came out for dinner," he cuts in, like a sullen schoolboy.

"Because Buckley *made* me, which I'm also livid about, because it smacks of sexism and the worst of 1970s behavior. What is wrong with you men? Grow up and get over yourselves." I hang up and then immediately block his number. My whole body is shaking. *I like it when you act tough.* What the actual fuck? I'm pure rage as I screech the car back onto the road.

38

I'm outside Caroline's house again, and once more not exactly sure how I got here. It's past five so I've been driving around the city for about two hours, raging in my head. Two hours? It feels more like thirty minutes. Have I had one of my lost time moments while *driving*? I bang my head against the headrest, angry and upset, and then close my eyes for a few seconds. I'm so tired. How can I think straight?

I look again at the terraced houses on the other side of the road. Why have I driven here again? I barely know the woman. I've only met her twice, and the first time I was rude and the next I basically forced her to have lunch with me. So why have I driven here? Is she the best option I have for a friend right now? It's a terrible thing to admit but outside of work colleagues and school mums I don't have many—if any—friends at all. I got caught up with Robert too soon, and I had too many hang-ups about people's transience after foster care. But Caroline did text me back, so she must have enjoyed the lunch a little bit. Maybe she's lonely too. I stare at the door some more.

This is stupid. I can't sit here outside her house all night, and neither can I bring myself to get out and knock. I should pick up a takeaway and go back to the hotel. Watch some TV. Hope to sleep. I'm about to start the car when her front door opens and she steps out onto the path, staring at my car.

Shit.

She comes a few steps up the path and pauses, frowning. Shit, she knows it's me. I get out, the only thing I can do other than drive away, which really would make me look crazy, and hesitantly cross the road.

"Caroline," I say.

"I saw you out here before, parked. I don't know what you—"

Oh god, she saw me.

"I'm so sorry, you must think, well I don't know what you must think, I just—well." I pause then. Her eyes are red and puffy. Has she been crying? "Are you okay? Has something happened to your mum?"

"No. No, nothing like that. Stuff at work."

She sniffs and I think she's only a couple of breaths away from sobbing again. "I'm sorry if I worried you," I say. "I was passing and basically just wondering if you fancied some company and maybe a takeaway. You tell me your problems, I'll tell you mine? I'm a lawyer. I'm perfectly normal. I promise."

After a long, almost awkward moment she gives me a wan smile. "Okay. I'm sorry I overreacted. I had a problem with a man once. He used to sit outside the house, right there. It freaked me out."

"It's my fault. I should have sent a text."

Once we've finished apologizing to each other, she leads me inside. It smells of clean paint and the hallway floor looks freshly polished and varnished. No wonder she's tired if she's been doing all this on top of nursing.

"It's a lovely house. And good paint job."

In the kitchen she takes a half bottle of white wine from the fridge and divides it between two glasses.

"Let's hope some buyers like it. I've got my eye on a flat down by the water. Shared ownership. Will be much cheaper on bills too," she says, and although she smiles, she doesn't look happy about it. But why would she? It must be upsetting to sell your family home for care home costs.

"What's going on at work? I may be able to help. If it's a legal thing?"

"Oh, you know how it is, a manager who doesn't like me. Can't do anything right." She takes a sip of wine and hands me the other glass. "I shouldn't let it upset me, but it's just relentless. I feel like she bullies me, which is stupid because I'm a fully grown woman. Nearly forty-three and she makes me feel like I'm back at school. I can't talk to her either. She brushes whatever I say aside."

"Have you been logging the incidences? If not, you should. And try emailing her—that way you have evidence of her ignoring you if you need to raise a complaint."

"I haven't been, but I'll start," she says. "Thank you." She pauses, and then smiles as if she's decided that maybe I'm not a weird stalker. "I made a curry earlier. We can have that instead of a takeaway? It's probably still warm and I can nuke some rice? Saturday nights are so slow on deliveries."

"That'd be lovely. Thank you." We're so polite. The awkwardness of strangers trying to make friends. There's a moment's silence and I see a small Bluetooth speaker on the side of the table. "Can I put some music on?"

"Sure."

I sync my phone and hit shuffle, quiet music filling the gaps in our conversation as she busies herself with the food. "What about you?" she says. "Are you sleeping better?"

"I wish." I sip some wine. "God, I don't even know where to start. So much shit going on."

"Tell me."

"You'll think I'm crazy . . ."

"I think most people are crazy, if I'm honest," she says. "Including me. The world is crazy."

And so, as we eat, I tell her. I don't go into details but I broadly share my phobia of turning forty because of my mother going mad and how she nearly suffocated Phoebe, and how now that my own fortieth is only a couple of days away, it's stopping me sleeping. The note under my windshield and my slashed tire. I tell her about my mother dying, waiting for CCTV to prove me innocent, and then about Phoebe's return and how she's worming her way into my family.

"She changed after what happened when we were kids," I say. "She's envious of me. I don't know what's going on in her head these days. I'm just so tired. I had to put a NightNight in my husband's tea so I could feel like he wasn't *studying* me all night. Of course, it sent him off to sleep fine, where my superstrength prescription did nothing for me."

"Do you think she slashed your tire?"

"Phoebe?" I push the last forkful of food around my plate. "I don't know. She was outside my house that night. I saw her, briefly. But I do have a client with an ex-wife who hates me. It could well have been her. I'm pretty sure she keyed my car, so this wouldn't be such a leap." She doesn't say anything, just watches me, face full of concern, and I sip my wine, feeling awkward.

"I'm sorry. I don't know why I'm telling you all this. I needed someone to talk to and I know this probably sums up my pathetic loneliness more than anything, but I felt like we had a connection. Two fragile people. It's stupid. Like a new friendship."

"I haven't made any new friends in a long time," she says and then raises her glass. "To new friends. And hopefully all our issues will straighten themselves out soon enough."

We clink glasses, and I wish I'd brought another bottle. Being around her makes me calmer.

"Oh god," I say as she takes our plates away. "I haven't mentioned this icing on the cake. I found out our seventeen-year-old daughter is sleeping with the father of a kid she babysits for. The couple are in our circle of friends. And I haven't told Robert yet. I meant to, but there's been no time. I'm hoping the fact that I know will scare the shit out of the guy and he'll finish it."

"That's awful," she says, eyes widening. "And you haven't confronted this man? Spoken to his wife even?"

"No, not yet. There's just so much other stuff going on, I don't want to drop this bomb in the middle of it."

"Yeah, I get that," she says, filling the kettle and getting mugs out. As much as I'd like more wine, tea is probably a better idea. I have to drive back to the hotel. Thinking of the drive makes me realize that my bladder is screaming.

"Could I use the loo?"

"Just along the corridor before the stairs. Tea? Milk and sugar?"

"Just milk please."

The downstairs toilet is actually a large disabled wet room with grab rails. Maybe her mum had moved downstairs before going to the home. In that respect Caroline and I are once again different. I barely knew my mother and her life has obviously been spent looking after hers in a lot of ways. So odd, how on paper we have nothing in common and yet I feel so utterly drawn to her.

The song is playing when I come back into the kitchen. "This is a cool tune," she says. "I like a folky sound." She puts the teacups down. "Can you play it again?"

"Of course," I answer and grit my teeth as the over-familiar melody starts. The song has killed my good mood in a moment. I'll drink my tea and go.

39

TWO DAYS UNTIL MY BIRTHDAY

I'd bought two large glasses of wine to take to my room when I'd got back to the hotel, and when I wake from my brief sleep, I'm fuzzy-headed and dry mouthed. Blurry with tiredness, it takes a moment before I can figure out where I am and then the penny drops. Not in my own home, the one I've worked so hard for. I've been banished from there. I sit up and check my phone. No messages from Robert or Chloe, and nothing yet from Darcy. I throw a text at Chloe: "Hope everything's okay. I love you all. Mum." *And have you dumped that cheating bastard yet* is what my hangover wants me to add, but I don't.

We'd played the song several times over before I

left—I didn't have the heart to tell Caroline to stop with it and didn't want to explain why. She said it was a melody of loss and haunting heartache and she loved it and by the fifth play even I could pretend that the tune was just a regular earworm. Maybe it is. Maybe it isn't entwined in my weird nights. I don't fucking know anything anymore.

The sleeping pills are still in the cupboard at home—I didn't see the point of bringing them as I have no intention of taking them—and I lay in the unfamiliar bed, awake until four, muttering my mother's numbers and trying not to think about what might be happening in my house without me there to check the doors, windows, and cupboards. Were the children okay? Was someone doing something bad?

At one point I'd got up and paced around the room, wanting to get in the car and drive over there, even though turning up in the middle of the night would hardly make Robert more inclined to think I'm sane. In the end I just drew the numbers on the wall with my fingers and tried some deep breathing until I settled.

Still in bed, I scan my emails, mainly crap sales shit, but then I see one from Hartwell Secure Unit. It came through yesterday evening and I must have missed it. It's from Senior Forensic Mental Health Nurse Debbie Webster. She's sorry for my loss and I'm welcome to visit and she'll help in any way she can. I quickly reply that I'll come today—before they start thinking of me as a potential murderer if the police decide I'm a proper suspect—and then get up to put the coffee machine on.

There's no answer from Chloe by the time I'm ready to head off and I try not to let it bother me. She's a teenager. She's surly, and ignoring me is probably a lot easier than trying to have a conversation. My not being there has let her off the Julian hook for now too, so she's probably relieved about that. I'm not at home to tell her father, and right now we've got bigger problems to deal with.

It's a beautiful day, and I open the window so the fresh breeze can wake me up along with the energy drink I've grabbed from the petrol station. Hartwell is an hour out of Leeds and I'm on the wrong side of the city, but it's a quiet Sunday morning, so it turns into quite a soothing drive, a sense of direction and purpose in my floundering life. Has Parker Stockwell told Buckley about my outburst yet? Probably, but sod him. I'm perfectly within my rights to tell him to back off and I've already fired a warning shot across the bow about inappropriate sexual politics.

That doesn't stop my seeing my partnership chances going down the drain. But at least Buckley can't fire me. Perhaps I should play the game and tell him about

Miranda's probable actions against me. My scratched car. The note. *Bitch*. The way she was waiting for me in the restaurant. Maybe both Buckley and Stockwell would be more forgiving then. I hate the idea of backing down or making myself look weak, but I also want that partnership. I mean I *really* want it. If Robert thinks I'm about to quit my career so he can play at running the Rovers Return, he's as crazy as he thinks I am.

I am not crazy. Worried, yes. Sleepless, yes. Haunted by the past to the point of distraction, yes. But crazy? No. I'm not that. As I get closer to Hartwell, I start to feel more confident. I'm facing my past. Taking charge. Acting like a grown-up. Maybe Dr. Morris is right. There are only two days until my birthday. In a week this will all be over, but if I can get to my fortieth without this fear that the same thing that happened to my mother is going to happen to me, then so much the better.

40

I'm not sure what I was expecting of Hartwell—maybe some nineteenth-century Bedlam—but not the bright, modern, cheerful-looking building that is ahead of me. If it wasn't for the high wire fencing, the place could easily be a school building. With blue port-hole windows against the cream walls, and some very Scandi looking sections of wood cladding, the whole aesthetic is designed to put you at ease, and as I buzz into the main entrance the feeling continues through to a bright reception room decorated with paintings and clay pieces I presume were made by the residents, interspersed with motivational posters.

"Hi." A woman in a blue polo shirt smiles at me from behind the pine counter. "I'm so sorry but our whole system has crashed this morning. Something to do with the server. Someone's promised to mend it, but they haven't arrived yet, so you'll have to bear with me for a moment—it's all back to pen and paper for now. How can I help?"

"I came to see Nurse Debbie Webster?"

"Ah, another problem there." She shrugs apologetically. "Migraine. She called in sick. Which I'll probably be doing tomorrow if the internet whiz kids don't arrive soon."

God, I hope I haven't driven up here for nothing. "She emailed me last night saying I could come and talk to her about . . . about my mother. She was a patient here. She just died. Patricia Bournett?"

Her faces softens into a warm sympathetic smile. "Oh Patricia. I'm so sorry for your loss. I can't actually believe she's gone. She's always been a part of Hartwell. We'll miss her."

Her soft tone puts me on the back foot. I don't expect anyone to talk like that about my mother. "I didn't really know her. I was very young when— Is there someone who can maybe talk to me about her? Show me her room or something. I just—I've been told I need to find some closure basically and . . . ." I can feel blotches coming up on my neck with awkward embarrassment. "Well, I thought this might help me."

"Of course. I'm sure I can find someone to show you

around. Especially as she was a low-security resident and—"

"Low? It was medium wasn't it?"

She gives me a gentle smile. "To start with, yes. But for a long time Patricia was only really in danger of harming herself, not others. She was moved to the Apple Tree Low Secure wing over a decade ago." I almost snap that as far as I was concerned, she was very much a danger to others, but instead I force myself to smile in agreement.

"I know my sister came to see her a few times this year," I say, after she calls through for a nurse to come and collect me. "Have there been any other visitors? If there were, I'd like to thank them, if possible." I'm doing my best impersonation of a grieving daughter, but I'm mainly curious.

Now that I'm here, the reality that this was my mother's life—her home—for the past thirty-five years is a lot to take in. Even if some of the staff have spent their whole careers here, she was still a resident for longer. It's a strange thought. This was her entire world. Such limited horizons. What did she think, if she ever thought of us? *Did* she ever think of us? Did anybody out there care about what happened to her? Did she have any other friends? How strange if she lived here all this time with not a single visitor until

Phoebe. Not much to say for the forty years of life she had before this.

"Until we have the computers back up and running again, I can't tell you." The receptionist breaks me from my thoughts. "But I'll make a note to contact you and let you know when I can. I'm sure Nurse Webster will call you anyway. And if you could complete this"—she slides a clipboard and pen over to me—"then I can register you as signed in."

By the time I've filled it in, a solid woman, Julie, is striding forward to greet me and lead me over to the Apple Tree wing. She takes me down the side of the building, talking me through all the facilities, pointing out the garden gym area—telling me there's a fully equipped indoor gym as well, but the fresh air is good for the clients—the picnic benches and the wonderful grounds and other exercise areas. I definitely feel like I'm getting a tour of some academy and that at any minute we're going to have to watch a chemistry class demonstration.

Only when we get inside the Apple Tree wing do I feel the tips of my fingers cool and my heart race.

"Did you know my mother?" I ask Julie as she leads me farther into the heart of the building.

"Of course. Everyone knows—knew—Patricia. I joined the team, gosh, about eight years ago now, and passing the Patricia test was like a test of character. If she liked you, then you were a good egg, that's what Debbie said at the time, and it's proved true."

I frown slightly. "But my mother was catatonic, wasn't she? How could you tell if she liked someone?"

"Trust me, even very locked-in patients, like your mother sometimes was, have ways of showing if they like a nurse or not. It can make dressing and undressing them very difficult."

"Like she *sometimes* was?" What does that mean? "Did she have periods of lucidity?" My mother collapsed in front of me when I was five and as far as I was aware had been entirely noncommunicative since then. They'd thought she'd had a stroke at first, it was that bad. And Phoebe said she wasn't talking when she visited too.

"Of sorts. Your mother's issues were complex. She didn't really fit into a defined bracket, but then people rarely do. There were long periods of time when she was definitely present. She just chose not to speak. But physically she was weak from so much inactivity and on the occasions, not so much recently, that she was out of her wheelchair, she would need a walker."

My mother was active? Not almost brain-dead? The past is rewriting itself and making my head spin as we finally come to a stop at one room. My mother's room.

I'm hesitant at first to cross the threshold, but the bed is stripped and the desk and drawers are empty of any possessions.

"She didn't have many things," Julie says. "Just her clothes and toiletries. There used to be a radio, but it would upset her. Mainly she liked quiet." Her voice is soft and as I peer into the bathroom, I see where a mirror over the sink has been removed.

"Is this where . . ." My throat is tight and dry. In my mind's eye I see her standing here, but as she was when I was a child, bloodshot eyes and greasy hair, slamming her forehead angrily into the glass.

"Yes." Julie looks pained and uncomfortable. "We all feel awful about it. There was no warning. She'd been more alert of late, but nothing to imply that she was going to hurt herself. She was such a placid soul, you see. You might not think of her that way, and that's natural given your childhood, and yes, she was damaged, but she was gentle. She hadn't done anything like that in twenty years."

"She'd done it before?" It all feels surreal. The void of my mother's life is filling up with these snippets of time.

"Not like that, no. But she did try to stab herself once. Long before my time, obviously. In fact, it was a whole different regime then, and this extension wasn't even built, but it was a terrible thing. To this day no one knows how she got hold of the piece of glass. Thankfully the nurses got to her in time and the wound wasn't deep."

I look back at the mirrorless wall and although I'm a long way from feeling any pity for her, I wonder how desperate she must have been to smash her head so hard against it. And why the long gap. Why now? It gives me a shiver. *Why at 1:13* A.M.*? And why did I wake up so full of fear and dread then?*

"Let me show you the art therapy area. She spent a lot of time in there. I think she found it soothing."

I'm happy to leave the empty room behind. I don't want to think of her on that mattress, night after night, for all those years. I'd pictured her as totally lost to the world, basically having to be turned and washed, but now I know that wasn't the case. Phoebe didn't tell me about that. She came here a few times. Was our mother alert during any of those times? Why wouldn't she say? Would I have wanted to know? Probably not, to be fair. But everything I've assumed to be the truth of her life is being rearranged and the world feels unsteady.

When we get to the large room where an art class is going on, it's the first time I've seen any patients at all. There are maybe eight or ten women of various ages concentrating on their work, some light pop music playing in the background. A woman with long gray hair swept up in a chignon, a heavy bead necklace, and an ID around her neck looks over and smiles, and even without the badge I'd know she was an art therapist.

"Patricia liked it in here," Julie says. "To be honest, we all like it in here. The calmest room in the building."

Another nurse peers in. "Ah, Julie? Can I have a word? I've got a problem in room six. Two seconds."

Julie looks at me apologetically. "Take a look at some of the art if you like. Some of it is quite impressive." And then she's gone.

Awkward, I stroll around the room, wondering where *she* would have sat and whether she ever painted anything and if she ever tried to draw her children. It makes me think of Will's drawings on the walls. Is he now also doomed to be haunted by that night from long ago? *Did* Phoebe tell him? Could he have overheard? I glance at the people concentrating on their art. All with issues. All damaged. Am I like them? *Those little slips of time. What do I do in them? Am I standing over my child's bed? Am I the one fated to repeat the mistakes of the past?* My birthday is so close now. I'm exhausted. *Am I going to snap? Like her?*

"You're not the one who came before."

The voice startles me and I find that a woman with

a saggy face, heavy bags around her eyes, and dark hair shot through with steel gray has appeared beside me. There's a hum of energy about her as she moves from foot to foot. Anxiety maybe. She's got paint dried onto her fingers, and there's a splash of white on her blue sweatshirt. No ID card. One of the patients. One of my mother's peers.

"I'm sorry?" I say.

"Pat's daughters." Her eyes search mine. "You look more like her than the other one. Got the same eyes. I'm Sandra." She smiles. She has surprisingly great teeth. Maybe she's not as old as she looks. "The other one was different."

Julie hasn't returned yet, but the other nurse in the room and the art teacher don't seem at all concerned by this interaction, so I don't see why I should be. I've spent all these years thinking of my mother locked in a facility for the criminally insane, it's hard to adjust to the realization that these people are mainly just troubled.

"My sister, Phoebe? Yeah, we're not really alike."

Sandra's face clouds over and then she looks up at me again. "Want to see my paintings?"

"Sure."

She has a whole corner of the room to herself, away from the rest of the group.

"We always kept space for Pat next to me. Patsy, I used to call her sometimes. Like off of *Ab Fab*. Love that show. She used to watch me paint. Even when she wasn't really here." She taps the side of her head. "Off wherever she would go. Somewhere, that's for fucking sure, but just not here. I don't think she liked it there. Her face would go odd. Tight, you know? I was always glad when she came back."

I know exactly what she means. I remember that "tight" face when Mum would be staring into the middle distance. She had it that night. *"Ah, there you are."* When she opened the under-stairs cupboard door.

"Look." Sandra pulls a few pictures out of one of the drawers. She's painted on boards, no crisp warped paper covered in poster paint like Will brings home. As I look at them, I'm surprised. They are actually quite good. Bright flowers and abstract butterflies. "I love the summer," she says. "I think my head would be all right if it was always summer. Know what I mean?"

"Yeah. I think I do," I say. "I don't suppose my mother ever painted?"

"Not exactly." She gives me a sideways, secretive glance. "I didn't show the other one, what did you say her name was Phoebe? I didn't like her. But I'll show you, Emma."

"Thank you." I pause, and frown. "How do you

know my name?" I'm pretty sure Julie didn't say it. Not in here anyway.

"The other one, Phoebe . . ." Sandra talks while rummaging back in the drawer. "She was sly. Didn't know I could lip-read."

"Sorry, I don't understand." What has lipreading got to do with Phoebe?

"Things happened when I was little. I don't talk about them." She suddenly tugs at her hair, pulling a few strands free before looking over her shoulder, guilty, waiting to be caught. No one is looking. "But I learned to read lips. Had to."

"You don't have to tell me about that. But what do you mean Phoebe was sly?"

"She smiled a lot. I never trust people who smile a lot when they visit here. It's not fucking Center Parcs." I laugh at that and she grins at me, before her face clouds again. "She'd sit there, holding Pat's hand, all calm and caring, but I watched her. Looked like she was just chatting away, telling her about life outside, things Pat was never going to understand or care about, and she probably didn't even know who your sister was. It's not like you two have been filling up the visitors' book."

She looks at me as if I might try to defend myself but I can't argue with that. "And it's not like she was exactly always mentally here," she finishes. "But anyway, that Phoebe was smiling and holding Pat's hand with the nurses all thinking the sun shone out of her skinny arse for coming here and forgiving the poor old woman, but all the time she's talking quietly and I could see what she was saying. *Bitch. Wish you'd just die. I can never forgive you. I hate you.* Those were the best things. There were worse words. Crude. Vicious."

I stare at her. "Phoebe? She was saying all this?"

Sandra nods. "I'm glad she hasn't come back. She's lucky we only have plastic cutlery 'cause I'd do her some damage with a fork if I saw her again."

"Did you tell anyone?"

She looks at me as if I'm the one who should be locked up for suggesting that and then pulls a sheet of paper out from her drawer. It's tucked into a folded drawing. Hidden.

"It's not a drawing. It's why I didn't show anyone. I don't think she wanted people to see it. I hadn't even noticed her doing it. It was just there, the other day, after she'd wheeled herself away to stare out the window."

She hands me the paper and with my heart pounding, I unfold it. My breath catches. The handwriting is all spidery scrawl, but it's my name, written over and over, in sharp, shaky capitals until it filled the page, the word overlapping, and a few had been scratched out.

Emma. Emma. Emma.

"That's how I knew your name." She shrugs. "Figured you had to be Emma."

"When did she do this?" I ask her, staring. My name. Emma. The last word I ever heard my mother say.

Sandra says nothing for a moment, chewing her bottom lip. "The day she bashed her brains out against the mirror. You must have been on her mind."

The world spins again.

"Sorry, for keeping you hanging around." Julie bustles in, smiling. "Ah, has Sandra been keeping you company? She's very good at making sure everyone is feeling comfortable. Now, where were we? I can show you—"

"Actually, I should probably head back now," I say, folding the paper up tight in my damp palms. Sandra doesn't ask for it back and I don't know if I want to keep it or throw it as far away from me as possible, but I can't get my fingers to uncurl from it. "It's all been a bit overwhelming." That isn't a lie. I am overwhelmed.

"Of course. I can imagine. I'll take you back."

I glance at Sandra. My hands are shaking again.

"Thank you. And your art is wonderful. Joyful. I'd buy one." Her face bursts into a genuine smile, and then she's back at her board and I'm following Julie's bustling figure out into the corridor while my head spins and my face heats up. When we leave the building, the breeze is a relief and I gulp in the fresh air, happy to be away from *her* air. Julie doesn't say much. Maybe they preferred Phoebe with her cool, controlled manner to me and my obvious unease.

At least she came before her mother died. And she was the one with the most to forgive.

41

There's a cold sweat under my T-shirt and I hold it together until I've driven away from the facility, but about a mile down the road I see a turnout and pull in, turn the air-conditioning up to high, and take some deep breaths as the cold air slowly calms me down. It's surreal to have been in the place where my mother lived—to have seen where she slept and ate and even socialized as much as she could—but none of that is what's tipped me over the edge.

Phoebe. Holier than fucking thou Phoebe. *Go and see her. . . it might do you good*—or whatever it was she said to me. What a fucking joke. I grab my phone to call her, and my fury quells my nausea as it starts to ring. The call goes to voice mail.

"Fuck you, Phoebe." I'm so angry my voice is shaking. "I've just been to Hartwell. I know what you were doing up there. The things you were saying while pretending to be all Goody Two-shoes. You think I'm crazy? What is wrong with *you*, Phoebe? What are you doing back here?" I'm about to hang up when my anger simmers over and I shriek, "And stay the fuck away from my family or I swear to god I'll kill you!" into the phone.

I'm panting loudly in the car. Where is she now? At work? At my house? I remember her and Robert hugging in my kitchen. Is she *comforting* my husband? As I pull away from the turnout I call Robert. Screw waiting for him to make the first move. He might not want me at home, but I don't want *her* there either. A new *her* in my head. No longer my dead mother, now my older sister.

"Hey," he says. "Look, I can't really talk now but—"

"Are you at home? Is Phoebe there?" I'm too sharp—*hysterical*—but I can't help it.

"No to both. I'm at the park with Will. I'll call you later. Or tomorrow. This isn't—"

"I don't want her in my house, Robert. Tell me you won't have her in our house. She's a liar. I know she is. I don't want her near Will—" I can hear myself and nothing is coming out right, just a splurge of paranoid ranting. I know I should be calm, reasoned, but I can't. "She's frightening him. She's telling him things."

"Stop it, Emma!" he snaps, sharp, irritated, before

calming down and speaking quietly. "Stop it." Has he stepped away from Will? I imagine my little boy, wondering what the hell is going on. Where his mummy is. Why his parents are fighting. It breaks my heart.

"Will isn't afraid of Phoebe, Emma."

"You don't know that—he's only little—he might not want to say—"

"He's not afraid of her. He's afraid of you." He pauses. "And right now, I don't blame him." He says it with such a cold disgust and finality that I feel like my breath has been punched out of me.

I hang up. What am I supposed to do now? Maybe I should drive to the house and wait for them. I want to see Will. If I'm honest, I want to grab him and run. Take him and run from Phoebe and my insomnia and Robert and everything that's making me afraid. He feels so far away from me, and that makes me fear for him more. I'm not a threat to Will, I don't care what they say. But I can't shake that something is. My nighttime fears are leaking into my daytimes as my dreaded birthday creeps closer. It's not me though. I'm not the thing my child is afraid of. I throw my phone into the footwell, full of rage and frustration, and head back to the city. I am not.

42

"She's out to get me. I'm sure of it. Phoebe's *always* been jealous of me, right from when we were little."

"Why don't you sit down? Please?" Caroline says. "I need to just finish this work text."

She was surprised to see me—*or was that shock*—at her door again, carrying fish and chips and two bottles of wine, I could see that, but she still let me in as I garbled an apology for being back so soon.

"I can't, I'm too wired." I take another large sip of the wine. I'm nearly a glass down already and I've only been here five minutes, ranting about what Phoebe had done at Hartwell. I wait while she finishes with her phone and then sits herself, carefully unwrapping one parcel of food.

"I can't believe I didn't see it before," I continue, ranting as much to myself as to her as I refill my glass. "Of course, she wasn't visiting our mother out of any sort of forgiveness. How did I believe that? Because she's always been able to make me feel guilty, that's how. Ever since that night. God knows what Mum was planning to do to me after suffocating Phoebe, but my sister's never forgiven me for not being the one she tried to kill first, even though I'm the one who saved her. Or at least if it wasn't for me, our mother wouldn't have stopped. I was five. I could have just run away, but I didn't. I went upstairs to get Phoebe. Not that she's ever acknowledged that." I look at Caroline for a response.

"Sometimes it's difficult to say things like that aloud," she says, eventually. "And maybe she felt ashamed for having bad feelings."

"You're sounding like a psychiatrist."

"Carry on. Get it all off your chest."

As if I need any encouragement. "Then she was jealous that there was a nice family who wanted me when we were in foster care. They were going to adopt me. They changed their minds, but the damage was done by then. It wasn't my fault no one would keep her. She had issues. She was older, and so moody and angry. But none of that was my fault. We *both* got moved around, not just her. The difference between us is that I worked hard for everything I had. Phoebe never tried hard enough. And there was the thing with Robert. I mean, at the time she said she didn't care, she even laughed about it."

Caroline looks at me quizzically. "What thing with Robert?"

"It sounds worse than it was, but Phoebe knew Robert before I did. I mean, barely, but yeah, but she dated him first. Only a couple of times, nothing serious." I stop pacing, take another long drink, and lean on the table.

"But I've been thinking about *why now*. Why would Phoebe suddenly turn up and want to hurt me now? And then it struck me. Me and Phoebe have both always been worried about what happened to our mother repeating itself with one of us. It's in our blood, that's what our mum said. Her great-aunt ended up in an asylum. And she used to say I'd go mad like her.

"But what if *Phoebe* went crazy on her fortieth? She disappeared off on a retreat and I've barely seen her since then. Maybe this has been a simmering plan in her head? How do I know *she* didn't suffocate my mother? Last I saw her, she was heading out of the ward with a nurse, and she told me she was going home for a while, but maybe she didn't? Maybe she waited, saw me leaving, and then took the opportunity to kill our mother herself?"

"But Emma—" Caroline's eyes widen, but I don't stop.

"Don't you see? That way it would have looked like *I* did it. And on top of all that stuff she was saying to her at Hartwell—I should call the police really. Let them know they *do* have another suspect."

"Devil's advocate here again," Caroline cuts in. "But you have only an inmate's word for that. Do you know anything about this Sandra's mental health problems? Does she hallucinate, for example?"

"I don't know. But she was so, well, normal. And why would she lie?"

"Hallucinating isn't lying. She might think that's what she saw. And if she was fond of your mother, maybe she was a bit jealous? I'm not saying it didn't happen, I'm just pointing out that it's not the most reliable evidence. You're better at least to wait until your friend Darcy has got evidence of you leaving the hospital and then you're in the clear yourself."

I feel deflated as I realize she has a point.

"And I know I asked if you thought she might have slashed your tire," she continues, "but this is quite a step further from a jealous sister having a moment."

"What if she's trying to turn my family against me? Or what if she hurts them?"

"What if she isn't and doesn't, which is the most obvious answer." She eats another chip. "You need a good night's sleep. You can't do anything today. She's not going to hurt your family. Why would she? They're her family too. And you're going down a really dark path with what you think she's capable of. You said you've already left one angry voice-mail message, so leave it at that for now." She looks at my wineglass as I drain it again. "Aren't you driving?"

"I'll get a cab," I mutter. "Or walk. Or go and sleep outside my house."

"Don't be silly." She pauses. "You're in no state to be alone. You can stay here tonight." It's a reluctant offer, I sense, but it makes me feel instantly calmer. Spending the night around Caroline. Inside her house. I might even get some sleep.

"Thank you," I say, embarrassed to find tears threatening to spill over. "I'll be fine in the morning. It's all been a bit of a shock."

"Let's have a cup of tea and then I'm going to get an early night, I think," she says. "I'm covering for a colleague tomorrow. You should probably try to sleep too."

After our tea—during which I get a disappointing text from Darcy saying he's got nothing yet—I follow her upstairs and then wait in the spare room while she showers quickly before using the tired disabled bathroom myself, brushing my teeth with my finger so my mouth feels at least a little fresh. When I come out, she's waiting in the corridor.

"There are some books in the back room if you want something to read. Ignore the mess in there. I've been meaning to get it all down to the dump or charity shops but you know how it is. Never enough hours. They're mainly crime novels or those Barbara Taylor Bradford 1980s family sagas, but plenty to choose from. My mum's."

"Thanks. See you in the morning," I say as she disappears into her room, and even though I'm not sure a book is going to do me any good, I figure I should take one to be polite. I've been weird enough as it is.

The third bedroom is down at the other end of the corridor, and it's chilly, the radiator turned completely off. I have a twinge of money guilt. It's been a long time since I've had to worry about the heating bills. There are also boxes everywhere. I can see framed photos poking out of one, as well as other decorative pictures and knickknacks—old china dolls and blown-glass animals that clearly aren't to Caroline's taste. They're not mine either, really, and yet there's something I find comforting and heart-warming about them.

How wonderful to have had a mother to love and be loved by and who you share all these boxes of memories with. For a moment I feel my own mother's cold dry fingers gripping my wrist in the hospital and remember how her eyes flashed open and terrified me. What did she see in that moment? Did she see me? Did she see anything at all?

Shivering, I turn to the stack of books up against a wall. Thick, well-worn paperbacks, bought from charity shops that they will no doubt now return to. There are several Wilbur Smiths, some Shirley Conrans, and then a lot of crime novels. I pick out an Ian Rankin, because at least I've heard of him.

I turn the light out and head back to my room. The shapes and shadows make me feel five years old again, the layout so similar to my mother's house, and I hurry along the landing, happy to get back to some light. Maybe reading will help me switch my brain off and sleep before dawn, although as soon as I'm under the covers I can feel my heart picking up its pace again. Alert. Awake. Worried. It's still early though, and so I open the book, determined to focus and start to read.

I'm five chapters in, and it's past eleven, when my phone lights up on the bedside table, the vibration making me jump. I see who's calling and my stomach knots. *Here we go.*

"Phoebe," I say, cool. No more hysterics from me today. I don't know what my sister's game is yet, but Caroline's right, until I'm in the clear I've got to hold my fire.

"I don't know what that voicemail message is all about." She's ice in my ear. "But it's not convincing me of your sanity. Nothing warrants that kind of reaction."

"Don't turn this around—"

"Something's wrong with you, Emma. Your secretary told the police about your Dictaphone. Mum's numbers? For God's sake."

"That's not what it—"

"What it sounds like? What is it then? From what I hear you've been losing your shit since Mum was in the hospital. Not your shit. Your *mind*." She lets out a long sigh. "Maybe you should check yourself in somewhere. Recalibrate."

"Well, I've had to since my husband asked me to move out." She's not mentioned what I said to her about Hartwell. The awful things Sandra said she was saying to our mother. She's just glossed over it like it doesn't matter, and I'll let it go for now, until I'm in the clear, but that's an admission of guilt if ever there was one. "Which I'm sure you already know," I continue. "Being as close to Robert as you are." I wonder if the acid from my tongue stings when it lands in her ear. If it does, she glosses over that too.

"I meant a facility. Somewhere someone can keep an eye on you until your birthday is over. All these accusations. So much paranoia."

She means a loony bin. Somewhere like our mother was, except a place for people who haven't yet committed their crimes. My face burns. She's calling me mad.

"It'd be for the best. For everyone," she says, softly. "For your family. You don't trust yourself at the moment. I know you don't. Because I know you, Emma. I'm your sister."

"Fuck you, Phoebe," I say, despite my promise to stay calm. "I know your game and fuck you." I hang up and turn my phone off, leaning against the cool pillow as my rage burns.

43

I am not mad. *I have not had a psychotic break. I am not out of touch with reality,* I tell myself over and over as I tap my fingers against the glass. No. I am not mad. *I. Am. Not.* I am, however, still wide fucking awake.

I'm in the third bedroom and a draft creeps in around the frame as I peer out the old window down into a dark garden below. All this started when Phoebe called me from the hospital. *Did it though? Didn't it start the night before? At 1:13* A.M. *when Mum bashed her own brains in and you woke up and haven't slept properly since? Isn't that when it started?*

Not with Phoebe's text at all.

The numbers start up in my head, and then I'm

muttering them over and over under my breath. *"One hundred and thirteen one hundred and fifty-five two hundred and eighteen two hundred and twenty-two."* I repeat them like a mantra.

Phoebe is my sister, the rational part of my brain thinks. We love each other. *Do you really?* the whispering voice immediately counters. *Does she love you? Why would she? You married a boy she brought home—the first boy she'd ever brought home and you've never known her to have another. Isn't that weird? Isn't she weird? She turns up and your life is now going down the drain and she's always, always there. And someone told Will what happened. Someone wanted to scare him.*

Maybe you're right. Maybe Phoebe did go mad at forty. Maybe she's the one who's like our mother.

I head back into the corridor, still muttering the numbers, and the song starts playing in my head. So much noise, making it so hard to think. Numbers. Lyrics. Mum. Phoebe. Me. This old house makes the past and present feel more closely entwined. I pause at the top of the stairs. I've already been down there. Pacing and muttering. *Nothing like her, I'm nothing like her.*

The banister post is round at the top, old-fashioned,

just like the one back then. "Look, look," I whisper, "A candle, a book and a bell." Did our mother pause here in her house that night? Like this? I feel her dry hand tight on my wrist and the glossed wood under my fingertips and our hands become one. I wonder if I'll see myself on the stairs if I look back down. I close my eyes and breathe deeply as the past threatens to drown me with memories in the dark.

We come in through the back door, Phoebe rattling the loose handle to get it to open where it sticks, and the daylight that peers in, curious, is as brief as the fresh air I manage a gulp of before Phoebe closes the door again and we're plunged into the stinky gloom of the house we know as home.

I look at the floor. A half-hearted attempt has been made to clean up the mess of broken eggs, but the tea towel she's used to scoop up the shells and their rotten contents has been dumped in the middle of the rest of the clutter on the kitchen countertops. Phoebe tries to wash up when she can, but there's always more, and a lot of the space is taken up with half-empty wine bottles or other spirits, spilled coffee, and random items Mum's taken out of the cupboards and not put back.

One whole end of the surface holds a collection of milk bottles from when the milkman used to come. Me and Phoebe aren't allowed to touch those. Mummy says if we touch one, they'll all fall down and smash. Then we'll have glass in our feet and won't be able to go to school. I don't understand why she doesn't give them back to the milkman and then he might start bringing milk again.

Phoebe tugs at my sleeve and points at the kitchen table. The fortieth birthday card we made—HAPPY BIRTHDAY MUMMY—is sitting in the middle, warped with dried egg, but displayed. We look at it, hopeful. This is the kind of thing Phoebe calls "a good sign."

"Mummy?" she says. "We're home, Mummy."

There's some noise in the hallway and I go first. To me, the events of the morning are further away than they are to Phoebe. She's eight. I think time is different when you get older. Anyway, Mummy picked our card up. She loves us. Maybe today is going to be a good day. Or at least a better day.

The floorboards creak under my feet and I frown a bit, my confidence wavering. Mummy's crouching in the hallway by the under-stairs cupboard, her back to us. The door is open and she's viciously scratching something into the inside of the door. Her head tics, erratic little movements, as she mutters fast under her breath.

"One hundred and thirteen one hundred and fifty-five two hundred and eighteen . . ."

Suddenly aware of us, she stands, spinning around to cover the inside of the open door, and drops the school protractor she's been gripping. She glares at me with wide, sleepless eyes, and even though I know Phoebe is only a few steps behind me, it feels like there's an ocean between us.

Mummy lunges forward and for the second time that day her fingers are digging into my arms, but this time instead of shaking me, she pulls me toward her. No, not toward her. She's dragging me to the cupboard.

"No, Mummy, please no!"

Darkness yawns in front of me. Hungry. And then it swallows me whole.

I'm in there a long time.

It's so dark and I'm pressed up against the wall, my knees under my chin. From somewhere far away— somewhere outside—I can hear a distant rumble of thunder. My face itches from tears and sweat and my breath comes in short, fast pants. The long hours since getting home from school have turned into an eternity, and even though I know the cupboard is small, all I can see is an endless ocean of black that makes everything shadowy when I shut my eyes. I don't know what I'm more afraid of, monsters that might be living in here, or Mummy out there. I can hear her in the hallway, pacing up and down, up and down. She goes upstairs.

She comes back down. Sometimes she pauses, right by the door, and I pull back tighter into myself.

I can hear her muttering.

"One hundred and thirteen one hundred and fifty-five two hundred and eighteen . . ."

Something thuds heavily, maybe a bottle dropping on the carpet, and the muttering stops. There's a long moment of silence and I hold my breath, and then there's the sudden loudness of the bolt moving and the cupboard door opens.

Mummy is crouching in the doorway, her smile too wide behind the ragged curtain of her hair. Behind her, the house is grainy dark. It's the dead of night. Neither of us moves, and the sound of the storm outside is loud, as if a door is open somewhere. A slight breeze confirms it. The back door maybe.

A flash of lightning illuminates Mummy. She's soaking wet. Her eyes are odd. Empty. Looking at me but not seeing me. Looking at something past me. I think she's more frightening this way. More "funny Mummy." I almost want her to shake me again so I know this is my Mummy.

Her head tilts to one side and there's a long pause before she speaks.

"Ah, there you are." Her voice is soft. Calm.

She stands up and pushes the door closed once more,

drowning me again in darkness, and I bite my hand so I don't cry out or scream and call for her to come back, to not leave me in here forever. The hallway creaks as she walks away.

"Back up to bed," I hear her say before the stairs I'm buried under start to groan with her tread. As she moves over me, I wriggle toward the door, the blackness in here now too much to bear, and kick it. It swings open easily. She didn't relock it. As I crawl out, my heart threatening to burst from my chest in fear that Mummy will somehow come out of the cupboard and grab me back in and we'll be lost in there forever, I see the scratchings on the door. Mummy's special numbers.

1 1 3 1 5 5 2 1 8 2 2 2 1 1 3 1 5

No monster grabs me to pull me back, and I drink in the fresh rain-damp air as more thunder rolls angrily overhead. I straighten up, my school uniform creased and my legs sore. There's an empty wine bottle on the dirty carpet. Farther along, an abandoned glass. I look back at the kitchen and see that mine and Phoebe's birthday card is on the floor again.

Phoebe. Has Mummy gone up to see Phoebe? The thought fills me with a dread that I'm too young to understand, something built deep into my DNA, a survival warning signal. Despite my fear, despite wanting to run out into the storm to find the nice lady and tell her Mummy is being funny again, like Phoebe did that time before, I force myself toward the stairs. Phoebe is up there. I need to get to Phoebe.

I grip the banister and start to climb, forcing one foot in front of the other. A flash of cold lightning makes me jump, but the upstairs hallway is empty. There are noises though, strange sounds I don't quite understand, coming from where my and Phoebe's bedroom is. I stare into the gloom, gripping the top banister, stuck, not knowing what to do.

"Mummy?" I say, so quietly it's barely more than my lips moving. No one answers. I gulp air into my dry mouth and start walking forward. I hear a gasp. Exertion. Something muffled. My heart beats faster until by the time I'm pushing the door open I feel like I'm going to explode. Not just my heart. All of me. And then my breath is gone. The implosion is internal not external as I stare, air whomping out of my open mouth and my ears humming like I'm underwater.

Mummy, beside the bed, is leaning over Phoebe, her hair hanging over her face, as she holds the pillow down, smothering my big sister. She grunts with the effort, because Phoebe is struggling hard. I can hear muffled panic coming from under the pillow, but all I can see are Phoebe's legs thrumming against the mattress as she arches and then they're up and wheeling as if she's trying to kick something away. Phoebe.

I take a step forward. The old boards creak. Mummy's head spins around, her eyes startled and wide.

"Emma," she says, surprised. She straightens up. And then suddenly, with no warning, she spins fast to one side and then crumples, as if dead, onto the thin carpet. And then all I can hear is Phoebe wheezing and sobbing, and then she's grabbing me and stumbling and pulling me away from the too still raggedy mess of our mother and out into the rain.

My fingers are tight on the banister and as I push the memory back into its box, I force myself toward my bedroom. It's nearly three. I'm wrung out, but I'll get a couple of hours sleep if I try hard enough. As I pass Caroline's door, I notice it's ajar. I get the sudden urge to check on her, to see that she's in bed, sleeping, the world in order, so I quietly push it open. She's on her stomach, one arm under her head, fast asleep and totally relaxed. Every muscle in my body is tense but I feel better for watching her. I breathe in and out. I do feel better. Maybe I'll stay for a while.

The next thing I know I'm back in the spare room—my room—and my feet are cold, and my lower

back aches, but my chest is warm. I'm hugging a pillow, hunched over and standing beside the empty bed.
My hair hangs over my face and I'm staring at the
mattress in gray dawn light. *Oh god.*

I'm hugging a pillow.

I yelp and drop the pillow, afraid, as reality sinks in
around me. What am I doing? How did I get here? I
glance back at the door. It's closed. I closed it behind
me, I must have. The last thing I remember I was
standing in Caroline's doorway watching her. A terrible fear grips me. Oh god. I couldn't have. Wouldn't
have. My head is still filled with Phoebe's kicking legs
and I'm about to run to Caroline's room when I hear a
deep rumbling snore through the wall. I collapse onto
the edge of the bed, breathless, a rush of relief.

After a moment I curl up in the bed and grip the edge
of pillow, now under my head. What was I so afraid of?
I feel sick. I know the answer to that. I was scared that
I'd hurt her. *No, not hurt her, suffocated her.* That I'd
done what my mother did to Phoebe. My head starts to
throb. Did I really think I could have suffocated her?

Could I have suffocated her?

44

ONE DAY UNTIL MY BIRTHDAY

I didn't sleep at all, but lay in bed, terrified for me and of me, as dawn ticked into morning, and then I got up and started to make a proper breakfast for Caroline of eggs, bacon, and tomato on toast. She's a bit taken aback when she comes downstairs to the smell of it all and me washing up, but I usher her to the table, where her full plate is waiting.

"You didn't have to."

I hand her a knife and fork. "Least I can do, and you've got to go to work." It's a half-truth. I'm not sure how *I was scared in the night that I'd accidentally suffocated you while I wasn't myself and a breakfast was one way of appeasing my guilt* would go down.

"Why don't you go and speak to your sister this morning?" she says. "She works in a pub, right?"

"Yes, the Hand and Racquet." I imagine Phoebe's face if I turn up at her work. We'd be throwing pints at each other in seconds and then the police would come and I'd be in trouble all over again.

"Then go and talk it out. I'm sure it's all a misunderstanding."

"You're right." I'm embarrassed for ranting at Caroline last night. I must have seemed so hyper, I'm surprised she didn't ask me to leave. "Maybe I will."

My phone beeps—an email from Debbie Webster at Hartwell. Their systems are obviously up and running again. She says my mother did have another visitor and did I want her to pass on my number to them if they want to get in touch. I fire back a quick, "*yes please*," curious but mainly disappointed that the message wasn't from Darcy. God, why doesn't he just—

The email has barely whooshed into the ether when my phone rings and his name is there on the screen and my heart is suddenly in my mouth.

"Good news," he says before I've barely got a "hello" out. "You're in the clear. The police just called. You're on camera leaving the hospital and you don't return through any of the other entrances. If there was any foul play, it wasn't you."

I'm flushing with relief, up on my feet and pacing, half laughing, half crying. I didn't do it. And whatever happened last night I didn't do anything then either. Holding a pillow is just holding a pillow. It doesn't mean anything. Does it?

"Thank you, Darcy. Thank you so much."

"I've got to go. But if you need me for anything else, just drop me a text. And let's grab that beer sometime, yes?"

"Yes. Yes, definitely."

"Good." He pauses. "It was good to see you again, Baby Spice." And then he's gone and I'm grinning at Caroline. "I'm in the clear."

"There you go."

She looks extremely relieved, and I guess I don't blame her.

"I should have asked him to check the footage for Phoebe," I say.

"Go and talk to her before you start throwing accusations around. She's your sister."

"Okay, okay," I say.

She doesn't look convinced.

"I promise. And I'll come and report back." I look away then to finish washing the frying pan and while she doesn't say *please do* neither does she tell me not to. Whether she likes it or not, she's my only friend in all this. And anything to save me from being alone in that hotel room. "But first I've got somewhere else to go."

"What are you doing here?"

It's not exactly a joyful greeting from my husband. "Don't look so surprised, it is my house."

"Our house." Robert's holding the front door open but isn't moving aside to let me in. "You look terrible. Have you slept?"

"There's proof I absolutely didn't kill my mother. They've got me on camera leaving the hospital." I'm trying not to look too smug but I can't help it. "So at least you don't have to think that of me anymore."

"Two things." His expression doesn't change. "I never *did* think you'd done that, and secondly I already knew. The police rang this morning. They said Darcy was going to tell you."

"But surely you're happy? Surely this means we can—"

"You moving out wasn't about that and it doesn't solve any of our other problems, does it?" He keeps his voice low and comes outside, pulling the door to, as I try to peer around him, hoping to catch a glimpse of Will at the kitchen island. "You think this makes everything else go away?" he continues. "Will still won't talk about his drawings. When I've asked him, when the therapist asked him, what he's drawing, all he'll say is 'Mummy.' Why would he lie, Emma? Why does he say your name?"

"I don't think he is lying. Of course I don't. But neither am I." I pause and then the words come out in a flurry. "It's Phoebe, Robert. It has to be. She says she was visiting our mother to make her peace? She wasn't. She was calling her names, being horrible to her, someone there told me."

"A doctor?" He frowns. "Why did they let her visit if—"

"It wasn't a doctor, it was a patient but—"

"For god's sake, Emma," he cuts in, exasperated. "Listen to yourself. You're so paranoid you're believing what lunatics tell you."

"Lunatic?" I have a flare of anger on Sandra's behalf. "Very PC. Be proud of yourself. And you know as well as I do that Phoebe has always been jealous of me, of *us*, of all this. Is it so crazy to think that perhaps she wants to take it away from me? She knows I worry about what happened to our mum. That it'll happen to me. She's playing on that worry. She's making you buy into it, and she's scaring Will. Maybe she's the one with a screw loose." I pace on the path, and my words are nearly a snarl. "And I bet even she didn't bank on how easily you'd believe it all. I'm a lawyer, Robert. I'm the most together person we know."

"You *were*. But these past few days? You're a different person. As if something's snapped. And as for belief? I believe our *son*, Emma." His voice is low. "I mean, Jesus Christ, I'm just trying to protect him. I love you. I want all this resolved. For my sake and for yours. But it's better if you stay away until after your birthday."

The wind goes out of my sails and my clenched fists feel the memory of standing by my bed in the night with no idea of how I got there, clutching that pillow. He's right. Maybe I should stay away until after my birthday. Is my feeling of dread about *me*?

"I don't want Phoebe here," I say. That much is true. I may not trust myself but neither do I trust her. We both have the same mad blood. "And I'm going to go and tell her as much."

"What's going on? Oh. It's you." Chloe's face is sullenly defensiveness as she comes outside. "I'll get the bus. See you, Dad." She barely breaks stride and I change tack, turning my back on Robert and going after her.

"Hey, Chloe, wait. I'll give you a lift."

"Not after last time."

"Oh, come on, we both know that wasn't my fault. At least slow down and let me walk with you." I have to jog to catch up with her.

"Have you ended it with Julian?" She doesn't answer but glares stonily at the ground. "Oh, for God's sake, Chloe, I'm going to have to tell Dad. I can't keep it from him forever."

She stops then, finally looking at me. "If you do, I'll deny it. And who's he going to believe right now?"

"Wow. That's quite something." I square up to her. I'm not taking this from my own child. "Shall we try it, Chloe? Because that might be how it goes at first, but trust me, he'll start to have doubts."

She strides away again, all pent-up anger, and I grab her arm.

"I don't want to fight with you, Chloe. I'm not the enemy. I'm just worried. About everything." I glance back at the house. "About you and this situation. About what's happening with Will. And Phoebe. Has she been here? Is she spending time with Will alone? Your dad won't listen to me, but she can't be trusted. I know her."

"Stop it, Mum! Stop it!" She spins to face me and I'm expecting rage, but instead she's on the verge of tears. "Please, just stop! Don't you see what you're doing? You're scaring us! All of us! Dad. Will. Me. You want me to end it with Jules? Why would I do that? I feel *safe* with him."

"You don't feel safe with me?" I take an involuntary step backward.

She half shrugs, half sobs. "How can I? It's like you've, I don't know, suddenly cracked. All this shit about Auntie Phoebe. You're acting so weird. Not sleeping." She takes a hitching breath. "Auntie Phoebe said this is what happened with your mum. The mum you never told us about. And other people in your family too. Some great-aunt or something, who got locked up for being mad."

"Sounds like Phoebe's been talking a lot."

"Maybe, but she's not making you act weird, is she? You're doing that all by yourself. And it's freaking me out."

This time when she hurries away, I don't follow. I can't bring myself to move, suddenly seeing myself as they must. Unhinged. Unkempt. Untrustworthy.

I should do what Caroline suggested. Go to see Phoebe. Find out what she's up to face-to-face. What else have I got to lose?

45

My whole body is jittery, and I stay in the car for a bit before I can bring myself to get out. Last night I had no sleep at all, and on top of my prior exhaustion I feel trippy. I probably shouldn't even be driving. I can't afford to crash the replacement car as well as my own. I've parked in the city center and I finally get out, the world shimmering around me, and find the Hand and Racquet pub on my phone. There are two in Leeds, but I recognize the logo of one from the top Phoebe had been wearing and let Google Maps start to guide me to it.

As I get within a couple of streets of the pub, I grab a strong coffee and a sugary iced cake from a café and take a seat outside. I need some energy to be able to think straight. I'm in a busy part of town, and as the day gets warmer the pavement fills up with people hurrying here and there, buses and cars streaming by, and somehow the noise is soothing. All these people going about their daily lives, oblivious to the mess in mine. I probably look like a perfectly normal person, a little tired perhaps from managing work and kids, but nothing more than that. I feel invisible. A ghost.

The cake is sticky in my mouth and I tilt my head to the sun. I've got time. The pub is probably only just opening and I don't know what time Phoebe works. I take a sip of my coffee and break another piece of cake off. Phoebe whispering bad things to our mother. Phoebe whispering bad things to Will. Phoebe maybe whispering sweet nothings to Robert. *Why, Phoebe? What did I ever do to you? Apart from save your life?* Phoebe, Phoebe, Phoebe. I close my eyes for a moment and relax.

"Phoebe!"

I startle. At first I think I'm the one shouting, but then my head spins as I come out of my haze, and the world is such a place of noise and movement around me that I almost lose my balance. I'm standing on the sidewalk, a chunk of cake sticky against my fingers where the icing has melted, and my mouth is dry. A man is staring at me and he tuts as if I've tried to push past him. What am I doing here? I was at the café. How am I standing here?

"Phoebe!"

With the second call of her name, I look back, the anxiety in the tone cutting through the city sounds like a knife. Cars have stopped. People have stopped. A little farther up and on the other side of the road is the Hand and Racquet pub, on the corner of what looks like a busy crossroads. Or it would be a busy crossroads if anything was moving. Why am I walking away from it? How did I get here?

"Call an ambulance!"

"I think she was pushed," someone says as I force myself forward. "She looked like she was pushed."

Phoebe Phoebe Phoebe. No. No.

My heart is in my mouth.

"She's still breathing!" A shout goes up from someone hunkered down in the road.

I force through the gawkers, and then I see her. She's on the ground, twisted at an awful angle, three people hovering over her. Oh god, Phoebe.

Someone grabs me, trying to pull me back, to keep clear. "Let me go! She's my sister!"

I fall to my knees, a woman in a pub T-shirt making way for me, and I see how pale and scared her face is as she moves back, embraced in a hug by an older colleague. I tug off my jacket and put it over my sister's hitching chest.

"Phoebe. It's me. It's Emma. Can you hear me?" Her lips twitch, but she doesn't get any words out.

"She came out of nowhere." A fat man is crouched on the other side of her, his face blotchy under his bald head. "I swear to Christ, there was nothing I could do. I was only going about twenty miles an hour. The light was green. It was like she threw herself into the road. Or someone pushed her."

Her hand—the only part of her I can risk touching without potentially hurting her more —is icy as I rub it, hot tears and snot running down my face. "There's an ambulance coming, Phebes. Any minute now." I'm trembling—shaking—all over. "Keep breathing, Phoebe," I whisper. "Please."

There's blood under her head, thick and red, and I want to grab her and pull her to me, but instead I rub her hand and watch her eyes, one pupil horribly dilated as they flicker, confused. "I'm here, Phoebe, I'm here," I say before turning to the gawping crowd. "Where's the fucking ambulance?" I scream, as her hand tightens around mine. "Get that fucking ambulance!"

46

Her blood is sticky as it dries. I should wash it off, but I don't. The bright color is a part of her, clinging to me as I sit in the cold hard chair and watch as more and more hospital staff hurry toward the room they've moved her to after the chaos of her arrival in the emergency room. I am a still, small body of calm as I stare ahead, impassive. They don't know what to make of me. No tears. No emotions. All that stopped when the paramedics and the noise took over and then I was pressed into the corner of the ambulance as they worked on her unresponsive body.

Not dead yet, though. She's not dead yet.

They think I'm cold, but I'm not. I've simply brought the shutters down. I did it back then. I remember now. Once we'd fled the house, out into the rain and thunder, Phoebe was calling for help, banging on a woman's door, and then there were ambulances and police and so many lights and so much noise that I couldn't breathe and I became very still. They carried Mum out on a stretcher and I never saw her after that.

The whirlwind of heat is inside me, just as it was back then when I came into our bedroom to find my mother suffocating my sister. Why did she choose her to die first? Just because she was older? Phoebe wasn't the one she said would go mad. Phoebe was her little helper. If it wasn't for Phoebe, social services would have already been aware of the mess our lives had become. Even before Mum stopped sleeping, there were forgotten dirty uniforms, unwashed dishes, Mum staring into space.

Much as I'm doing now.

How did I get to the pub? What was I hurrying away from?

How did Phoebe end up in the road?

I am afraid of myself.

Is this how my mother felt? Were these thoughts she had? *What am I capable of? Do I really know? Am I the thing I dread?*

Forty tomorrow.

Tomorrow.

There are broken bones, a punctured lung, subdural

hematoma. Phoebe's brain is bleeding, just like Mum's did when she smashed it against the Hartwell mirror. I'm forty tomorrow, just like Mum was. My lips are moving silently, muttering her numbers. Is this shock? Or is this madness?

Phoebe might die this time.

She looked like she was pushed.

Not by me. It wasn't me.

Emma. Emma. Emma. I stare down at my own name scratched hard in black lines on the paper. Maybe my mother didn't even write it. Maybe it was Sandra. I don't know anything about Sandra except that she paints happy places. Why would she write it? How would she know my name? I look at the scrawl. Really look at it. It's my mother's writing. I know it is. Letters full of jagged sharp edges.

I crumple the paper back up as a shadow falls across me.

"Why didn't you call me?" It's Robert and I haul myself to my exhausted feet so I don't feel so small with him looming over me. "Is she okay?" He takes in the blood and dirt on me. "Are you okay?"

"No, she's not okay. She's sedated while they figure out how to save her." My eyes are dry. All my emotion a nuclear ball inside me. "How did you know?" I didn't call him. I haven't called anyone. This is family business and right now Robert doesn't feel like family. "Who called you?"

"The police." He doesn't move to hold me, and instead we stand face-to-face like awkward strangers who've had a one-night stand and now don't know how to behave with each other. I don't mind. I don't want him to touch me. Or pity me. He asked me to move out of my house. So much for in sickness and in health.

The police. Of course. I guess our names are in a system somewhere, and, as if by magic, like a genie summoned, Hildreth and Caine appear in the doorway of the waiting area. "What were you doing there, Em?" Robert asks.

"I went to talk to her. There are things I wanted to talk to her about."

"And you got there just as she was pushed?"

My eyes flash upward. *Oh no, you don't, Robert Averell. I may get to question my own sanity, but not you.* "Nice passive aggressive accusation there. If you've got something to say, come out and say it."

"I'm only trying to understand." He can't meet my eyes. "It's your birthday tomorrow. I know you're feel—"

"You don't know anything about how I'm feeling," I snap. "And as for my birthday, I'm very well aware of that. And I just held my sister's hand while her broken body bled on me, and she might be dying, and thanks for all your concern." My words drip sarcasm. "But if you don't mind getting out of my way, I'll go and speak to some people who are marginally less hostile to me than you are. The police. But thanks for being so determined to think the worst of me once again. Just the support a woman wants from her husband."

"Emma." He sounds like he's talking to a troublesome child. "I didn't mean—"

"Oh, fuck off." I spit the words back loud enough for the police to hear, but I'm past caring. I pause at the nurse's station and say, "I'm Phoebe Bournett's only next of kin. My husband and I are currently estranged, so please only contact me with any updates on her wellbeing, is that okay? You've got my number."

"Of course. We would only ever contact next of kin and the police." She gives me a warm smile full of sympathy, and only then do I have the first tightening in my throat that threatens tears. The kindness of strangers will kill us all. I walk away before I actually weep and join Caine and Hildreth, a pair of ghouls, once again wanting to talk to me about someone hurt in my family. My heart races despite my cool appearance.

I think someone pushed her.

What if a witness saw me do it? What if I did it?

I can't trust myself.

Hildreth looks me up and down and I'm surprised to see a glimpse of sympathy in her eyes. "Problems at home?"

"You could say that. Men. They're like children." I give Caine, as representative of his sex, a withering glance. I'm afraid, but I'm also feeling bullish. I'm going to confront them head-on.

"I presume Robert said that I'd been angry at Phoebe?" I take charge of the conversation and it makes me feel stronger. I'm a highly respected lawyer. I'm a success story. I am not mad. I don't wait for an answer.

"That's true. I was. I'd also been to Hartwell House to talk to them about my mother. Get closure, as the Americans would say. While I was there, someone —I'm damned if I'm saying who—told me that Phoebe had been less than pleasant to our mother on her visits. Quite verbally abusive, in fact. So it made me wonder if maybe Phoebe is the one with the unresolved issues. And, as much as I don't want to think it, maybe *she*—"

"You think she might have suffocated your mother and then thrown herself in front of a van in a fit of remorse?"

Has it occurred to them too? "I'm saying it's a possibility."

"No, it's not," Caine says bluntly.

"Oh, so you can suspect me, but—" I protest, and

Detective Sergeant Hildreth holds her hands up, a defensive plea for quiet.

"Take a breath," she says. She looks as tired as I do in the harsh hospital lighting. "When we checked the security footage at the hospital for you leaving, we didn't only check *your* whereabouts."

"What do you mean?" I frown.

"We also checked the hospital cameras to see if Phoebe was where she'd said she was—in the Starbucks concession. And she was. She didn't suffocate your mother either."

I'm not sure what I feel. Relief definitely. A great wash of it. Neither of us killed her. Faces flash in front of me—Robert, Chloe, Caroline. All their polite disbelief. Their accusations of paranoia are shadows clinging to me. Am I paranoid? Or is paranoia just a good gut instinct? Something's wrong and I can feel it. It's like a worm burrowing inside me.

"So no one killed her?" I finally ask. "What about the fibers in her mouth and nose?"

"Inconclusive," Hildreth says. "We're running some more tests, but we probably won't be able to prove anything either way." She pauses. "I know this is a difficult time, but I do want to ask you some questions about this morning. While it's still fresh. Did you see your sister before the van hit her?"

"Oh, I see." I smile and the expression feels cut into my face with razor wire, no humor in it. "First you think I killed my mother and now you're wondering if maybe I hurt my sister."

"I'm not wondering anything. We're just trying to get a clear picture of what happened."

"I was on my way to see her, and then I heard the commotion and there she was on the road."

She eyes me thoughtfully before speaking. "Passersby say they thought she might have been pushed."

"I wasn't close enough to see." My hackles rise. I'm too tired for this shit. "But if you're suggesting that I could have done it, then unless you have a witness . . ." My heart is hammering now but I keep my eyes steady. "I would be careful of making unsubstantiated accusations. You've met my lawyer. If you want to come at me again, then you'd better bring some actual evidence."

"Mrs. Averell?"

We all turn. A doctor, middle-aged and serious, hovers a few feet away. "If I can . . ."

"Yes. We're done here." I turn my back on the police as if they no longer exist, and as far as I'm concerned, they don't. My pulse thumps in my ears, strong and loud and alive. They don't have a witness. No one saw me push Phoebe. Relief floods through me. Now I feel like I could cry. Relief. *You're relieved only because you were worried. And you were worried because you don't know if you pushed her or not. You don't trust yourself. Forty tomorrow and maybe going mad. You don't even know if you're to blame for your sister being . . .*

"Is Phoebe . . . is she . . . ?" I can barely get the words out.

"She's alive. But she's in very critical condition. We'll be taking her into surgery as soon as she's prepped and we're ready. We're waiting for Mr. Harris, the neurosurgeon, to arrive and then a team will be working on her."

"A team?"

"She's going to need several procedures, and we want her in the best hands for each. She has several hours of surgery ahead, and even if it all goes without any problems, which of course we're all hoping will be the case, she won't be able to have visitors at least until tomorrow. You can choose to stay here if you want to, and the staff will do their best to make you comfortable, but I would advise you to go home and we'll call you as soon as she's out of surgery and back in intensive care." He looks at the state of my clothes and then at my tired face. "Get some rest. There's nothing you can do here for now. We'll take good care of her."

"And you'll call me if there's any change? Straight-away? And me first and only me?"

"Of course."

I don't even know if Robert's still here, but he can't stay all day anyway. He's got Will and Chloe to look after, since he doesn't want my help. For some reason I don't like the idea of him sitting and waiting for Phoebe all day. He doesn't have that right. She's my sister, not his.

"Okay. Thank you." I reach for his hand. "Please don't let her die."

"I'll do my best." His grip is firm and safe.

I guess that's all I can ask for.

47

I'm in a taxi heading back into town to collect my car when Buckley's secretary calls asking if I can "just pop in." She says it in a tone of voice I've heard her use on other people, one that means *I'm sure Mr. Buckley can do this another way, but it may be better for you to be able to defend yourself in person.* I almost tell her about Phoebe's accident—*I think somebody pushed her*—and that I can't possibly make it, but I don't. I hear myself saying I'll be there in about fifteen minutes.

What else have I got to do anyway? Sit in my hotel room and wait for a call from the hospital? I don't even have my sleeping pills, so I can't double dose and hope to sleep for forty-eight hours, until my birthday is over. I may as well face whatever music this is with Buckley.

I get the cab to drop me at the office and I'm still

trembling, but I stand tall as I take the lift up and head straight to Buckley's office.

"I'm not sure of the legality of calling someone in when they're on compassionate leave," I say, standing in front of his desk. "Are you okay? Need my help with something?" He looks at me somewhat aghast. My clothes are dirty. The blood has darkened but there's no doubt as to what the sticky patches on my hands and clothes are. I imagine my hair is a mess and my eyes are bloodshot and sunken. If Phoebe thought I looked like our mother before, what would she make of me now?

Phoebe. She'll be in surgery now. I look at the clock on the wall. It clicks between one ten and one fifteen, and then for a moment there's only blackness and I'm sure that I'm rattling the door handle of my kitchen. My heart thumps and the world spins and then I can see Buckley, and also the door handle, one laid over the other like tracing paper. *Look, look, a candle, a book and a bell* . . . I flinch, the burst of song loud in my head.

"Emma?" Buckley is up on his feet. His mouth's moving and I can read his lips, but I can't hear the words. "Emma? Are you all right?"

I close my eyes for a moment and when I open them again, thankfully my house has vanished and only the quiet office remains. My right hand, however, is hovering out in front of me. I've been rattling an invisible door handle in front of my boss.

"Sorry," I mutter and drop into a chair opposite his desk. "I've had a bit of a morning. My sister was hit by a van. I've been at the hospital." I cover one hand with the other. What was that? A hallucination? Forty tomorrow. Going not so quietly mad. Tread carefully, Angus Buckley, who knows what I'm capable of?

"If this is about Parker Stockwell and how I spoke to him when he called me, then I'm sorry, but I shouldn't have to be sexually harassed at the weekend just for the firm's benefit. And—"

"It's not about Parker Stockwell." He clears his throat. "And for the record, I agree. I'm sure he didn't mean it that way, but no one on the team should be made to feel uncomfortable by a client. And I apologize if having you at the dinner made you feel that way."

I sit up a little straighter in my chair. This must be serious if Buckley's been reading up on sexism in the workplace. Covering his own ass before he guns for mine. "So what is it?"

"These reviews." He slides a printout across the desk at me.

I look down at the paper. Trustpilot and Google. Four reviews. All with the header of my name.

"I've never been spoken to so rudely by anyone in my life. I expected sympathy when I said my husband wanted a divorce. Not to be laughed at and told it was probably my own fault."

"I'm actually in shock! How is this woman qualified? I was honest about my situation and she called me a slut and hung up. Sick woman. I should complain to the Law Society but I've got enough problems to deal with. I'll go somewhere else. Don't use this firm!"

Stunned, I look up at Buckley. "Surely you don't believe any of this? I mean . . ." I look at the paper again. "I never said these things. I don't know who these people—" I stop. There *is* a familiarity to the names. They ring a bell.

"You rang them. They were client inquiries. Rosemary has their names in her records."

"Well, whoever they are, I never said these things."

Buckley lets out a long sigh. "Why would they lie?" His voice is soft and he leans forward. "Rosemary told me that on the day she gave you these, there was an incident with some letters on your Dictaphone. An odd recording."

"That's different," I say. "That's . . ." How do I explain that? I look back at the papers. "This is . . . this is slander. These people. How do we even know they're real? I mean, it could be someone out to make me look bad. It could have been my sister even. Or Miranda Stockwell. Or anyone."

"Why would anyone be out to get you? It doesn't make sense. I rang one of these women and she confirmed the whole exchange. She's going to Milborough & Brown. I checked with them. They have had a preliminary meeting with her and she's looking for divorce representation." He stares at me. "You're clearly going through something. Some kind of breakdown. And while I have every sympathy, we can't have this here. And these reviews—well, you can imagine the damage they could do to the firm. We have to be seen to take action."

The silence hangs heavy with meaning. "You're firing me?" Even sitting here in my sister's blood I find that hard to take in. Some time off, yes, but letting me go? I was supposed to be made partner. That's what my future was. And now this. "Wow."

"We really have no choice. I'm very sorry."

I say nothing for a long moment and then get up. He doesn't look sorry at all. He looks relieved. A quiet calm settles on me.

"I understand." I'm not going to scream and shout at him. I find I'm not even that surprised. My personal life is crumbling, *of course* my job would be next. I walk out of Buckley's office without another word. I remember calling those women. I'm sure I do. The day Michelle came in. The day of the Dictaphone. Perfectly normal inquiry calls. I listened and told them that they could have a free thirty-minute consultation and then could proceed from there. All pretty standard. I'm sure it was. But even as I think it, I doubt myself.

I go straight to my office and gather up what I can that's mine. No family photos on my desk—not great when you're dealing with people's breakups to remind them of what they've lost—but I take my diary and contacts book, and a few other bits packaged into a box. I'm sure there's plenty of other stuff in here that's mine, but I can't be bothered to go through it all now. I just want to get out. My face burns and I notice that Rosemary has made herself scarce. So much for all that warmth and care she emits. A fair-weather friend.

48

In the lift on the way back down, so soon after arriving, I don't know whether to laugh or cry. Maybe Robert *is* going to have to pay the bills for a while if my name is mud in legal circles. Our savings certainly aren't going to be blown on his midlife crisis bar. Maybe we'll have to downsize. Tomorrow I'm forty. Maybe these things will no longer be my concern if I go the way of my mother. *What happened back there? One glimpse of some of Mum's numbers and your mind starts to slip? One daughter may be dead by the morning, the other mad by nightfall. Our mother would be so proud.*

"Emma."

It's only when she appears in front of me that I realize she's been calling my name. Miranda Stockwell.

"Miranda." This I do not need. "I'm having a shit

day—no, in fact I'm having the mother of all shit days—and I really don't have time for—" I try to barge past her, but she stops me.

"Please. I don't want to cause any trouble, I just want to apologize. I'm so sorry for how I spoke to you. How I've behaved. And following you to the restaurant and threatening you. I was—well, frankly, I was out of order and drunk. And hurt. I appreciate you were just doing your job, and I shouldn't have behaved that way. Now I'm sober and—" she stops and frowns, bright eyes studying me. Her eyes linger on the dried blood, and then looks at my face. Maybe I've got some there too. "Are you okay?"

I almost laugh at that. "I am so, so far from okay, Miranda. So if you'd move, I can get on with examining the wreckage of my life."

She doesn't move. "Do you want a coffee? You look like you need a coffee."

"Actually, what I need are some answers. And I need you to be honest, because I'm not going to do anything about it, but I really have to know. Did you key my car and leave a note calling me a bitch? And slash my tire and leave false Google reviews about me?"

Her eyes widen. "No, I didn't. Is Parker saying I did, because that's exactly the sort of game—"

"No, no, he didn't say anything. I just presumed . . ."

"It wasn't me. I can understand why you might think it was, but it really wasn't." She takes the small box of possessions I'm carrying from me. "I may have *been* stupid when dealing with my divorce, but I'm not stupid. You look like shit. Come on."

Twenty minutes later and we're in a trendy bar-cum-diner that has enclosed booths that give us some privacy, so no one will stare at my bloodstained clothes. My surreal day has taken a turn into something weirder. Here I am having lunch with Miranda Stockwell. And she's the one pitying me. How times change so quickly.

We've got coffees and I've also got a large brandy—I needed it, telling Miranda about my morning—and we've each got roast beef sandwiches. I don't feel at all like eating, but Miranda insisted—especially when I added the brandy to the order—and I've got to drive so I probably should. Energy. I definitely need energy. I'm forcing it down as she speaks. It's a revelation to hear her side of the divorce story, but it all kind of makes sense.

"I expected him to behave like an adult," she's saying. "Instead, I let him wind me up like some toy and play games with me that made everyone think I was crazy. He'd get me to a point that I'd be ranting down the phone and coming in the house looking for him, and then when I left, he'd pay one of the staff to cut up all his clothes and then it looked like I'd done it. So many things like that until I believed I *was* crazy. A jobless crazy nearly forty-year-old having a breakdown."

"That would make two of us." I raise my brandy glass in a toast as my coffee goes cold.

"And he did it all to keep our boys. He doesn't even want them around, but he doesn't want me to have them. He wants them to hate me. And I'm the crazy one? Thankfully, my boys are bright, I've realized. They bought themselves disposable phones, so they can speak to me without his knowing. I try not to say awful things about him—I feel bad enough for all the fighting that came before and everything we, as parents, have put them through, but god, it's hard because he's such a bloody psychopath."

"Why did you marry him?" My mind is half here and half watching the large train-station style feature clock in the center of the room as it ticks past two fifteen P.M. I take a sip of brandy and it sounds like her words are underwater. "*Ah there you are,*" I hear myself whisper as the hand finally clicks toward the twenty. For a moment, all I can see is darkness and I think that maybe I *am* my mother or she is me, and then I'm back in the bar and Miranda is saying something about being young and easily impressed and how he was handsome then.

"I think I'm going mad," I say, suddenly. "Not just a breakdown. Fully insane. It's in my blood. DNA. Whatever. Runs in the family. My charming husband thinks I am too." I look at her, expecting her to interject with the usual platitudes, but she doesn't. She just listens.

"I have this feeling," I continue, "right in the core of me, that someone is out to get me and hurt my family. It's stopped me sleeping. But now I think maybe everyone's right. Maybe it is all in my own head? Maybe I am the one I'm afraid of. You know, I have no idea if I pushed my sister in front of that van. I don't think I did, but I don't know. That's got to be a definition of madness, hasn't it? And last week, when I wanted to take Will to school instead of Robert, he went out to get the milk and cut his feet on broken milk-bottle glass. I said it was probably kids. But it's too coincidental."

"Coincidental how?" She's not eating her sandwich now either. "I don't get you."

"My mum kept all our milk bottles, some still sour with milk, stacked up on the kitchen side. She wouldn't put them out. She said someone might smash them and then we'd get glass in our feet and we wouldn't be able to go to school."

I look at her and sip some more brandy. "And then that's what happens to Robert when I *know* he always goes out there barefoot to get the milk. I wasn't sleeping. I wanted to go into school. I've been thinking about my mum and all her crazy and I must have used that tic of hers as some kind of inspiration for some madness of my own. I must have smashed the milk bottle, knowing he'd probably stand in it."

"Or," she says, "someone smashed your milk bottle and it was just one of those things."

"There have been so many of those things."

"Then maybe you are going mad."

She's brutal in her honesty, I'll give her that.

"How would you slash a car tire?" she asks.

"What?"

"Quickly. How'd you do it?"

"Bread knife," I say suddenly, and she snorts with laughter.

"Okay, maybe not. I don't know, a Stanley knife?"

"Do you have a Stanley knife?"

"I don't know. Maybe somewhere."

She shrugs and sips her coffee. "I don't think you slashed your own tire. If I'm honest, you sound like the worst tire slasher in the world. Before you ask, I haven't ever slashed a tire, but I'm not going to lie, I did google it a couple of times before Parker and I broke up."

"But none of it makes sense. There is definitely something wrong in my head. I'm missing bits of time. Doing things I don't remember."

"Insomnia will do that to you. And look, having just gone through a mini-meltdown myself, maybe you are going a bit cuckoo. Happens to a lot of people. More than you'd think. And I don't mean *crazy* like you do. I don't think you're insane. Just struggling. It's actually why I'm going to train to be a counselor. This world can be a mean place. I mean, we've both struggled and we're in lucky situations. But that's a conversation for another time. Anyway, my point is that you're looking at this as an either or." She signals a waiter for the bill. "When in fact, why can't it be both?"

I look at her, perplexed. "What do you mean?"

"I mean that yes, maybe you are going through some incident with your mental health. But that doesn't mean that someone isn't fucking with you too." She shrugs again, as if she's French and we're discussing the dullness of a lover rather than my potential insanity. "I mean, just because your sister got hit by a van doesn't mean she didn't slash your tire, or do any of those other things, does it? Two separate actions." She taps her card on the machine and the waiter vanishes.

"And she knew about the milk-bottle stuff as well as you, I presume?"

Once again, my suspicions of Phoebe start to swirl around my head. "Yes. Of course."

"So all I'm saying is, trust your gut. If you think there's something wrong in your head, there probably is. But also, if you think someone is out to get you, I'd say trust your gut on that too. My divorce has taught me that much. People can be slippery shits when they want you out of the way."

She's right. I look at the clock. *Look, look, a candle, a book and a bell.* Maybe I am going mad. But someone's still out to get me. Two equal truths. Could it still be Phoebe? Maybe when she's out of surgery she'll tell me. I look down at her dried blood on my hands as if it has some answers. It stays silent. It doesn't tell me if I pushed her either. It holds its secrets close.

49

"**P**hoebe got hit by a van," I say.

Caroline's in her nurse's uniform, professional and dependable, and I look the complete opposite. A low-rent version of Carrie from that old Stephen King book standing on her doorstep. Less blood but the same level of crazy. Her face pales.

"What?"

"I know. Insane. I was on my way to see her and there she was in the road. She's in the operating room now." I called the hospital on the way here and there's no real news on how she's doing. There won't be till the surgery's all over and she's in recovery. Hopefully she's in recovery. No promises there. "Can I come in?"

"Um . . . sure." She backs up and I come inside. "Is she okay?"

"No. No she's not."

The song is playing on a loop in my head, making it hard for me to look anything but irritated. "She may not make it." *Look, look, a candle, a book and a bell, I put them behind me. Oh look, look, A candle, a book and a bell. There to remind me . . .*

The song's got louder since I rang the hospital—*she's in surgery; more complicated than we thought*—going around in my head all the while as I drove, thinking about what Miranda said. Phoebe being run over doesn't mean she wasn't out to get me.

"Look at these." Once we're in the kitchen, I take the reviews out of my bag, the paper crumpled, and hand them to Caroline. "Do you think Phoebe could have done them? I do."

She looks at the pages and then at me. "Why would she do this?" She frowns as she shuffles the papers around. "What's this?"

She holds up a different piece of paper, one I didn't plan for her to see, that must have got tangled with the others in my bag. My mother's page with my name written jaggedly all over it. "Oh, that's nothing. Will did it ages ago." I take it back and hurriedly stuff it into my bag. "But those—I mean who would do that?"

She studies the reviews. "What happened that day? Did you speak to these people?"

"I wasn't rude to potential clients," I snap. "That's what happened on that day."

"I was only asking." She hands the papers back carefully and I half expect her to anti-bac her hands, as if paranoia is a virus she can catch from them.

"I'm sorry," I say. "Just came as a shock. And they've fired me. Not good for the firm apparently. But this *could* have been Phoebe. Maybe she made the calls to my work. How do I know the women I spoke to weren't all her?"

"Isn't that a bit of a leap? And surely now isn't the time to be suspicious of her. How did her accident happen? Did she go into the road without looking?"

"Someone said she was pushed, and of course I'm sure the police think it was me. Not that they've got any proof." The words are coming out fast. It's hard to get clarity with the song so loud in my head. "She's so jealous of me and there's the way she is with Robert, I can feel something's off there." I crunch the paper and flinch as more lyrics blast loud in my head, without warning. I press a hand to my temples.

. . . Sees through a glass, darkly. Can I have an opinion. To trigger this loop . . . Look, look, a candle, a book and a bell . . .

"Emma." Caroline says, awkward, and the crashing music suddenly stops, leaving my head ringing in blissful silence. "Your sister is in the hospital. You're in shock. And you're tired. Why don't you go back to the hotel and get some sleep?"

I stare at her for a long moment and then from nowhere, I burst into laughter. *Get some sleep.* Oh god, that's funny. I snort as I laugh harder. "Get some sleep," I wheeze, my bloodstained hand covering my mouth as I laugh.

"Why are you laughing?" she says, and I know I need to get it together, because this isn't funny and this isn't both of us giggling together but just me, rocking backward and forward, lost in a terrible private joke.

"You make it sound so easy," I splutter before laughing again. I can see her watching me, blurred through my watering eyes, until finally I get myself together, gasping for breath.

"I'm sorry," I say. "I just. God, I wish I could sleep. Maybe I'll sleep when tomorrow is over. The big four-oh." I pull a jokey scary face, but she doesn't laugh, keeps on studying me, worried and thoughtful. I can't blame her, really. *Tomorrow. It's finally here after all these years. And here I am, turning into my mother.*

I look down at my clothes. "I can't go back to the hotel like this. I hate to ask, but could I have a shower and put these in for a quick wash and dry?"

"I was just on my way out," she says, flustered. "I've

got two more house calls to do." Her face looks tight, as if she's trying to appear natural but failing.

"Please," I say. I'm begging and she knows it. "I won't touch anything and it's not like you don't know where I live." I try to make a joke of it, but I smack of desperation. "When all this is over, I promise I'll make it up to you."

"Okay," she says, eventually, although if I'm honest, she looks cornered rather than willing. "I'll be back soon. The washing powder is under the sink."

"Thank you so much." I want to hug her but not in these clothes.

"It's fine." She flashes me a smile and for a moment I relax, and then I catch the way she glances back at me as she heads out the front door.

As soon as she's gone, I head up the stairs and I want to cry. I know the way she was looking at me.

Awkward. Afraid. As if I'm somehow disturbed and dangerous.

Maybe she's right, I think again, as I watch the pink tinge of Phoebe's blood disappearing down the shower drain as the hot water batters my exhausted body. Miranda's logic seems far away now. I am the common denominator, after all. God, I'm so tired. I just want to sleep. *I just want to sleep.* I remember my mother hissing those same words at me all those years ago, and for the first time in my life, as I start to weep, I find I have some pity for her.

Once I'm dry, I take the Ian Rankin book back to the spare room. Idly curious, I pull out one of the framed photos sticking out of another box. A woman in a wheelchair smiling in front of an old cathedral. A younger Caroline, maybe around twenty years old, standing behind the chair. The woman in the chair has to be Caroline's mum, the resemblance is too uncanny. Caroline's not looking at the camera but down at her mother, watching over her perhaps. She looks awkward. Maybe they'd asked a stranger to take the photo. One of them together on a mother-daughter break.

I browse a few more, mainly of Caroline, a few of a cat that must once have been a pet. At the bottom is an older family photo, judging by the clothes taken some time in the nineties. Caroline, maybe six years old, in a neat school uniform, a private school uniform maybe, old-fashioned in its look, and also slightly too big. First day of school photo maybe, her mother, slim and pretty, standing on one side of her and her father on the other, both beaming with pride. She's never mentioned her father and I'd assumed that her mother had become infirm only with old age rather than something that happened to her earlier. We all have our family secrets, I suppose. The scars that we don't want to tear open.

I put the picture back and head downstairs. I've got enough problems with my own family history to spend any time thinking about hers.

I'm finally back in my clean, dry clothes, and with my hair and skin scrubbed I feel halfway to human and sane. Sane enough to be staring at my phone and wondering how to go about checking myself in to a clinic for a few days to be assessed. I should ask Dr. Morris, but I don't want to. I want to find out anonymously. What if I speak to someone and then that's it, no turning back, I'm locked up and I can't get out? *What if something happens to my family?* Nothing's going to happen to my family. It's a ridiculous thought. It's a *paranoid* thought. I look up effects of insomnia on my phone and immediately wish I hadn't.

. . . Going without sleep for long periods of time can produce a range of experiences, including perceptual distortions and hallucinations. Many questions, however, remain unanswered regarding whether symptoms worsen over time toward psychotic decompensation . . .

Perceptual distortions. Hallucinations. Psychotic decompensation.

I take a deep breath and am about to dial Dr. Morris when my phone rings. My heart almost stops with fear. I don't know the number but it's a landline. *The hospital.* Phoebe. She shouldn't be out of surgery yet. What's happened? Is she . . . I stare at the screen, my mouth dry, as it keeps ringing. Eventually, I force myself to answer.

"Emma Averell speaking." I sound surprisingly normal, even though my other fist is clenched. *Please be okay, Phoebe. Please.*

"Oh hello. Emma." The voice at the other end says, "I hope this isn't a bad time. Hartwell gave me your number and told me it was all right to call you? I'm Nina Harris. I was a friend of your mother's."

50

"Emma."

I thought Nina would be about the same age as my mother, but as soon as she opens the door I realize she's about a decade younger, mid-sixties, and with shoulder-length gray hair and in her yoga pants and flowing Indian top she has an air of ease about her. Her face bursts into a delighted smile. "Oh, I'd recognize that beautiful dark hair anywhere. So much like Patricia's. Please, come in."

"Thank you. And thanks for seeing me." I follow her inside. The house is stylish and not inexpensively decorated, and under the waft of sandalwood candles I'm pretty sure I can smell weed. She looks like a middle-class hippy and as I pass the bookshelves in the hallway, my thoughts are confirmed. There are vegan cookbooks, meditation manuals, and I'm sure I spot books on spiritualism and another titled *Astral Projection and How to Do It Safely.* It makes me smile. I don't believe in all that stuff, but I like that she does.

"Oh no, it's an absolute joy. I think about you often." She ushers me into the kitchen and then out into the garden, where a table is ready in the gazebo with a beautiful oriental tea set. "I made Chinese tea. Is that okay? I have wine or beer or of course coffee if you'd prefer. I don't do much caffeine myself, nor alcohol." I see the rolled spliff in the ashtray and she shrugs. "I know I'm too old, but it's always been my thing. It gives me my zen and keeps my joints loose. I teach yoga and Pilates and meditation. At the holistic center down by the park." She's chatty and lovely and I take a seat as she pours.

"I was never sure how much you remembered—or wanted to remember—about your early childhood," she continues. "Phoebe must remember more than you do?"

I nod. "So she says. I'm not so sure how much she really remembers of *before* everything that happened. That night. The few weeks before." I have no intention of telling her about Pheobe's accident or any of my problems. I've put makeup on and I'm clean and fresh from the shower and I may look slightly tired but other than that I can pass for normal, I imagine. "We don't really talk about it much. We don't see each other that often. Not in recent years."

"That happens. I think I've seen my brother only three times since he moved to Australia forty years ago. But we were never close like you two." Her face clouds over with sadness. "You wouldn't let each other go that night. Clinging so tightly together. I remember a policeman trying to separate you and Phoebe screaming at him to get off. I wrapped you both in the same blanket like you were Siamese twins, then I called the ambulance for your mum."

I stare, surprised. "You were there?"

"Gosh, you really don't remember much." She pulls one knee up under her chin, all fluid and catlike, and then lights the joint. "Yes, you came to my house. You ran through the rain. Soaking and terrified."

"The nice lady," I say, as pieces of the past fall into place, and I look at her, eyes wide. "That's what we used to call you."

"Did you? That's lovely to hear. I lived in a little downstairs flat at the other end of the street. Your mother was very kind to me. We looked after each other. It's why, I suppose, in the aftermath, I spent so long wondering if there was something I could have done to stop her. I don't think there was. It was such a shock. But I do wish that they'd let me keep you both.

It made me so mad they wouldn't even let me foster you. Especially after the tragedy with that family, and then you both ended up in different foster homes and you could have both been with me all that time. I would have loved you like my own."

My head is spinning. This I wasn't expecting. "You wanted to keep us?"

"Of course! I loved your mum. I loved you. I said I'd move, if necessary, because of the proximity to your old home." She shakes her head slightly.

"But the social services weren't having any of it. I was a twenty-nine-year-old domestic violence survivor, and there were police incidents on record from before I'd fled my marriage. A miscarriage he caused, leaving me unable to have children of my own." She speaks matter-of-factly, but I can see ghosts of a life that could have been in her gray eyes behind the wisps of smoke. "Even though I was the victim in that situation, I wasn't considered emotionally stable enough to tick all the boxes on their forms. I didn't have a big enough home. Didn't earn enough money. Was too big a link to your mother. Basically, they'd just decided I wasn't good enough and that was that."

"I did come and find you though." She looks over her tea. "When you were at university. You were pregnant. You looked so happy and you and Phoebe were living together, and I wasn't sure bringing the past back into your lives was the right thing. So I never actually said hello. Maybe that was a mistake. It's always so hard to know things in the moment, isn't it? I suppose that's why hindsight is so wonderful."

This is all a revelation and I feel a small flicker of optimism. Maybe if she helps me understand the past, I can shake this fear that I'm going to repeat it. "You didn't have any idea that our mother was going to do what she did?" My lawyer's brain is struggling to believe it. "How? Surely you could see she was falling apart? Not sleeping?" I try not to sound accusatory, but it's difficult. I don't understand it at all.

"I know. I can see that from your perspective it must seem crazy, but I'd known your mum from before you were born. She was my best friend in a lot of ways. When your father was there, I didn't see her much, I don't think she was allowed out very often—she was too beautiful to live with such an angry man. He was older and resented her beauty, just like he resented Phoebe when she came along, and even though Patricia didn't want a second child, he insisted that she have one. And then as soon as you were born, he vanished. Tied her down with all this responsibility and left her. He disappeared down south, to Cornwall I think, to live with someone he met on one of his work trips. Died in a boating accident a couple of years later. It's how she managed to cope on her own when she started struggling. His life insurance paid off the house."

I don't ask any more about our father, although it's strange to hear of him as an actual person rather than just a noun. Father. No shape or meaning to him, but even after everything, it still hurts to hear her say so bluntly that my mother didn't want me.

"I'm not surprised she never wanted me. Phoebe said that's when she changed, after I was born. She must have hated me."

"Oh god, no! Never think that!" Her eyes are wide, surprised, as she leans forward. "She loved you fiercely. So, so much. From the very moment you were born. She loved you both, but you—you were her special girl. There was something about you that made her like a tigress. She wanted to protect you. She hadn't wanted a second child because—well, there was a history of second children in her family having . . . problems."

"You mean going mad?" My stomach churns and my mouth is suddenly greasy. "She used to tell me I'd go mad like her."

"Madness is a strong word."

"I'm not sure you can call what she did to Phoebe anything else."

"Maybe." She tops up my tea. "But she was such a

kind woman. So thoughtful of other people. *Attuned,* I guess is the word. But she was always a little fragile. Maybe *fragile*'s not right. Ethereal. She said sometimes that she thought she was *put together wrong.* That she had bad genes. Her own mother wouldn't let up on it: whenever she misbehaved, it was because she was the second child. Bad blood. It left Patricia haunted by the past. She was so afraid of it. But oh, she loved you. So much pride in her eyes when she talked about you. How clever you were. How you could read earlier than all the other kids in nursery school. How you made her laugh. How you could get Phoebe out of her black moods."

I wonder where all these relatives evaporated to when we were left orphans. My mother's siblings and parents. None came to claim us, although I'm sure the social services would have tried them. Maybe because there were two of us. Maybe they didn't want anything to do with the second child with bad blood. At least if I do totally lose my marbles, I think wryly, I don't have to worry in that regard. Phoebe is more than ready to step into the shoes she's forcing me out of and take over my family.

"So, what happened to her?" I ask. "What changed?"

"I'm not really sure." She lets out a long sigh. "I mean, this second child thing, it doesn't even make sense and she knew that. As if your genes know which number sibling you are? It's ridiculous, isn't it? She'd laugh about it and talk about how messed up her family must have been to believe it. It's not like it even happened to *every* second child. Sometimes generations skipped completely. And I figure, if you look at most families, in every generation there's someone who finds coping in the world difficult at some point, so it's not exactly a curse on the Bournett name."

"That's a nice way of putting going insane." I sip my tea. I'm glad she's got thick ceramic cups like you get in a Chinese restaurant. Anything more delicate and I'd probably break it, I'm gripping it so hard.

"She was filled with dread. Specifically, for you. Looking back, it did start after you were born. Little things at first. Worrying about where you were all the time. Even though Phoebe was the far more accident-prone and adventurous child, she would panic if you were out of her sight. As if some danger might befall you. Then she'd have odd moments when I'd find her staring into space and have to snap her out of it. She'd say she was lost in her own thoughts and laugh it off and that was that. I didn't question it. But in that last year, those episodes got more frequent, and I could see she was worrying about them." She takes another long inhale on the spliff.

"The day I realized there might be something

wrong with her was the day she almost set the house on fire. I popped over one afternoon to return a book, let myself in—she always left the back door unlocked at that point if she was in—and found the chip pan smoking and about to burst into flames. She was upstairs, staring out the window in the hall that looked over the garden. You were tugging at her legs, crying and so distraught. You were shrieking by the time I reached you, so loud I thought you'd seriously hurt yourself. Your face was bright red and you were shouting "*Mummy, Mummy*" over and over, but she didn't even know you were there. She was like a statue, just staring out at the garden, her hands pressed against the glass, her mouth open. Only when I shook her, and I mean *really* shook her, did she finally snap out of it."

My skin is prickling all over. I have no recollection of that day and yet I've bought a house with a beautiful window that looks out over the garden and I've stood at it at night, just as Nina is describing my mother did, my hands pressed against the glass, my mouth open. I cringe, remembering Will finding me like that. And did he hear me—

"That was the first time I heard her say those numbers too," Nina says, cutting through my thoughts, and I want to cry. I was saying the numbers when Will saw me at our window. Time once again folds in on itself, me and my mother, mirror reflections of each other. Did Nina shake my mother by the arms like I shook Ben? Like she shook me? *I just want to sleep!*

"She was appalled. And frightened," Nina continues. "I went with her to the doctor and they did all the tests but found nothing wrong with her. Nothing physical anyway. She withdrew a bit after that. Worrying. Do you remember the practice drills?"

"What practice drills?" I scan the files in my head but nothing pops out.

"She worried that something like the chip pan would happen again and she made you and Phoebe practice running down to my house for help. And if I wasn't in you were to go to Christine Wright—the librarian who lived on the next street whose husband was always home because he'd had a spinal injury at work."

I remember Phoebe gripping my hand as we ran through the rain to *the nice lady's* house. Phoebe has never talked about any drills. She must remember them, surely? But how much do we remember of anything? Memory. We rely on it so heavily for everything we know about ourselves and those around us, but actually we remember so little. Just wisps of emotions or a smell or a moment. Corrupted files in our heads. Pages missing, torn or burned. Disks unreadable. Memories are like time, constantly slipping from our grasp.

"How long before her fortieth birthday did all this happen?"

"It was only in the last few weeks that things began to build. It probably felt longer to you, because you were so small, but it really wasn't very much time at all. I loved Patricia, but if I'd thought you were in any danger, I'd have called the social services in a heartbeat. And so would the school. And she would have thanked us for it. No, it all happened fast. She started locking the back door, which I took as a sign that she didn't want me around so much. I think she'd stopped looking after the house properly by then, so maybe it was partly that, but then it became something else to her."

"What do you mean?"

"She came to see me a week or so before it happened. She'd lost weight and she was tearful. She said she was going to get some help—medical help at a mental health facility like the one they'd put her great-aunt in or something. She wasn't sleeping, she said. She had a sense something was coming. She said she'd become obsessed by things. Broken milk bottles. These numbers she was always muttering. Checking the back door. She often wasn't sure who she was or where she was. She was having more blank space moments, as if her entire head emptied, and then when she came back to herself she was in a different room. She said she'd been so worried that something bad was coming, or someone was going to hurt you, and now she was starting to think that the bad thing was her."

Oh god, oh god, oh god. I wish I hadn't come here.

I don't know what answers I was expecting, but everything Nina says is like a knife in my gut. I *am* going mad exactly like she did. The same tics. The same fears. The same blank spaces. I'm my mother's daughter. The second child. Somewhere deep in my mind, I've remembered it all and now I'm repeating it. Like an abused child who becomes an abuser.

"I told her that this was probably all down to her insomnia. I'd known a speed freak who didn't sleep for a week and they got paranoid and sleepwalked in the day and basically nearly had a full breakdown until we got some downers in him and he slept for forty-eight hours straight. She said she'd tried pills but they weren't working. She said she felt like she didn't know who she was anymore half the time, and there were things filling her head that she didn't understand." She looks down at the ground. "I told her to give it another couple of days and if she still wasn't sleeping, then I'd go back to the doctor's with her and you girls could come and stay with me for a bit while she sorted herself out."

She looks up and I'm not sure if it's because of the cloud cutting across the late afternoon sun or the weight of her story, but she suddenly looks older. "Of course that didn't happen," she continues softly. "We ran out of time. She loved you so much, you know. I think that's probably what caused her to collapse when you found her with Phoebe. The realization of what she'd been doing was too much for her fragile mental health to cope with."

"Maybe," I say. "I don't suppose we'll ever know. But I wish I'd remembered you. And I wish I'd got to thank you for looking out for us before this." She looks up at me with such relief that I don't blame her for anything, and it breaks my heart. The ripples out from what our mother did touched so many lives. "And I wish we'd got to come and live with you. It would have been really good for us and I think you'd have given us both really happy childhoods." Tears spring in her eyes and she takes my hand in hers across the table.

"Thank you for that," she says, voice full of emotion. "Seeing you has brought it all back. She'd be so proud of you. Of both of you. I know she would."

I smile back, but I'm sweating under my top. I can feel the damp in my bra line. I know I should probably do the same as my mum was going to. Check myself in somewhere. If I needed any more evidence before this visit, the conclusion is obvious. I'm the danger to my family. I'm the one going mad. But still, *but still,* even after hearing all this, my body hums with paranoia that someone is out to hurt me or my family. If I'm locked away, what will I be able to do about that? I've seen enough movies and TV shows to know what these places are like. Even if you check yourself in voluntarily, it doesn't mean you can leave when you want, and so what would happen if I changed my mind? I can't be that far away from my children. I just can't.

". . . and of course once she'd moved to the low-security wing I was allowed to visit her more freely." I realize Nina is still talking, and I try to focus while taking subtle deep breaths to calm myself down from my panic.

"I hoped that maybe chatting to her would bring her back to us, but although there were odd glimpses in her eyes that something was registering, I never felt like she was truly present. She'd locked herself up so tightly in her mind that I don't think she could get out even if she wanted to. And then of course I saw Phoebe there a few weeks ago. I'm surprised she didn't tell you? She was leaving as I was arriving. I went to say hello and introduce myself, and she got so angry at me for abandoning her. She called me all sorts of names. I felt so bad. It's why I chickened out of actually coming into your office after seeing that piece about you in the paper—the divorce case. I loitered outside in an alley but then changed my mind."

"I saw you!" I say as the memory slots into place. "From my window." It was the day Michelle came in. I saw the older woman in the alley opposite. "I wish you *had* come inside. I really do."

"Well, fate brought us together anyway. And after the way Phoebe reacted to me, I didn't want to cause any more problems. Thankfully her husband was with her and calmed her down and I—"

"Sorry, wait," I cut in, not sure I'd heard correctly but fully focused on her now. "Did you say she was with her husband?"

"Yes. Although maybe just her boyfriend? Good-looking man with sandy, kind of blond hair? Late thirties? Probably about six feet tall?

I stare at her, all thoughts of my own psychosis evaporating, my shock overriding everything else.

A good-looking man with sandy-blond hair in his late thirties.

Robert. Phoebe was at Hartwell House with Robert.

51

For now, at least I am wide-fucking-awake. I'm parked and pacing beside my car as my brain races. I can't take it in. I'm looking at everything through a prism. I lay the new information out in clear sentences so I can grasp it.

Phoebe took Robert to see our mother weeks ago. Robert had known Phoebe was back. Robert had known about our mother and what she did. Even as he asked me why I'd never said anything, feigning surprise that she'd been alive all this time after the police visit, making me feel bad, he *had known* all along. Why didn't he tell me?

Secrets.

Pieces of the puzzle fall into place in my head, forming an awful picture. I'd been thinking that Phoebe's been out to get me on her own. What if she was in it with someone else?

What if my sister and my husband planned this together?

I lean against the car, dizzy, as thoughts come thick and fast. If Robert was with Phoebe at Hartwell, then he knew *everything*. The numbers. What my mother did. *He* could have told Will about the suffocation. He could have encouraged him to do those drawings, and if he knew our family history, he'd know what it would do to me, seeing them. He'd know I'd worry I was going mad. And more than that, other people would think it. No wonder Will hasn't been himself—torn between two parents.

Robert's with him all the time. If anyone knows how to manipulate our little boy, it would be him. *Don't tell Mummy.* It's not such a leap that Will wouldn't say anything. All childhood abuse stories are about secrets kept. We didn't tell anyone how bad our mummy had got. If Robert told Will not to say anything to me, he wouldn't. He'd be scared and confused, but he wouldn't tell.

The cooling evening breeze is fresh against my hot face as my brain races. If Robert and Phoebe were in it together, she could have snuck in during the night when I was upstairs and written the numbers on the board and recorded over my Dictaphone letters. Robert could have given her a key. It's a big house, I wouldn't necessarily have heard her if I was so tired and finally falling asleep.

I was sure someone was watching me from outside. It could have been Phoebe. Maybe Robert's been putting something in my food to make me stop sleeping. What was it Nina said? She knew a speed freak once who stopped sleeping. Something like that? Just enough to make me paranoid that I'm going the same way as my mum did?

Even what Sandra said about Phoebe makes more sense now. Was she saying awful things to our mother to try to prompt some kind of reaction? To do something that would get her into the hospital and force me to face her? Another thought strikes me. Robert was late to the school for the meeting after I'd seen my mother in the hospital. No one checked for *him* on CCTV. What if he went in and suffocated her while Phoebe was drinking her coffee?

Could he really do all these things? My head whirls. Could Phoebe? And why would they? Phoebe may have her messed-up reasons from our complicated relationship and jealousy but why would Robert?

Money.

The word pings into my head instantly. If it's not

love, it's money. That's what we learned in law school—the two main motivators for any action. Sure, there are more, but most of what people do is driven by one or the other. Robert's been unsettled for a while—we've both felt it. Unhappy being the stay-at-home husband, wanting his midlife-crisis bar, wanting *more*, whatever that is, and resenting my career. But without me working, whatever money we've got, even if we sold the house, wouldn't last long and certainly wouldn't give him any kind of luxury lifestyle unless of course—

The conversation comes back at me in a flash. *Oh, just sign those papers, it's for the insurance renewal. That's gone up a bit, hasn't it? Yeah, but this is gold-standard stuff. Worth it for the peace of mind!*

I was shocked by the premium when it came through last week. I was going to talk to him about it, then got distracted by the talk of my birthday party. What kind of insurance did he take out? I didn't read it, I just signed. Maybe not just death. Is there an insurance for income protection for loss of earnings due to mental health issues? Is he banking on having everything—the house, a big payout, and still more cash? He doesn't know I've been fired, but maybe he'll back the claim if I lose my shit and go bonkers tomorrow.

Money *and* love.

Does Robert love Phoebe? Or did he just use her?

I think someone pushed her.

Oh god. Did he get her to do what was needed then try to get rid of her? He knew I was going up to see her that morning. Did he get there first and push her into the road? Maybe they were walking together. If he's known she's been back all this time, then he'd know where she lives and where she works and what times. Chloe said he's been out a lot. With her? I can't begin to compute it all. Who have I been married to?

My phone rings and I startle. It's Caroline.

"Hi, Caroline. Listen—" I start.

"Hey," she cuts in, quietly. "Just checking you got back to the hotel okay. And that the tumble dryer—"

"It's not me. Any of it. I think it's Robert," I say. "Or him and Phoebe together. He knew all about my mother and what she did. Phoebe took him to meet her and he never told me. Don't you see? They must have—"

"Look, Emma . . . ," she says. "You need to get some help." She sounds odd, slightly muffled and distant. Maybe she's in the car. I remember how she looked at me earlier, like I was crazy. I need to make her see— point out the logic of what I'm saying.

"No, listen. It all makes sense. He knew about the milk-bottle thing, he could have smashed them himself and trod on them. He would have known about her numbers. Maybe he's been keeping me awake at night by drugging me, knowing it would make me think I'm like *her*—"

"Hang on, *you* were the one putting sleeping pills in his drinks, weren't you? "

"Only NightNight and that barely counts, but they could have been giving me something to make me manic. And what if he suffocated my mother and then pushed Phoebe in front of the van because he didn't need her anymore and wanted all the money to himself? Or because she changed her mind and wanted to tell me? These new insurance policies—"

I hear something in the background. Three long beeps. I pause and frown. My whole body stills. That can't be. Can it?

"Oh god, sorry, I'll let you get on with work," I say. "I shouldn't babble on. Not your problem. And thanks again for letting me shower and stuff."

I hang up before she can say more and get in the car, my blood boiling. I know exactly where I'm going. I know exactly where Caroline is.

52

I let myself in and head straight for the kitchen, the hub and heart of family life, and where our enormous American fridge door beeps three times if left open for more than a couple of seconds. The kitchen is currently the broken heart of my house, even though everything seems frighteningly normal. There are potatoes bubbling on the stove and the oven is on. I guess kids still need feeding, even if you've kicked your wife out and tried to kill her sister.

"What the hell are you doing here?" I ask, staring at Caroline, who's holding a coffee mug—my favorite coffee mug in fact—and sitting at the kitchen island. At first I think she's watching something on YouTube, the sound of talking coming from her phone, and then I realize it's *my* voice. I'm talking about Phoebe—*ranting* about Phoebe. For a second I don't understand, and then it clicks into place. The conversation we had the other day, when she had to send a text to work. "You recorded me?" I say, aghast. "But you're my friend!"

"I like you, but I'm not your friend, Emma. I barely know you." She looks at me, nervous and pitying. "All I did was bring back your wallet and you've *fixated* on me. The insistence on lunch and you keep turning up at my door. Texting me. I was placating you, but it's not normal. None of this is. I recorded you to play it back to *you*. So you could hear how you sound. But after what happened to your sister . . . I'm a medical professional, what else was I supposed to do?"

"Oh, get over yourself, Caroline, you're a district nurse not a doctor, and you're right. You don't know me."

"But *I* do."

I turn around to face Robert, his face cold. "You drugged me, Emma? I mean fucking hell. You *drugged* me."

"Come on, it's hardly like I roofied you—" How am I on the back foot here? Why am I always the one in the wrong? At least Caroline looks like she wants the ground to open and swallow her whole. The back door is open. Will must be in his playhouse in the garden. I stare at the door handle, fighting the urge to go and rattle it. They think I'm crazy enough as it is. And perhaps I am, but as Miranda said, that doesn't mean someone isn't out to get me.

"And one of our friends' husbands is abusing our daughter and you didn't tell me?" Robert's voice is rising now, filled with so much anger and loathing that I take a step backward. *Oh god, Chloe.*

"Abusing is a strong word."

"She's seventeen!" he snaps. "What would you call it?"

"I told her to end it. I was giving her time. And we had enough trouble. Have you told Michelle?"

"Of course I've bloody told Michelle. She's devastated."

"And where's Chloe? Is she upstairs?"

"She's not home yet. And not answering her phone."

"You should have bloody waited! Who knows where she is now? She won't want to come home, that's for sure. Or maybe that's what you want? Something else to help flip me over the edge? Is that it?" I want to strangle him. "You knew everything! All along! And you never said." I'm leaning forward and spitting words at him in my rage. My husband. My love. My enemy. "You lied to me. Did you kill my mother, Robert? Did you push Phoebe? If I check our insurance policies, will I find that I'm insured to the hilt against losing my mind? Is all this because you're tired of being a stay-at-home dad? Jealous of my work? The work that's kept you for twenty years and now you want to blow it all on a midlife-crisis bar and are ready to kill for that?"

He stares at me for a long moment before he speaks. "Jesus Christ, Emma," he says, and shakes his head, exasperated and so patronizing that I want to grab one of our kitchen knives and stab him in the eyes with it. "Listen to yourself. How paranoid do you sound? And you wonder why we're all worried about you? Yesterday it was Phoebe's turn to be the psycho and today it's me, is that it?"

"This isn't paranoia!" I'm shaking all over, trying to contain myself. "You knew!"

"Yes, yes I did!" he says. "And I didn't tell you because Phoebe said you wouldn't forgive her for it. You want to know about this big conspiracy against you? Well, this is what happened. I bumped into Phoebe *by accident*. I'd been for a job interview—yes, that's right, I didn't tell you about that either—and I saw her in a coffee-shop window. She'd been back a while by then. She didn't want you to know. She didn't want you to think she was worrying about your birthday. But she thought I should know the truth about your past. Just in case you started acting strangely—"

"Oh, that's charming—"

"No, she didn't mean losing your mind—not like

this—she meant you might be odd because you were afraid. She said she'd been afraid but it would be worse for you. Always had been. And then she told me why. And yes, Phoebe did tell me everything. And then she took me to see Patricia. I went only the once, and I've spent the past few weeks waiting for *you* to tell me about her. But no, I guess I've never been important enough for that. And as for the insurance? Yes, yes, I have insured you to the hilt. And can you blame me?"

He's pacing as he rants, the words an angry barrage of machine-gun fire. "As my attempts to get any kind of worthwhile jobs have shown, after nearly twenty years as a stay-at-home dad, I'm not exactly employable. And we have two kids. School and university to pay for. A home to maintain. Of course I wanted us protected if you got sick like she did. So yeah, if that's my crime, I'm guilty. But as for secrets? You kept that one for our whole marriage. I didn't keep a secret from you, Emma. All I did was find out about the one you kept from me."

"You told Will about what she did. Made him draw those things to scare me. And you knew about the numbers and—"

"For god's sake, Emma, stop it! You're my wife. I love you. But this is madness."

"What about the scratches on my car? The reviews

left about my work? The note?" I look from Robert to Caroline. "What about those?"

"Are you sure you didn't do them yourself?" Caroline asks the question softly in the silence that hangs after my question. "I know you believe someone else did it, but are you sure it wasn't you?"

My mouth moves, but I don't get any words out. I was so sure of everything when I got here, all my accusations ready, so *sure* that Robert and Phoebe had planned all this together, and now? Now all I am is confused. Everything he says is so reasonable. It's all so explainable. And here I am again, looking like a fool.

"I don't think anyone's out to get you, Emma," Caroline says. "I really don't."

"So you tell us, Emma," Robert says, his tone a lot less sympathetic than Caroline's. "What happened to Phoebe? You were there, weren't you? Did you push her?" He holds up Caroline's phone. "Because it sounds like you wanted to."

"So I'm crazy for thinking it could be you, but it's fine for you to think it's me?"

"Mummy."

The small voice startles me and makes us turn to the back door. It's Will, my darling boy, standing there. Suddenly all my accusations and theirs are forgotten and I just want to sweep him up and cuddle him so hard and never let him go. My baby boy. My light. My life. He comes closer, if a little wary, and I smile at him, a big grin, even as I'm sure I'm about to cry. My perfect boy.

"I made you a birthday card," he says, inching toward me. Robert won't tell him to stay back, however much he might want to. He can never be seen as the bad parent. "For tomorrow, if you're not here."

"Oh, thank you," I say softly. "I didn't expect that." When he's only a couple of feet away, he brings it out from behind his back and holds it up to me. It's not the big excited cuddle I'd love, but I'll take a card. If he made me a card, that should show Robert I'm not all bad.

"It's *your* card," he says.

"Thank you, Will, that—" I stop, my words sucked away from me as I stare at the card made from folded paper. He's carefully written an uneven "Happy Birthday Mummy!" on it, but below is the drawing again. A woman, hair hanging down in front of her face, holding a pillow and leaning over a little boy's bed.

"How did you know about this?" I drop the card, and I crouch, my hands on his upper arms. "Who told you to draw this card, Will? Who told you about this? Was it Auntie Phoebe? Was it Daddy?" He says nothing and I shake him. "Who, Will? You have to tell me."

He wriggles to get away from me as Robert steps in, pulling him free from me.

"Enough!"

"It's your card," is all Will says, and then bangs at the side of his head with his palm as if trying to shake something free. "It's your card."

"You bastard." I look up at Robert. "You're doing this. You! I know it. You and Phoebe." Will's starting to sob now and I go to comfort him and Robert holds out one arm to stop me.

"Stay away from him, Emma. Or I swear to god, I don't know what I'll do."

A door slams in the hallway and I turn to see Chloe storming toward me, face blotchy and nose running, a mess of emotions. "You bitch!" she says loudly. "You told. And now he's staying with her and I hate you. I hate all of you!"

I take a step back, alarmed, and my arm touches the handle of the pan on the stove. I turn to try to grab it and accidentally knock it and find myself scrabbling at thin air. I see Caroline dart forward from her stool and Robert wrap himself around Will, as all the boiling water and potatoes launch into the air. I close my eyes in panic, and then Will is shrieking and Robert is swearing and the pan clatters to the floor. There's a long moment.

Oh god, oh god, oh god. Please god.

"Get out, Emma."

I open my eyes, my chest heaving. "Are you okay? Is Will? Did you—"

"I said get out."

I see the damage now. Will is crying mostly from shock, I think just a few splashes of water on his thighs below his shorts, but Robert's arm is red. It's going to be a nasty burn.

"I'll get my bag, it's in the car," Caroline says, already headed to the door.

"It was an accident," I say, "I didn't mean—"

"Just get the fuck out of here!" Robert shouts, on his feet and looming over me. "Or I will have you committed!" He lets out a long rattling breath as I retreat into the hall and he picks Will, sobbing now, up. "It's okay, just a little burn. Let's get it under some water," he says to our son soothingly, before looking back my way. "Maybe I will anyway," he adds quietly. "For your own good."

As Caroline comes hurrying back inside, a stranger more welcome in my house than I am, I back away, defeated. Chloe looks down from the top of the stairs. "You've broken everything," she says, her voice thick with heartache. "I hope you're happy."

I hold it together until I get to my car, and then I start sobbing. Even Caroline is against me. I'm all alone now.

53

I stop at an ATM and take five hundred pounds out of the checking account and then from my credit card and don't go back to the Radisson Blu. If Robert does try to track me down to commit me, I don't intend to be easy to find. Instead, I choose a small hotel near the station, one that's a step up from a B and B but definitely not branded, and the woman behind the narrow counter in the hallway doesn't ask me for any ID before taking my cash and handing me a key attached to a big slab of wood.

It's the kind of key that in some hotels is a "feature" but here is just old-fashioned and practical for stopping any guests from leaving with it. She tells me my room is on the top floor and there's no lift, so I wearily trudge up the narrow staircase and musty smelling carpet until I find my haven, a room that just about fits the double bed and wardrobe, and there's a small shower room attached. It's stuffy, the heat apparently fixed in the on position, and I open the old sash window and let in a humid breeze and the traffic noise from below. At least there's a kettle tray and it looks clean.

I'm so tired. Tomorrow is my birthday. Only just over a week ago my husband and daughter were planning a party for me and now here I am, alone, outcast, and still fizzing with worry. At least Phoebe is out of surgery, I think as I pull out the bottle of wine and packaged sandwich I picked up on the way after the hospital rang. *Comfortable and in recovery. Still critical, but we're cautiously optimistic.* What will Phoebe have to say when she wakes up? Will she condemn Robert or put him in the clear—from pushing her anyway. I've wondered about them working together, and as I fill a mug with warm white wine, I realize that there are more options. Yes, maybe one or the other is out to get me. Maybe both together.

There is of course another possibility. Maybe it's both of them, but separately. Unaware of the other. And Phoebe's accident could be just that, an accident. Maybe she was distracted. Maybe Chloe warned her I was coming. Or Robert did. There are so many *what ifs* and *maybes,* a person could go quite mad trying to figure out all the eventualities.

Quite, quite mad.

Which of course is yet another possibility, in a strand on its own.

That all of this persecution complex is simply a product of my own paranoia. No one is coming for me. I am the only danger with my second-child madness from dirty blood. I am turning forty. I am turning into my mother.

I lock the door and then stand on the chair to put the car keys and room key right at the back of the dusty top of the wardrobe. I don't want it to be easy to leave the room tonight. I take two pills for my headache with a large swallow of wine and then sit on the side of the bed. I don't unwrap the sandwich. It's getting late and outside the heavy overcast sky is turning to night fast, the sun lost behind the thick clouds. I drink my wine and feel my head start to whirl, a crazed merry-go-round of numbers, music, and tics. I drink some more and hope I'll pass out. I wish I had my sleeping pills to add to the mix, but I'm not sure I could trust myself not to take too many. I'm so desperate to sleep.

Night falls.

I don't sleep. And yet I'm not entirely awake. The night passes like a fever dream, my anxiety ratcheting up as the clock goes past midnight. I pace the room. I rattle the handle. I press myself against the window. I do these things and yet I'm not entirely sure I *am* doing them. I drink wine and my head buzzes and as I rattle the locked door, I'm sure my hand is not my hand.

I drink some more. At around two, I have a moment of clarity and realize I'm soaking wet all through my clothes. It feels right. It feels important. Why is it important that I'm drenched? I drink some more and then find myself standing, staring at the bed. I'm mumbling lyrics and clap my hand over my mouth to stop from screaming them. I stare at the pillow, full of fear, and then finally allow myself to tumble through the cracks in my mind. I can't fight the night.

In the night I am mad.

54

MY FORTIETH BIRTHDAY

It's the phone ringing that brings me back to myself. It's ten thirty A.M. The night has vanished and the morning is well and truly here. Forty. I'm forty.

The big day.

The first thing I realize is that I'm freezing; my sodden clothes are clinging to my skin. I'm still standing in the small space at the end of the bed, and my legs almost crumple under me as soon as I take a step forward, they're so tired and stiff. I can hear the shower running and I go to turn it off. The water's freezing, set to cold. I have no recollection of being in the shower, only of being wet. The phone starts ringing again. Michelle. I don't answer it. I can live without her ranting at me as if it's all my fault that her husband sleeps around. And if she's not ranting, I don't have the energy for her emotional upset. Let her talk to Robert. He's her friend after all. I've got enough of my own shit to deal with.

I glance at the mirror above the kettle. The numbers are written in pink lipstick in three lines. 222113155218222. I vaguely remember doing that. A flash of my reflection, hair hanging over my face as I muttered and scribbled. I could have been my mother. I look back at the unslept-on bed. The only thing disturbed is the pillow on the floor.

I start to cry then, and I keep crying as I peel off my clothes and stand in a hot shower trying to warm up, my whole body shivering and shaking. Fractured moments of the night come back to me. Pacing. Singing. *Look, look, a candle, a book and a bell* . . . Staring out at the night. It's me but not me.

The truth is clear in my head. They're all right and I'm wrong. I am the cuckoo in the nest. I am the threat to my family. What will I do to them tonight? What am I capable of in these lost moments? Is this how my mother felt? This terror?

"I just want to sleep," I whisper, over and over.

Finally, the tears stop. I know what I have to do. I'm going to go and sit with Phoebe. I'm going to hold my sister's hand until she wakes up. *Please wake up, Phoebe.* Then I'm going to apologize to her, tell her I love her, tell her how grateful I am that she was my big sister and made me feel safe when I was small. I'm going to tell her how sorry I am that we lost our way, and then I'm going to drive myself to the nearest private psychiatric facility, hand over my credit card, and tell them to keep me for my own and everyone else's safety.

I feel calmer as soon as I've made the decision. I'm *not* my mother and I have the benefit of hindsight. I know what she did and I will not repeat the mistakes of the past. I'm numb as I start to dress, going through the motions, my new zen doing nothing to ease my crushing exhaustion.

My own family can wait until I'm better. I won't try to speak to them today. No good can come of that. As long as my children are safe, that's all that matters. I need to get past tonight. Somewhere safe. Somewhere locked up.

There are two birthday texts on my phone, one from Darcy and one from Rosemary. I don't answer either. I don't have space for other people. I barely have space for me.

In the end, I don't even try to clean the mirror but leave a twenty-pound note under a cup for whoever does the rooms. The rest isn't too bad. The bathroom floor is wet from the shower running with no curtain and I've shoved my soaking clothes into the bin, so I'm sure there'll be plenty of discussions at reception about the strange woman who stayed in room sixteen, but in this price bracket and this close to the station, they'll have undoubtedly seen worse. And at least they don't know my name.

It's quiet in the hospital and almost deathly silent in the room where Phoebe lies so still in the bed. A few days ago, my mother gripped my arm from her hospital bed, and here I am, gripping Phoebe's hand, as if she, with her bandaged head and broken body, can somehow be an anchor for me. Maybe I should go outside and throw myself under a bus. Break my bones. Keep my family safe. Whenever I close my eyes, I see my hands on a pillow. And I see that pillow going over Will's face.

"What's happening to me, Phoebe?" I whisper. "I can't keep hold of anything in my head."

She doesn't answer, and I go back to singing softly. I know all the lyrics, but I don't know how. My throat is dry. I must have been singing quietly for hours.

"Look, look, a candle, a book and a bell. There to remind me."

Beside the bed there's a cup of tea a nurse brought me a while back. It's gone cold. I don't think it's the first. They're worried about me too. I've been here for hours, not moving. My hand is numb in Phoebe's, but I'm scared to let go. That if I do, I'll be lost and won't find my way back. I don't want to hurt my family, and yet I can feel the cotton of the pillow and a cold rage in my heart, and if I don't stay focused, what's in my head will be real.

Maybe I can jump from a window somewhere here? End it. Outside, night is falling. The night of my fortieth birthday.

Help me, Phoebe, I think. *It's getting late and I'm afraid.*

She's stays silent, a broken sleeping beauty. I hold her hand and I drift as time washes over me. What will be, will be. The music is my companion. Hours pass. I drift again.

"Emma?"

My eyes flash open. I don't know where I am for a minute. Did I sleep? Was I *absent*? My hand is still gripping Phoebe's, but now she's gently squeezing back. I look at the clock. It's past midnight. My heart thrums and I feel spaces in my head cracking, wanting me to fall through again, but I focus on my sister. She's awake. This isn't some weirdness in my head. This is real.

"Phoebe?" I lean forward, tears filling my eyes in an instant. "Oh god, Phoebe." Her eyes are open but bleary, still woozy with drugs and no doubt a lot of pain. She swallows carefully.

"Do you want anything? Water? Shall I get the nurse?" I want to burst in this moment of joy. She's woken up and she's here. She can talk. She can think. Maybe there is no permanent damage done.

A barely imperceptible shake of her head. "I saw you," she whispers, and my heart drops to my stomach as she pauses for breath and energy. *Was it me? Did I do it?*

"You were farther along the road, I saw you coming and then someone pushed me. Were you there or did I dream it?"

I almost laugh with relief. I didn't push her. It wasn't me. I bring my chair closer. I want to be as close to her as possible. My darling big sister, who held my hand as we ran to safety. "I was there," I say, kissing her hand. "I wanted to say sorry." It's a lie, but if I could change the past that is what would happen. "I'm sorry for accusing you of all those things. I don't know what's wrong with me, Phoebe." I'm snotty with tears, and she gives my hand another weak squeeze.

"Nothing's wrong with you, Emma." She's struggling to get the words out, wheezing them as much as speaking. "Some of it was true. I said some terrible things to our mother. I couldn't help myself. I get so angry about it all still. I didn't expect her to . . ." Her face distorts slightly, emotional, so unlike Phoebe, and I wish I could scoop her up and hug her tight.

"It's not your fault. Nothing is your fault. Shit just happens. You didn't know what she'd do."

"I didn't kill her."

"I know. I didn't either."

She closes her eyes again, as if this has brought her some peace, and I can see her sinking back into oblivion. I won't be here when she wakes up again. I'm going to get the nurse and then go to Bayside Residential, hand over my credit card, and get myself locked in. Happy birthday to me.

I'm just about to carefully pull my hand free of Phoebe's when she speaks again, soft and sleepy, her eyes barely open.

"You were singing Mum's special song," she says. "Weren't you? Or did I dream that?"

I freeze. "Mum's song?"

She sighs, caught between waking and the sleep that's dragging her back down. "Hmm, yes. She sang it all evening that last night. You were in the cupboard, you probably didn't hear."

"How did it go?" I ask, my heart pounding in my rib cage. "Can you remember?"

For a moment there's only silence, and I think I've lost her to sedated sleep, and then very quietly, she starts to hum, whispering the lyrics I know so well.

"Look, look, a candle, a book and a bell, I put them behind me. Look, look a candle, a book and a bell, there to remind me . . ." She smiles, a drugged half laugh. "When I heard it, I thought it was then and she was here with me. But when she was good."

And then she's gone again, leaving me with my head spinning.

55

I go into the corridor, my breath coming fast, trying to make sense of what Phoebe said. How can my song be our mother's song? It can't be. I tell a passing nurse that Phoebe's woken up and she goes to get a doctor and I retreat to the family room to Google the lyrics again. I see a text from Robert sent hours earlier.

"For god's sake give Caroline her spare house keys back. And why would you threaten her? Please get help. Anything else like this and I'm going to have to call the police."

I stare at it. What's he talking about? I don't have her keys. And I never threatened her. What's *she* talking about? I'm about to text a tirade back when I stop. I need to check my bag in my car first. Maybe I did somehow pick the keys up or something. I haven't slept at all in two days and barely at all for nearly two weeks. I can't be sure of anything. I didn't push Phoebe though, and this makes me feel stronger. I didn't kill my mother and I didn't hurt my sister. Whatever is wrong with me, the only person I've damaged thus far is me. Robert can wait, and Caroline's keys can wait. The song is bugging me. It can't be the same one. It just can't. I click on the info link.

It's not a cover. Sweet Billy Pilgrim, "Candle Book and Bell." Released 2015. Written by Tim Elsenburg. It doesn't make any sense. How can a song written in 2015 have been sung by my mother back in the mid-eighties? She couldn't have known it. How can this song that fills my head have filled hers too? It doesn't make sense.

A nurse pops her head around the door. "A police-woman is on her way in case Phoebe wakes up again. She'll probably want to ask you some questions too when they take her statement."

"Sure," I say. "I just need to get something from my car. I'll be back in a minute."

Those keys are bugging me almost as much as the song. Why would Caroline lie? *She recorded you.* The thought swirls in the background. *She recorded you and then went to your husband's house and played it back. That's not normal either.* I need to know if I have them, and if I don't, what does that mean?

Why would Caroline be out to get me? She's just a random woman who brought my stolen wallet back. I want to punch myself in the face. This is the paranoia everyone tells me I have. Caroline is a stranger. Why would she want to hurt me? It doesn't make sense. And how can my mother's song be the same as mine? Fresh air is what I need. And to find those keys. No one is out to get me. I'm having a breakdown. *Call the clinic. Check yourself in.*

I don't want to bump into the police coming the other way, so I head up toward the geriatric department, because I know the way out to the car park from there. It's late and although the lights in the corridors are bright, the hospital feels out of time in the stillness of the night, patients asleep or quietly awake in the gloom listening to the struggling breaths of those around them, the smell of disinfectant trying to suffocate the stench of sickness. The occasional cough or cry. Everyone waiting for the optimism of dawn to roll around. I know how they feel. The lights are dimmer in the corridor that leads down to the private ward. I pause. It feels like a lifetime ago that I fled from my mother's grip.

I stare down the corridor and my skin prickles. Everything started going wrong after I came to see my mother. Internally, I may have started feeling odd the night before I knew she was hurt—and that's something else that's taking shape in my thoughts—but all the physical things started after that hospital visit. The note. The scratch on my car. My wallet being stolen. The sense someone was watching me. My alarm bells started ringing then and they haven't stopped.

I push open the door to the ward and creep forward, my heart in my mouth. Up ahead, a door to one of the rooms is open and I can hear nurses soothing a patient. I hurry to the desk and quickly scan the visitors' book. I don't have to look far. She was here a few hours ago.

Caroline Williams.

I go back through the pages—she comes here every day. Caroline. The random stranger. She was here the day I first visited. I look behind me at one of the rooms near the entrance. I remember shouting my name at the nurse who wanted me to sign in. I remember there was a woman reading to an old lady in a bed, and she paused. I thought I'd disturbed her, but was it my *name* that had disturbed her?

My whole body is shaking. But why? Is she the ex-wife of a client? Was I focusing on Miranda when a different crazy ex was in front of me the whole time?

I quickly leave the ward before the nurses return and then hurry out to my car. The night air is thick with moisture and from the distance comes a rumble of thunder. Just as the first heavy raindrops fall, I open the trunk and empty my bag. I check through all the sections and in my washbag and makeup bag and then check my coat pockets. In the car, I look behind the back seats in case the keys have slid down there, and do the same in the front footwells and then the side wells. It doesn't take long—it's a hire car, there's none of the clutter that gathers in a family car. There are no unusual house keys here. I haven't stolen anything.

So why is she lying? Who is she? What have I done to hurt her?

Something is scratching at the inside of my exhausted brain. Something someone said. Something that almost got my attention, and then I got distracted. What was it? What— My eyes widen as lightning flashes overhead. Nina. It was Nina.

"They wouldn't let me foster you. Especially after the tragedy with that family."

I had been so surprised that she'd wanted to give us a home, I hadn't paid attention to the rest. What tragedy? I get out my phone, only one bar of signal remaining. It's nearly one o'clock in the morning, but there are things I need to know, and she's the only one with answers.

A tragedy.

My mother's song.

A picture forms in my mind. A truth. A story weaving everything odd that's been happening together, and it makes no logical sense, but at the same time makes impossible sense. My head feels clearer than it has in days.

I need to talk to Nina. My foot is tapping. What's the worst that can happen when I ask her what I'm thinking? She thinks I'm mad? So what? She can get in the bloody line on that one.

A bright flash of lightning cuts through the rain and the phone rings in my ear before the thunder catches up. We're not in the eye of the storm yet. My knuckles are white, gripping the steering wheel. I blink and see knuckles in the gloom clutching a pillow. I blink it away. I am not mad.

But maybe I am my mother's daughter.

56

Nina picks up after four rings. "Emma? Are you okay?"

"I'm sorry to call you so late. I know it's the middle of the night—"

"Oh, I'm never in bed before two. I'm a night owl, not an early bird. It's fine. But what's the matter?"

The warm night rain is coming down so hard now the car is steaming up. I start the engine and blast the fans. "Are you in your car?" she asks.

"Yes, I'm at the— It doesn't matter. I'm not driving. I need to ask you a couple of questions. They're important. One was something you said yesterday that I didn't really grasp at the time." I go with the saner question first. The one that will give me something concrete.

"When you said that social services wouldn't let you foster us, you said something about *especially after the tragedy with that family.* What tragedy? I don't understand."

"Oh my gosh." I can hear her shifting at the other end, and then the click of a lighter and a soft inhale. "I always presumed you knew."

"About what?"

"The family that were going to take you in. What happened to them."

"They changed their minds." I remember the house mother at the children's home sitting me down and telling me that unfortunately I wouldn't be going to a new home that day. I remember how heartbroken I felt, having to unpack my little suitcase, and I remember Phoebe's victorious look. Was it victorious? I look at the memory again, this time analyzing it with an adult's eye. Yes, she looked pleased. But maybe she was pleased we were staying together for a little while longer. Perhaps she was hurt that I'd been so happy to be going off to a new life without her. All that anger she'd shout at me about going mad, that was all just hurt and rejection.

"No, that may be what they told you—and I can understand why, given all that you'd been through—but that's not what happened. It was awful really. Such a tragedy. They were coming to get you when they were in a head-on collision. The husband was killed outright. The wife was lucky to survive but was left paralyzed in both legs."

My mouth is dry and my head is spinning. "Did they have any children of their own?" I ask.

"Yes," she says, and I know the answer before she speaks. "A little girl. A couple of years older than you. She escaped the accident unhurt, thank god. She was in the back seat. Although I imagine it probably didn't leave her unscathed. The other driver didn't stay. She was left there alone with her dead father and severely injured mother for about half an hour, I think it was. Must have been terrible."

Enough to drive you mad.

Everything falls into place as I think of the disabled bathroom Caroline hasn't updated yet, from sharing a house with her mother. The transition from teen carer to qualified nurse was probably the most practical career choice if that's what you've been spending your life doing anyway. I remember her first-day-of-school picture. They all looked happy and proud. A complete family. Then I came along and broke everything. How must she have felt when she was reading to her mother and heard me call out my name in the hospital. Not my married name, that wouldn't have meant anything to her, but *Emma Bournett*? A person who'd been the cause of her family's ruin, her father's death even, right there in the same place. Brought together by coincidence. It wasn't my fault—it obviously wasn't my fault—but for thirty-five years I bet Caroline has blamed me.

"Emma?" Nina cuts in. "Are you still there?"

"Yes, yes I am. Sorry, thank you. That's very helpful." I pause. "There's one other thing. And you'll probably think it's crazy and maybe it is."

"Go on."

Lightning flashes, and a loud crack of thunder hammers the sky only a second later and another sheet of water crashes against the windshield.

"Do you believe that time is always linear? Or that maybe it's all happening at once and there can be glitches?"

"Well, that's a big question for the middle of the night." I hear her take a long toke on her joint. "I don't know so much about the physics of it, but I certainly think our brains are capable of a lot more than we've ever used them for. Attuned to more. And time is a concept that even scientists don't fully understand. I know of people who've had dreams of a friend saying goodbye and have woken to find out that they'd died. I know some people think déjà vu is when we experience a flash of the future. Tarot card readers—and I don't mean the charlatans—operate on *sensations* of the future rather than visions. People in extreme emotional states often claim to have glimpses of crisis coming. Fishermen's wives who've begged their husbands not to go out to sea because of a dream or a sense of dread, and the men have never come home. Why do you ask?"

"Do you think maybe these glitches, these flashes of premonition, can run in families?" I think I know the answer, but I want to hear it from someone else. Someone with books on all kinds of weird shit on her shelves.

"Oh, for sure. I would say almost definitely. DNA. That kind of thing."

"Thank you," I say. "Thanks very much. You've been a great help. I've got to go."

"But Emma, wha—"

I hang up and stare breathlessly out of the window. What do I do? Go back into the hospital and try to explain to the police there that this time I'm not being paranoid, this time I know there is someone trying to hurt my family and that they have to send someone right away? I dial Robert's number and it rings and rings and rings. I try Chloe's. It goes straight to voice mail. Caroline is at my house. That's why she said I still had the keys. She's gone to Robert's as a safe haven from his mad wife, who could turn up at her door at any time. *She's in my house. She's going to hurt my family.*

I think of my mother. Of me. Of Will's drawings.

I have been so worried about repeating the past, but what if I've been looking at it all the wrong way around?

What if the past was all about the future?

Phoebe said I was singing our mother's song. A song that was thirty years from being written when our mother sang it. So there's only one way she could know it.

It's all been a warning. Flashes of something terrible happening in the future.

I look at the clock on the dashboard.

It's just past 1:00 A.M. and I'm at least half an hour from home. I think of my mother's numbers as I put the car into drive and pull away fast. 113155218222. More jigsaw pieces slotting into place: 1:13 A.M. 1:55 A.M. 2:18 A.M. And 2:22 A.M. I have to get home before 2:22. *I'm running out of time.* I drive into the storm.

57
Caroline

I'm soaking as I come back into the kitchen and drop the empty honey jar into the trash. I've left honey-sweet surprises outside that will sting like a bee. My clothes are slick and heavy against my skin and my long hair is drenched, but I don't care. The rain was invigorating. Perfect weather for my plans. I am the storm come to wreak havoc.

I close the door quickly, but rain has still blown hard inside, wetting the floor. It's a wild night and I love the sound of the rain beating at the house, attacking from outside, while I attack from the inside. I lock the door and pocket the key. Everything is ready. I can relax.

I don't know what Emma was complaining about with her insomnia. It's very calming to be the only person awake in a dark house. Sometimes the night is the only time any of us can truly be ourselves. And here I am. At last.

Emma.

Sweet Emma. Pretty little thing. You'll love her. You really will.

Well, you were wrong about that, parents dearest. I wasn't exactly keen all the way back then, before I'd met her, and now I have nothing but disdain for sweet Emma.

She stole her sister's boyfriend and married him. Her husband is kept on a leash. Her daughter is a slut. But, of course, everything's all about Emma. Take, take, take. Always gets what she wants. The career. The house. The family. And such a whiner. Not so sweet after all.

I sit at her pretentious kitchen island and sip from my glass of wine. No need to rush. They've all drunk their hot chocolates. Everyone needs a soothing drink before bed in times of stress, don't they? That's what I said. Something to help get them off to sleep. Everyone trusts a nurse. Especially a grateful one who's sharing their concern.

No NightNight this time.

I found her sleeping pills when I went upstairs to shower. Crushed a few and popped them in a tissue in my pocket. Easy to add. Robert wasn't watching me. I'm not his crazy wife. I'm a health-care professional. Chloe was in her room, all red-eyed because she hasn't managed to wreck a marriage, and Will is just a sullen little boy. I made sure I saw them both drink it. Down the hatch. Robert took his mug up to bed. I checked on him. It's empty. Used to doing what he's told, I expect.

I can't believe he let me in. *Oh, I'm a bit nervous. She has my keys. She threatened me. Can I—well, I know you don't know me—but could I stay here? I didn't want to call the police. I'm sure she didn't mean it. She's got problems but I don't want to get her into trouble.*

Only a man would believe that shit. If a woman feels threatened, she calls the police. End of. But you can always count on white-knight syndrome to put the blinkers on a man. And he thinks she's crazy anyway. He's bought into that hook, line, and sinker. So much for love.

And now here I am, alone. Taking a moment, as they say, looking out at the storm in the gloom.

I swallow more wine. A Sancerre. Much nicer than I can afford. Of course it is. There's two more bottles in the fridge. I'm not surprised she drinks too much. She's that type.

I should probably get started. They'll be dead to the world upstairs. I open up iTunes, put my earbuds in, and press play. "Candle Book and Bell." My song of the moment. She at least gave me that. It fills my head and I hum along as the haunting melody starts.

I look at the clock on the oven. It's 1:13 A.M. Lighting flashes outside, harsh white light, and I go to the back door and rattle the handle. A double check. Good. It's locked. I rattle again to be sure. I murmur along to the song, set to repeat, as the lyrics kick in.

"Choices, broken-backed / Become the facts / Distract the heart from the hand / That signs it off . . ."

I meander through her home, her life. Her office. I've seen her in here. From outside, looking in. In the living room, a vast soulless space where it's clear no family time is spent, I check the windows and the patio doors. Locked. I can see the broken glass glittering on the ground in the rain. Just in case.

I turn back inward and tip some wine onto the backs of the elegant sofas. No one really wants sofas like these. They're not comfortable. Nothing about them says warmth and welcome. They're simply prestige. *As long as your house looks like you've made it, that's probably all that matters, isn't it, Emma? At least it will look good on the news. If they get to take photos inside.*

I head back into the corridor and drop the wine bottle, but it doesn't break, landing with a deadened thump by the understairs cupboard. I ignore it as it slowly dribbles its contents onto the wood. There's more wine in the fridge.

Look, Look, a candle a book and a bell . . .

Maybe I'll get a little top-up now. There's time. The night is mine. I open the fridge and grab a fresh bottle of their posh piss, twisting it open and taking a long gulp. It makes my eyes sting. I put it back inside, cap off, and take out the eggs. Now that I'm letting myself go, I feel like a child again. *You can't make an omelet without breaking a few eggs.* That's what my dad used to say, often apropos of nothing and entirely in the wrong context.

I'm making an omelet now, Daddy, I think. I stare out at the brilliant storm and open the box. As the music plays, I take an egg and hold it in my outstretched hand. It falls and smashes on the ground. Much like Daddy's body smashed. I try to time the crack of the next one with a crack of thunder. *Crack. Crack. Crack.* When I've finished, the floor is a mess. I wonder what the police will make of that.

Maybe they'll think I'm mad. That might not be a bad thing. A psych ward could be preferable to a prison. I've made my peace with prison, but that could be an upgrade, even though prison would be quite comfortable. And a lot more relaxing than my current life.

The song starts again, and I sing along. I suppose I should get this party started. I go out into the hallway, the music loud in my ears.

I'll start with the boy.

58

Emma

It's one forty-five as I screech to a halt, abandoning my car in the street, and run through the hard rain to the front door. My mind is clear. The impossible made possible as time merges around me. My mother, me, and Caroline. All here. We've always been here.

The future, past, and present colliding.

This is the apex. The everything. The moment I can't lose. Time hangs in the storm. Lightning and thunder, in unison, threaten to break open the sky as my key fails, the door deadbolted from the inside, and I hammer at the solid wood. Ring the bell. Nothing. No answer. Robert's car is here. He's home. They all are. I run back into the street and see Caroline's car parked past the next house. She's inside. I know she is. I know, because this night has leaked through time, a warning seeping into my mother like a brain bleed, driving her mad, and seeping into me too. The bad thing is here on the night of my fortieth birthday. It's come for my family.

And I have to stop it.

I call the police, shouting through the rain, saying who I am and that there's someone in my home, trying to hurt my family, and I then hammer on the front door again. "Open up, Caroline!" I shriek up at the bricks. "I know what you're doing!" The storm sucks away my screams and drowns them in thunder. It's futile. I scream once more and then take a breath. I need to think. There is no way in from here. I have to get to the back.

The side gate is high, nearly seven feet, and I'm only five foot three and there's no way I can just pull myself over. I look at the space beside the garage, where we keep the tall green garden waste recycling bin. I drag it to the side gate and haul myself up onto the thick lid, the plastic surface slippery with rain and the hard edges scraping my hips. I grunt as I climb, out of practice at these activities of childhood, and then grab the top of the gate. I immediately yelp and bring my hands back. They're bleeding. I pull out shards of pain. Broken glass—*is that another milk bottle, Caroline?*—

has been balanced along the top. How can that be, in this weather? I reach out carefully and touch it. The glass is held in place with something thick and sticky. I bring it to my nose. Even in the storm, the sweetness is there. Honey. Robert's manuka honey.

I pull down my sleeve and push as much of the glass away as I can and then throw one leg over the gate, the remaining glass pricking sharp through my top as I lean forward and then close my eyes as I swing my other leg over and drop hard to the ground. My bones clatter up from my spine with the impact, but I stay upright and stumble to the back door. I grab the handle and rattle it, but it's locked and I kick it hard twice, but nothing gives. I need help. Where the hell are the police?

I pull my phone out of my already sodden jeans pocket and dial them again. "Police. Police, please . . . I need help. My name's Emma Averell. I called five minutes ago. My family. There's a woman in my house . . ." The line crackles and I shout some more down the line and then it cuts out. I go to dial again, but all I hear is dead air. I'm on my own. I have to get inside. My children. I have to get to my children. I have to get to Will.

59
Caroline

The boy is not in his bed.

The hot chocolate cup is empty beside it as it was when I checked on him earlier, but I can see now where he tipped the contents down between the corner of the bed and the wall. Sneaky, sneaky little boy. He drank some of it, I know that for a fact because I made sure of it, so wherever he is, he's going to be sleepy. There's nothing under the bed but a plastic dinosaur staring back at me. He's not in the closet. I search every corner, but he's not in his room. More lightning flashes outside and I murmur along to the song as I search.

Can I have an opinion / To trigger this loop . . .

Look, look, A candle / a book and a bell.

Are you allowed music in prison? I reluctantly take the

earbuds out, the music now tinny around my neck. I listen hard. Nothing. I come out into the hallway and peer into Chloe's room through the open door. She's slumped on her bed, still dressed, the dregs of her drink spilled on her duvet. Judging by the patch of spit and mess on her top, it looks like she may have been a little sick. She's lucky she's sitting up. Gets to breathe a little longer. Underage drinking perhaps. Not a good mix with sleeping pills.

I leave her to her stupor and go around the corridor away from the children's bedrooms. Where would that surly little shit go? To Daddy? I go to Robert's room and I can hear him snoring already. Sleeping like a baby, hugging one pillow like a teddy bear. The other lies cold on the empty side of the bed. It's tempting. Maybe I should do him now? No. The plan was smallest first, and I don't like that I don't know where the boy is.

I look in his parents' bathroom, and he's not there. The same with the family bathroom and the spare rooms. The house is beginning to annoy me. How much space do these people need? I go back to Robert's room to do another sweep and look in the laundry basket in the corner. No missing boy in there. He can't have got outside, because I locked the back door behind me and kept the key with me just like the front door keys. *Come out come out wherever you are,* I whisper and sit on the edge of the bed. I'm getting irritated now.

As if in response, I hear a heavy thud from the other end of the corridor. I frown. Too heavy for a small boy, surely. I come back out and peer down toward the large window. A small moan wafts toward me, carrying self-pity and confusion in it. I must have disturbed Chloe when I went in there.

I watch as she comes into view, leaning against the wall to keep herself upright. Her head keeps lolling down, but she shuffles forward. She's clearly determined to make it to the stairs, and I'm wondering whether I should stand out of view and let her fall and break her neck, but then her hazy eyes see me. They widen momentarily with alarm as I smile at her, and she lets out a sob. I wonder how I must look. Soaking wet. My long hair hanging over my face from looking under beds. Smiling at her in the darkness.

Her knees give way slightly, but she keeps herself upright and tries to turn back. She stumbles toward the window as if there can be help that way.

"Oh Chloe." I sigh. "You really are a troublesome teenager. Just give up. You'll be asleep again in a minute. I can see it from here and if you think I'm going to drag you back to bed, you're very much mistaken."

I watch as she presses herself up against the glass as if she can somehow get out that way.

60
Emma

Astone. A stone from the rockery. That's what I need. Something, anything I can smash glass with. The wind whips hard lashes of rain at my skin as I run down to the end of the garden, feet slipping on the muddy grass, until I'm on my knees and tugging at the heavy rocks, cursing us for being the kind of couple who "get people in" and don't have odd bricks lying around from a half-finished job.

I'm breathless and sobbing with impotent rage as I realize that they've been cemented together to create their pattern. I can't pull one free. I look at my watch. It's 1:54. What happens at 1:55? Focus, Emma, focus on getting inside. Think. My heart leaps. The pond. Our forgotten pond in which all the fish died and we haven't bothered to get filled in yet. There are big pebbles in the pond. I'm slipping across to the other side of the garden, trying to make out the water in the darkness and downpour when a flash of lightning illuminates the night. It's followed by a second and I glance up at the house, half expecting Caroline to be charging out toward me. But that's not what I see.

Chloe.

It's 1:55 A.M. Perfectly lit in lightning, Chloe is pressed up against the cathedral window, her hands up by her face, with fingers spread, as if shoved up by a policeman while being arrested, and her mouth open in a wide O.

Time collides. I can feel the glass under my own fingers. Feel the carpet under my toes. I've stared out that window sure there was someone below looking up, someone out there trying to get in. Can Chloe see me? Has it always been me down here looking up and trying to get in?

What was my mother seeing when Nina found her pressed up against a window exactly like Chloe is now, muttering her numbers, exactly like I have? Even so long ago, was she here, in *this* 1:55 A.M.? As I was tugging at her legs and screaming at her, was she seeing me, *now*, in the garden too?

I slide into the pond, the slimy cold water reaching

my thighs, and I crouch, scrabbling at the smooth rocks at the bottom. *I'm coming, Chloe,* I think, as I watch my precious girl slide down the window, *Mummy's coming. Please hold on. Please hold on, baby.* 2:22. I have to get in by 2:22. Every fiber of my being is screaming the truth of that to me. I think of my own mother. I feel her strong hand gripping my wrist in the hospital. I channel her strength now and tug a stone free.

61
Caroline

I lower Chloe to the floor and leave her sleeping, propped up against the wall, head forward and legs splayed, like the drunk slut she is. Maybe I'll finish her like that too. I'm not sure she deserves any dignity. Her mother's daughter, that's for sure. Want, want, want. Take, take, take.

A dead weight is heavy, and I stretch my back. In a flash of lightning something catches my eye through the window. A figure stumbling across the lawn. *Emma.* Well, well, well. She's carrying something. What is that? A rock? "Mummy's home," I whisper to a finally unconscious Chloe, and then turn to go back downstairs to greet my guest.

The storm is raging and as lightning flashes again

and I come toward the kitchen, I see her face, full of rage and fear, soaking-wet hair a mess, on the other side of the glass. She doesn't see me, but turns toward the back door. As I get closer, I hear her exertions as she heaves the stone. She couldn't do my job. She wouldn't last a day. The rock thuds against the thick glass, but nothing happens. She tries it again, harder this time, grunting like a Wimbledon champion.

The glass will break. And when it does, I'll be ready.

62
Emma

I launch the stone over and over at the door and finally, finally, the glass in the back door smashes. I punch at the broken edges and reach through. The key isn't there. I stretch my fingers, scrabbling for the kitchen counter, maybe the key is there, but it's too far. There's no time. I launch myself in through the broken panel, edges of the glass slashing at my torso and tearing through my jeans and into my thighs but I push through, collapsing in a soaking heap on the kitchen floor. I scramble to my feet, the floor slippery—*eggs, there are broken eggs on the floor, crack, crack, crack*—and I'm stumbling forward when I hear—

"Hello, Emma."

I turn, shocked, to find her there behind me. Caroline. Grinning. Her long hair hanging loose, long and straggly, hanging over her face.

"What the hell are you doing, Caroline?" I ask.

"This." She suddenly steps forward and before I can recoil, she punches me hard in my side. I stagger backward, clutching where she hit me. I'm surprised to find the liquid I touch there so warm. How can it be hot? And sticky? As my legs give out under me, I raise my hand in the gloom. My fingers are dark. Blood. It's blood. Oh god.

I crumple to the floor and as I grab for her legs, she kicks my flailing arm away. I lean back up against the kitchen cupboard, and press my hand against the stab wound in my side. *She's stabbed me.* Blood pulses out between my fingers and I bite back a sob. As the shock fades, the pain comes. This isn't good. Not good at all.

"What have you done to my family?" I ask. *Keep her talking. Where are the police?* I press harder, trying to hold the cut closed. Caroline puts the weapon down on the island. It's a thick shard of glass, only a few inches long. Maybe I'll be okay. Maybe.

"Nothing yet. But I'm just balancing the books, Emma." She opens the fridge and pulls out an open wine bottle, taking a long sip of wine as she sits at the breakfast bar. "You did it to my family first."

"I didn't do anything." My stomach feels cold. Like there is ice melting in my insides. "I was five years old."

"Mum always talked about fate after the accident," she says. "*Don't be bitter. We have to deal with what Fate gives us. You can't change it.* She'd say that shit so many times that as much as I adored her, I wanted to throttle her for it. Always so cheery. *That's what Dad would have wanted*, she'd say. She was wrong, of course. I think what he'd have wanted would be not to have died in agony with his lungs crushed by a steering wheel before he was forty-five." She laughs a little and sips more wine.

"It wasn't fate that caused any of that, though, was it? It was me and Mum *not being* enough for my sainted father. He wanted to share our home with another child. He thought Mum had spoiled me. He thought I was cold. Lacked empathy. Needed someone to look after. My mother obviously didn't agree. She loved me as much as I loved her. But she loved him too, and he wormed his ideas of a cuckoo in our nest into her and she went along with it. And then suddenly everything was "Emma, Emma, Emma." She glances at me then, face filled with sudden rage.

"And look where that got them. A coffin and a wheelchair. I was so angry, strapped in that back seat. I remember it so well. The bright sunshine. All Dad's excited chatter while I nursed my rage. I'd thrown a tantrum before we left. I'd screamed and I'd broken things, but for once none of it had gone my way. *She's so sweet. Emma. A pretty name for such a pretty little thing.* They were in love with you—even my mother— and expected me to love you too. Like I cared about your tragic life? They were *my* parents. There was no space for you."

My insides—*I've been stabbed, oh god I've been stabbed with a shard of glass just like Mum stabbed herself with a shard of glass*—throb as I picture what would have happened if I'd gone to live with her family. Caroline as my big sister instead of Phoebe. What accident would have befallen me there? Out of the frying pan and into the fire. Frying pan? Can I maybe ease a pan out of a cupboard? And do what with it?

I lift one hand away from my wound to open the cupboard next to me, but she moves fast, stomping my fingers with her shoe. The pain is white hot and I shriek as I yank my hand back.

"Then the other car smashed into ours and everything changed," she continues, as if nothing has happened, as I wheeze in agony on the floor. "In the aftermath, as I listened to my father gasp out his last breaths and heard my mother's rattled sobs as she drifted in and out of consciousness, and before I'd realized just how much my own life would be fucked from then on, I wanted to lean between the seats and say, "*Well there you go. That'll teach you.*

"Fate. No, I never believed in it. Not until *that* moment. Hearing your name in the hospital corridor. *Emma? Patricia Bournett's other daughter?* I couldn't believe it. Emma Bournett. It was like a bucket of cold water on my head. I'd been too young to remember your surname, you see. I'd heard it only once or twice. I'd searched my mother's paperwork, but she'd got rid of anything from the foster agency after the accident. After a while, I'd made my peace with never knowing who or where you were. But then as soon as I heard it in the hospital, it came right back to me. *Emma Bournett.* That was your name."

"None of this is my family's fault," I say. "It's not my fault. I didn't even know about the accident. I—"

"Oh, stop fucking whining, Emma, this is my moment." She glances at my wound. "And you can press that as much as you like, I'm pretty sure I got your liver. Sadly. I was hoping you'd survive. Take the blame. But hey ho." She tosses me a tea towel. "In fact, this may help keep you alive a little longer. I want you to hear this."

My liver, oh god, my liver. I press the towel hard anyway. Maybe she missed. I twisted slightly as she came at me. Maybe I'll be okay. *Maybe, maybe,* I think as the cold creeps outward from my belly.

"I followed you. I had to see what you'd made of your life after so casually annihilating my mother's and mine. Within an hour I'd already seen you argue with Phoebe and then some poor woman outside your work. Hardly wearing your feminist spurs. *As long as you're all right, Emma,* I remember thinking as I keyed your car. *Then fuck the sisterhood, eh?* I scribbled the note and left it under your windshield wiper. Crude, for me, but to the point. BITCH. It felt good. Fate had brought us together for a reason. So of course I followed you home. I saw this house. The husband. The children. The friends. All so fucking perfect."

"Nothing's perfect," I say. *Except my children.* Oh, my babies. Where are they? Where is Robert? Why wasn't he protecting them?

"Some people don't deserve what they have," she says. "They take everything and just breeze on by, untouched. You weren't going to breeze past me, untouched. It was so easy to pay those kids to take your wallet so I could meet you face-to-face. To slash your tire. Following Robert was a godsend too. That bar? Perfect. And then I had this elaborate plan to maybe become a client or make friends with you, but you were so needy you did it all by yourself. Texting me.

Then the first time you turned up and stayed in the car, I thought you *knew*. But no, you were just pathetically trying to make me your friend."

"Don't hurt my children. Please. They haven't done anything to you." She's got the knife within reach and I'm in no position to rush her. I'm not sure I could even get to my feet. I have to do something. But what? I was so *drawn* to her. I felt safe around her. I felt safe because when I was with her it meant I knew where *she* was and what she was doing. That leaking future at work again.

"I watched your sleepless nights from the bottom of the garden. They were a gift. I just had to feed your paranoia. The broken milk bottles, the call to the school about you shaking that kid. And it was easy to make those client phone calls to your office and then set up meetings with other firms in case anyone checked. Everything ready to leave those reviews just at the right moment. To send you over the edge." She grins at me from behind her wineglass. "Just like I sent Phoebe over the edge of that sidewalk in front of the van. Nurses are strong. We shove hard."

Phoebe. Poor Phoebe, once again nearly dead because of this night.

"And, of course, there was Patricia," she says. "It was a matter of moments to put her out of her misery.

All I had to do was go along the corridor from my own mother's room and take care of business once you'd left. She didn't put up a fight as I pressed the pillow over her face. Her arms twitched. That was it. I've had worse."

The internal cold is reaching my toes and I start to shiver. She killed my mother. She tried to kill Phoebe. She's going to kill my family. I look at the clock on the oven. It's 2:08. The next significant time is 2:18. Maybe there was never anything I could do about it. We look for meaning in everything and maybe there isn't any. A glitch in time with no purpose. The random chaos of the universe. One of my hands, fingers like ice, drops away from holding the tea towel in place, and flops on the floor. I don't think I'll see 2:18. I think maybe I'll have died here on my kitchen floor by then.

63

Caroline

I go over to where she's slumped on the floor and crouch beside her. Even in the gloom I can see how sickly pale her skin has become.

"Not long now, Emma," I say. "You know, I wasn't going to hurt them. That wasn't the original plan. I thought you'd be arrested for killing either your mother or Phoebe, and that would be that, but fate had other plans. On reflection, this is so much better. If you hadn't told me about your mother's birthday and how you'd been so afraid of repeating what she did, I'd never have had the idea. You told me some, and Robert filled in the gaps. I'm going to do those things for you. I'm going to suffocate them all. On your fortieth birthday. Happy birthday, Crazy Emma."

"You'll get caught." Her words are barely more than a whisper. Our talking time is nearly over. She can barely keep her eyes open. Unconsciousness and then the endless sleep are waiting for her. Her other hand falls away from her wound and her breathing is slowing.

"Oh, you know, I don't mind that so much. Selling the house will leave me with nothing. I've maxed out my bank cards. And over the years I've taken my frustrations out on a few older people and not always as smoothly as I could have. I've noticed some 'concern' when I take on new elderly patients. People are starting to look when one dies, and you know people, when they look, they will find. Prison will be perfect for me. Private space. Heating bills taken care of. Only my own arse to wipe. So, please, let them catch me."

I see her fingers twitch against the ground. Her eyes close. I listen for a moment. Silence. She's stopped breathing. I look at the oven clock. *Time of death, 2:16* A.M., *Doctor.* I get to my feet, my knees cracking—*yes, prison will be better for my joints too*—and turn to face into the house. Time to find the boy.

I'm about to go to search their ridiculous living room when I see the wine bottle I dropped on the hallway floor. I look next to it. A small door to an under-stairs cupboard. Of course. Where else would a child hide?

I'm right. He's pressed himself against the wall,

his knees up under his chin. Lightning flashes bright behind us. I tilt my head to one side, looking at him from behind long strands of my wet hair.

"Ah, there you are," I say, soft and calm like I'm talking to one of my patients. I shuffle back on my heels and hold out my hand. He looks at it for a long moment, and then reluctantly comes out. I smile down at him as he takes my hand and I block the view to the kitchen, where his mother's dead body lies. Children are so strange. They nearly always do what they're told, no matter how much they think they shouldn't. Get in a stranger's car. Eat the sweets. Hold someone's hand. I lead him to the stairs, and he comes with me as I start to climb. They creak beneath us.

"Back up to bed," I say softly. He doesn't reply. I put my earbuds back in and smile.

"Look, Look, a candle, a book and a bell . . ." I feel calmer already. Soon it will all be done.

64

Emma

I am not dead.

As soon as she's moved away, hand in hand with Will, I gasp in a lungful of breath and twist around onto my knees. Stars swirl and threaten blackness in a wave of nausea and pain, but I don't have time to stop. At 2:18 A.M. she found my boy in the cupboard. I've got four minutes to get upstairs.

My head fills with pockets of time. A memory.

Mummy is crouching in the doorway, her smile too wide behind the ragged curtain of her hair. Behind her, the house is grainy dark. It's the dead of night. Neither of us moves and the sound of the storm outside is loud, as if a door is open somewhere. A slight breeze confirms it. The back door maybe.

A flash of lightning illuminates Mummy. She's soaking wet. Her eyes are odd. Empty. Looking at me but not seeing me. Looking at something past me. I think she's more frightening this way. More "funny Mummy." I almost want her to shake me again so I know this is my mummy.

Her head tilts to one side and there's a long pause before she speaks.

"Ah, there you are." Her voice is soft. Calm.

I crawl to the cupboard, then and now merging. They'll be nearly at his bedroom now. The cupboard yawns wide in front of me. Another memory. Recent this time.

"Don't tell anyone, but that's Mummy's secret hiding place." His eyes come back to me. "It can be your secret hiding place too now, if you like," I say. "But the thing about secrets," I whisper, hoping I'm making it sound fun, "is that you can't tell anyone about them. Not even Daddy. Okay? It has to be just us. It's a safe space. A special place."

I reach inside and grab a golf club and haul myself to my feet, before pulling myself up the stairs as fast as I can, clutching the banister as I go. I reach the top. As I grip the balustrade, I hear strange noises coming from farther around the corridor.

"Mummy," I hear. It's barely a whisper. Chloe is

slumped up against the wall, barely able to lift her head. She's trying to signal toward Will's room, but I don't need her help. I've been in this moment since I was five years old. I move faster now, not caring if I'm bleeding out, not caring that I can barely feel my legs. I hear his feet thrumming against the mattress and I push his bedroom door open—

Mummy, beside the bed, is leaning over Phoebe, her hair hanging down over her face, as she holds the pillow down, smothering my big sister. She grunts with the effort, because Phoebe is struggling hard and I can hear muffled panic coming from under the pillow, but all I can see are Phoebe's legs thrumming against the mattress as she arches, and then they're up and wheeling as if she's trying to kick something away. Phoebe.

I take a step forward. The old boards creak. Mummy's head spins around, her eyes startled and wide.

"Emma," she says, surprised. She straightens up. And then suddenly, with no warning, she spins to one side before crumpling into a pile of silent bones on the thin carpet.

Caroline is leaning over Will, her hair hanging down over her face as she holds the pillow down, smothering my son. He's struggling hard and she grunts with the effort, and one of her headphones falls out, tinny music like the whine of a fly against Will's thrumming legs.

I raise the golf club and take a step forward. The floor creaks. Her head turns toward me, her eyes startled and wide.

"Emma," she says, surprised. She straightens up and as all my rage comes out in something between a scream and a grunt, I swing the club around as hard as I can. It smashes into the side of her skull and she spins away and then crumples onto the carpet.

"Fuck you, Caroline," I mutter, breathless, as I stand over her, the club raised in case she moves. "Fuck you." Her skull is dented. Her eyes flicker from side to side. She's not going anywhere.

I collapse onto the bed and pull Will in close to me. "It's over, baby." Outside, through the sound of the storm, I can hear sirens. I hug my baby tighter, my other child stumbling in from the hallway and resting her head on my knee, and with both my babies close, I start to sob with relief as unconsciousness comes for me. They're safe. It's finally over.

65

I take out the dying flowers from the small vase at the base of the gravestone and replace them with bright fresh pansies. Nina says Mum used to find them joyful. I'm learning a lot from Nina, drinking it in, trying to get to know who my mother really was.

I get up, satisfied, and dust down my knees and coat, ignoring the ache in my side. I was lucky. I did twist away just enough that she missed my liver. I'd lost some blood but I was home within a couple of days.

Sometimes I go and put flowers on Caroline's mother, Jackie's, grave too. I'm glad I had a chance to meet her. She was full of warmth, even in her grief. She cried and I cried and we talked about all the loss and what a waste it all was. There was a lot of love in her. She had a massive stroke and died two weeks after my fortieth birthday, days after it came to light that Caroline was also under investigation for the deaths of several patients in her care over the past few years, as well as the attempted murder of my family.

A lot of people want answers from Caroline, but they won't be forthcoming. I hit her hard with that golf club and caused her serious brain damage. She's not quite in a vegetative state, but she's close. Sometimes I almost feel bad about that, but I don't. I can't. I doubt she'll ever face trial for her crimes, but I've already given her a life sentence. That brings me peace.

I turn the heat on in the car and drive out of the quiet cemetery. Phoebe normally comes with me, but she has physio today. She's recovering quickly too, but maybe that's because she's got a new sparkle in her eye. Darcy has been visiting her in the hospital, and I think that whatever feelings he may once have thought he had for me have gone. He and Phoebe spar with each other, and I like how much that makes Phoebe laugh. I think they're a good fit. It's good for her. She's lighter now that she's had to let all that anger out. We all are. Kinder to one another. She doesn't want to talk about it much anymore, and I respect that. Everything is now about moving forward, and I can't blame her for not wanting to look back. And we're getting closer too. Talking more. Opening up about who we are. She's my big sister again now that all that anger filling her up has gone. We have each other's backs and I'm glad she's not running back to Spain. She's thinking of training as an art therapist, and I've noticed her own work is so much better than it's been for years. It's freer. She may even make a modest living as an artist, as was always her dream.

Robert and I are moving forward too, albeit in separate directions. We've sold the house, and he's gone into business with Alan. Good luck to them both. It might be the making of him. I have a feeling he and Michelle may get together for a while. They spend a lot of time in each other's company. I don't see her anymore. She hasn't forgiven me for not saying anything about Chloe and Julian.

Julian and Chloe didn't survive the night of my fortieth birthday, which came as no real surprise to anyone but Julian. Once Michelle kicked him out, he of course turned to Chloe, but she'd grown up a lot by nearly dying and that ship had sailed. She's stayed local for uni, which I'm glad about, but to be close to the rest of us, not for him, and I'm pretty sure she's dating a boy her own age called Darren, whose name seems to come up an awful lot in conversations and even Will has started to giggle when he's mentioned.

Will's taken mine and Robert's divorce pretty well, and we're determined to keep it as easy as possible for him after everything he's been through. His dark, quiet moods have lifted and he's back to being my bouncy little boy. I guess now that my birthday is over, he hasn't got a "fuzzy head" anymore.

We're both second children, just like my mother.

No one told him about what my mother did to Phoebe. Not Phoebe or Robert. No one was telling him what to draw. He was getting flashes of the future too, even if, like Mum and me, he didn't know what they were. They clogged up his head and made it fuzzy was the best way he could describe it. He had to draw it to feel normal. It shut him down.

Patricia, me, and Will. All stuck in that moment, the future bleeding into us. My poor tragic mother, who died thinking she'd gone mad and tried to kill her child. She had the strongest "gift" of all of us. The future was leaking into her. All those lost moments when she acted out events that hadn't happened yet. Her own fuzzy head. She'd never wanted to hurt Phoebe. She was caught in that moment in the future, trapped in Caroline's actions, overwhelmed by them. None of it was her at all.

I still think about how my mother grabbed my wrist in the hospital. Did she know then? Had she figured it out on her death bed? As my birthday got closer, did all the madness of her past make itself clear to her? Was she wanting to warn me? I still have that piece of paper Sandra gave me. I look at it sometimes, my name written over and over. Deep inside, she still carried that worry for me, even if she didn't know why. She did love me. She loved both me and Phoebe.

I try not to think about it too much anymore, but sometimes, like today, when I've been at her grave, I remember Nina, sitting on my new balcony, sipping wine and talking about the Ouroboros, not long after my birthday.

"This whole thing is an Ouroboros," she said.

"What's that?" I'd asked.

"A symbol. A circular image of a snake eating its own tail. Where does the snake begin and where does it end? It's an endless loop. A paradox."

She was looking into the middle distance, thoughtful. "I see the Ouroboros when I think about what happened to you. That's a paradox too. Don't you see?"

I shook my head. I hadn't had time to analyze it all, I'd been too busy with the police and separations and tears. "Explain."

"Okay. So, let's start with your mother. If Patricia hadn't been plagued by time from the future leaking into her subconscious, then she wouldn't have tried to smother Phoebe and then collapse and been put in the secure unit. With me so far?"

I nodded.

"And if she wasn't in the secure unit, then you and Phoebe wouldn't have gone into foster care," she continues. "And therefore, Caroline's family would never have come to adopt you, and so would never have had the car crash that crippled Caroline's mother. And if Patricia hadn't beaten her head against that mirror, not only would you and Will not have inherited this glitch in time, but, more important, Patricia wouldn't have been in the same hospital ward that Caroline's mother was in, and so Caroline would never have seen and come after you." She took another sip of her wine.

"You would have grown up entirely differently, in a different time and place, with no exposure to the danger of Caroline because nothing would have happened to bring you together or to make her hate you. None of it would have happened."

She lifted her wineglass and ran her finger around the wet circle underneath. "You see now? The events of the future couldn't possibly have existed without Patricia being plagued by it in the past. It's an Ouroboros. Where is the beginning and where is the end? Your life running in a circular loop, like the snake eating itself. And I can't get my head around that," she said. "Your poor mother. If only she'd known what it was."

No, I try not to think about it too often. There are some things you can't try to understand.

You'd go mad trying.

Epilogue

Just in time for my four P.M., I get back to work, where Alma, my new receptionist-cum-assistant, greets me with a cup of coffee and a smile. Our premises are small but cozy, and I have a sense of pride as I settle into my office. I've set up on my own.

Despite the apologies and incentives, there was no way I was going back to the firm. Fresh starts and brave choices, that's what I've decided life should hold for me, and as it turns out, I haven't been short of clients. It seems I'm pretty well respected and connected and word of mouth recommendations have kept me busy. My first client to sign on was Miranda Stockwell, and now she has joint custody of her children. Darcy sends plenty my way and this afternoon's prospective new client is the colleague Dr. Morris had mentioned before. I guess not even psychiatrists can make marriages work every time.

Alma buzzes to let me know he's here, and I tell her to send him through. I stand up to greet him, smiling. "Dr. Martin," I say.

"Please, call me David."

"And I'm Emma." I find myself wishing I'd refreshed my lipstick, as I nod him toward a seat. He's Scottish and handsome but there's a slightly haunted look about him.

"And this is?" I look at the little boy beside him, maybe seven or eight years old.

"Adam. My stepson," Dr. David Martin says. "We're in a difficult situation. I want to divorce my wife, Adam's mother, but Adam wants to stay with me." The little boy hasn't yet let go of his hand.

"Okay, that is unusual," I say. "But not impossible."

Adam glances at David, hopeful. There's a story here, I think, curious. They appeal to me, these two, and I want to help them.

"His dad died in an accident a year ago. Adam was lucky to survive. It's been difficult and my wife, she, well, she can be unstable. I want to know that if I divorce Louise, he won't be left with her."

"You don't want to stay with your mum?"

"No." The little boy shakes his head, adamant.

"She's changed."

"Do you want to go and see Alma in reception? She's got some toys and comics out there, and, if you tell her I sent you, there may even be some sweets. Okay?"

That seems to cheer him up and we wait until the door is closed before continuing.

"Do you think you can help us?" David says.

"Why don't you tell me some more? Then I can see."

Half an hour later, I'm looking out the window, watching them leave. David glances up and smiles and I feel a flutter in my stomach. He is handsome. And interesting. And from what he's just told me we've both been through the emotional wringer. Everyone else is moving on. Maybe I should too. Unlike with Parker Stockwell, if Dr. David Martin asks me out for dinner, I think I'll go.

After all, what could go wrong?

Acknowledgments

First and foremost, a massive thanks to Jess Burdett and Suzanne Mackie for our fabulous night away talking about the struggles of working women in all situations, trying to balance families, guilt, men, etc., and just how tiring it is, and yet kills our sleep. It was also an absolute blast of wine and laughter, and this book would not exist without it. Let's do it again please, you're clearly my muses.

Following on, I have to also thank Luke Woellhaf and Jemima Jennings at Left Bank Pictures. Developing the TV version while writing the book challenged us all and you guys were, and continue to be, amazing. Once again, this book would be nowhere near as good without your thoughts and insights. Also of course, Andy Harries, for making me feel so much like part of the Left Bank family and being irritatingly good at spotting problems in scripts.

Big thanks to Junot Diaz and Nikita Gill for letting me steal some of their words, and Tim Elsenburg for allowing me to use one of his amazing songs in this crazy tale. If you haven't got any Sweet Billy Pilgrim albums in your playlists, readers—rectify that!

A big thank you to Baria Ahmed, Gonzo to my Duke, for passing her legal eye over the text to check for accuracy. I still find it astounding that you're such a doofus and yet so professionally astute but I love you for it. Let's adventure again please.

As ever, a huge thank you to my patient editors, Natasha Bardon and David Highfill and their great respective teams at HarperCollins UK and Willam Morrow. An extra thanks to Julia Wisdom and Kathryn Cheshire at HarperFiction for early reads and great notes. I owe you both wine or the cocktail of your choice—at least one!

To Veronique Baxter and Grainne Fox, my agents on either side of the Atlantic, you two keep me sane, and put up with all my rubbish and I am forever grateful for your support and friendship. Big thanks also to the foreign rights team at David Higham for helping spread me around the world!

It's been a crazy time in the world, and with all the

traumas so many people have been through I'm just grateful to anyone out there still picking up books and supporting writers and hopefully enjoying our wares, so a big thank you to all you readers. It's said often, but that's because it's true. You really do make it all worthwhile. And of course, a thank you to Teddy for being the absolutely best dog and keeping me company throughout the various lockdowns and making me leave the house and clear my head in the park. You are a very good dog.